A Habit of Mind

A HABIT OF

Jim Newman

NORTH STAR PRESS OF ST. CLOUD, INC.
Saint Cloud, Minnesota

Copyright © 2015 Jim Newman

Cover design by Joel Bechtolt
conradbechtolt.com/about

ISBN 978-0-87839-818-8

All rights reserved.

This is a work of fiction. Names, characters, places, and incidents are the products of the author's imagination or are used fictitiously. Any resemblance to actual events or persons, living or dead, is entirely coincidental.

First Edition: May 2015

Printed in the United States of America

Published by
North Star Press of St. Cloud, Inc.
P.O. Box 451
St. Cloud, Minnesota 56302

www.northstarpress.com

Chapter 1

Doug Pepper stood near the glass doors in the television station lobby. He knew that any average Joe—somebody who didn't know the business—would see nothing on the floor but the backpacks, cords, and microphones, technical whatnot a professional uses everyday. But Doug understood that this particular pile was obsolete crap foisted unfairly on someone who deserved better.

Every day, Doug had to load a cruiser—load it and then unload it—camera, tripod, light case, and tons of other shit. It took time he would never get back.

It was heartbreaking. He wished he could share his feelings, but no one was interested.

Doug might have opened his heart to the news director, Bob Tratcher, who resembled his late father in some ways. But Bob Tratcher made Doug work nights. Mind you, videographers left the station all the time. They sometimes got fired, sometimes they were hired at Channel 5, sometimes they—whatever. And yet, though their day slots duly opened up, did Doug get a day shift? No! So he remained a mere camera-monkey shooting fires and traffic tie-ups every night. He never got to do interviews, except quick-and-dirty sound bites.

Ironically, though, and unbeknownst to anyone, Doug had partly beat the system loading microphones and cords and wireless this-and-thats mainly for show.

He'd begun using his smart phone camera for video of the fires and freeway smash-ups, and flooded streets. It saved time and energy.

Doug would have locked up the big professional Sony digital camera forever except it had a great zoom lens. He rarely needed it. But he kept it in the back seat, just in case.

It was 3:30 p.m. Technically, Doug was late for work. Management thought he should be on his butt in the cruiser at three. Should Doug himself become a news director someday he would never be that anal.

Through the double glass doors in the lobby, the glare hurt his eyes, and Doug could tell the sun was blistering now. The heat would crush him the minute he walked the two blocks to the parking ramp. He'd have to go back and forth several times, too, since he had so much shit. It was a recipe for heatstroke.

The alternative, of course, was to park in front of the building and load the cruiser. But that was asking for a ninety-dollar ticket. Bob Tratcher would have his ass.

Doug's head hurt. He could use a little sack time, he knew, with the shades drawn. Still, last night was worth it.

"Pepper! Here you are in the lobby!"

"Oh!"

It was Tanya Thorpe. He didn't need to look. Her picture was up there on the wall right above his head with the other "WEE-3 News" stars. Tanya had blonde wavy hair and shiny white teeth and a tasty tongue.

Doug ignored her. He crouched over his backpack, pretending to concentrate.

Doug was startlingly handsome by most accounts, a fact confirmed easily enough by any mirror, and when he smiled with teeth on full display, the effect was like wearing a starched white shirt.

He turned his 10,000-watt teeth on Tanya.

Predictably, Tanya didn't smile back. Lately, she was at pains to telegraph indifference. In a way, Doug sympathized. To be fair, she had a lot to live down. Specifically, the way she used to scream into his eardrums and then bite him.

There wasn't any point in bringing that up.

"Bill and Ruby tried to call you," said Tanya. "You aren't showing up on the map. Now I see why."

Bill and Ruby sat in a glassed-in room in the newsroom and tracked the news cruisers on computer screens. Every videographer and reporter had his own blinking blue dot. It didn't matter if you were in Minneapolis-St. Paul or somewhere outstate. You logged in on your shift and—bam!—your individual blue dot tracked you from then on. If you pulled into a coffee shop maybe or parked by the river just for a breather, you were sure to be in the shit. Bill or Ruby'd be right on you to ask what-the-fuck was up?

Doug frowned. "My dicroic is missing," he said. He picked up a loop of cord and examined it as if it could be a dicroic, then tossed it back into the pack. "I can't go out on the street like that."

"A what?"

Doug didn't actually have a dicroic, which was some kind of fancy light filter you could put on your lens for some reason. He for sure didn't need one to shoot train wrecks. "Somebody swiped it," he said, zipping and unzipping his pack.

"I don't see how you find anything in that mess."

"I can't go out unprepared, Tanya," Doug said, fingering the zipper. "And I'm real busy right now."

Tanya folded her arms across her breasts. "Too busy to change shirts, I see."

Doug was wearing a red-and-white Verizon "t"—which was fine.

"This is fresh, Tanya, just F-Y-I. I got two the same," Doug said. "And I wore the other one yesterday. So, your mistake. I can't afford a lot of fashion in this job."

"Oh. 'Cause, you know, we're all representing the station, right? I guess it's those identical pit stains and that godawful smudge that made me think you wear the same shirt every day. Good to know you change clothes."

Doug breathed out, slowly. There could be no clearer proof she remained shamelessly hot for him. She was keeping track of his sweat. Once that would have been a huge turn-on, but now it was mainly just sad.

The sidewalk reflection was a laser beam. What's-her-name—Doug's date from last night—turned out to be quite a drinker and now his head was paying the price for whatever they did. He decided he would bring the car around to the front of the building and load up that way.

Tanya needed to go back downstairs and let him get on with it. He rubbed his scalp, pretending to think. Tanya didn't move.

"Tanya, the mayor's office is calling!" said Theresa, the receptionist. "Do you want to take it here?"

"Go talk to the mayor," said Doug.

"Send it to voicemail," said Tanya, glancing over her shoulder at Theresa.

"But they said to page," said Theresa.

"Fuck 'em," said Tanya.

Doug cringed. Theresa was some kind of Christian, as was common knowledge. Theresa mumbled something and routed the call.

"Hope you find your . . . uh, 'dicroic,'" Tanya said in an unconvincing tone.

The elevator, which drained the upper floors of the WEE-TV building, opened with a pained mechanical whine. This was exactly why Doug tried to minimize his time in the lobby. At any given moment, for no reason at all, the elevator would just open, and management would come spilling out. They were judgmental, these people, and mean, and disliked Doug personally, which was obvious. If it weren't for Tanya nonsensically delaying his departure he'd have been long gone. But there it was: him on his haunches looking stupid, and nothing but suits crowding the lobby. A voice set his teeth on edge.

"Ha ha ha ha ha!" Vern Balstad! The big man moved through the people like a creature let out of his cage. He was laughing probably at his own joke. Tanya backed up.

All Doug's crap seemed more and more like crap blocking the doorway.

"What the . . . ?" said Mr. Balstad. He stopped dead. He folded his arms and kicked hard at Doug's red backpack. "Stow this!"

"Yessir, Mr. Balstad," said Doug. Doug grabbed the tripod, and set it a few inches closer to the wall. He kicked the big backpack and the smaller one to the side.

"*Meh, meh, meh, Mr. Balstad,*" Mr. Balstad, said quietly, in a sing-songy imitation of Doug. "See, Foster," he said, shaking his head. "this is just what I said. Labor in upheaval. Low pay, but equivalently unskilled." Doug adjusted the tripod so it wouldn't tip and grabbed the light case to move it somewhere.

"Put it on the goddamn sofa, you fool!" Mr. Balstad said, in a menacing growl.

"Yessir, Mr. Balstad," said Doug. He balanced the entire load on the narrow love seat and pulled his hand away. Nothing fell. "Okay. Sorry, Mr. Balstad." Doug wiped his forehead.

"You looking fine, doll," said Mr. Balstad, smiling at Tanya.

"Mr. Balstad."

"This little girl is the jewel of the WEE-TV crown," Vern Balstad said to a distinguished white haired man.

"Hi, Mr. Balstad!" said Theresa the receptionist.

Mr. Balstad pointed at her with his meaty hand and said, "You looking fine, girl!" Theresa laughed and showed her gorgeous teeth, and Doug wondered if being Christian and pleasing God made you look grateful at all times, which in Theresa's case, was a good look.

"Get this shit *the fuck* out of here now," Vern whispered softly to Doug. Then, smiling at Tanya and Theresa, Vern and company left the building.

"Yessir," Doug called to Mr. Balstad, as the door shut. Tanya was headed down the stairs. "Tell Bill and Ruby to hold their load," Doug said.

"Whatever."

Doug didn't dare relax. What, exactly, he needed to do wasn't too clear.

"Can I help in any way?" said Theresa.

Doug ignored her. She was just so Jesus-prone, and you couldn't justify putting serious time into a girl like that. Doug picked up the Sony camera and held it an inch from his face examining it with a show of concern he hoped demonstrated he had no time to talk. He was a little sorry for Theresa. By rights she should have him in the palm of her hand, even though he was just as hot as she, with his great body, skin, cheekbones, you-name-it. What could he do? She was angling for heaven. Doug knew he wasn't going to win with competition like that.

Chapter 2

The WEE-TV studios were a block off Hennepin Avenue, where the bars drew attractive gals from all over the Midwest like bug-zappers drew bugs. The Chute, for instance, had great DJs and was only a block North of the station. It was mainly gay of course—but who cared? Doug had learned to enjoy being hit-on from all directions and some of the guys at the Chute were satisfyingly graphic in their proposals and, truth to tell, not a little convincing.

Doug had even stopped saying "fag" though that was mainly because of having dated Tanya, who turned out to be a flaming liberal on top of everything else. But, as far as Doug was concerned, she was water under the bridge.

Doug got off work early. He switched to a ring tone to show he was on call but that was a joke. In Minneapolis clubs, not even the bartenders could hear over the music. Anyway, he was free from Bill and Ruby's computer until tomorrow.

Felice was a great club at the Target Center, an easy stroll away. The sidewalks were wet because it had rained, and the neon on Hennepin bounced off the pavement in a colorful way. The clamminess, along with the hellish heat, had disappeared. Felice made itself known long before you saw the flashing sign. The management was getting shit from nearby condos since its sound system carried for blocks.

Good ol' Dumbo was at the door, and Doug got in free. The air conditioning hadn't kept up with the sweating bodies. Doug rolled his short sleeves over his delts to cool off, and suddenly there was Seth Peterson, whom he'd just left at work. Seth was staring at him with a needy look. *Fuck me*, Doug thought.

He liked Seth fine but not in Felice! Tonight, in fact, Seth had called Doug off a worthless brush fire story, saving him hours on the freeway. Seth didn't have to do that. He was a good guy. However, Seth, being a supervisor, was not welcome here.

Doug sat down by Seth at the bar. "Night out?" Doug said, with a big smile.

"More like forever," said Seth, glumly. "Princie and me, technically we're on the skids. I thought that was common knowledge."

It probably was, thought Doug. On nights, he never heard a thing. He nodded sympathetically. "Yeah, well, I'd hoped."

"Thanks, man," said Seth.

"Rough on the kids."

"Well, there's just the one, Francine, you know. In school."

"Yeah. But. You know. What goes around comes around." It was so awkward meeting Seth outside office hours. Doug had never even really looked at him before. Now, here he was in a friendly situation with mainly a stranger. He could see the little hairs on his face. "Uh . . ."

Seth signaled the bartender. "What're you having?" he said. "On me."

"Double scotch, Glenlevit, neat," Doug said, knowing his way around a bar. An eighteen-dollar scotch, give or take, was pushing it. But Seth's mood was a subtle green light—that and the fives in front of him. Doug, in any event, was as good a listener as anyone. "Appreciate you waving me off the Pomfret Farms fire," Doug said. "Bill and Ruby would of sent me to Hinkle without a blink, had they been left to their own devices."

Seth waved his hand. "They're okay," he said. "Don't breathe a word," he went on, "but the hammer's coming down."

The DJ's thumping dance beat interfered with Seth's exact meaning, but it was a notion that made Doug's skin crawl. "Yeah, is that right?" Doug said, displaying his teeth.

"What's right, is Vern Balstad's long-term vision," Seth said.

Doug sipped his drink, which was as strong as you'd want. He watched the dancers' shifting shape under a strobe. He looked directly at Seth. "Big things, I guess," he shouted.

"Just what you've heard," said Seth. "Only, times two."

"Feely, feely fi fo fum," Sami Lou Demon crooned, as if she was saying real words. Doug watched the dancers. Seth seemed to think Doug knew what he meant.

"Matter of time, I guess," Doug said, leaning in.

"Don't take it that way," said Seth, his eyes blazing. Boom, boom, boom, went the bass line. Doug wished he and Seth were on a park bench at Lake of the Isles batting away bugs and talking in peace. You could miss a word here and there and say the wrong thing and fuck things up.

"So what do you think?" said Seth.

"Of what?"

"'Of what?' The whole enterprise, is what." Seth made a gesture. "The whole enterprise, if you will."

Here was this guy, Seth, from the suburbs, cramping Doug's style on First Avenue. How many nights off did Doug get, anyway? Sure, quite a few, if you meant late. But how many nights did he get off early and with cash-in-hand? Doug didn't make a lot. And now, on a perfect night, and pretty flush, he was listening to a sob story when his coke dealer was out there on the floor dancing with a complete babe. Doug didn't actually have money for coke. But it was the principal. The night was slipping through his fingers. Other people were getting theirs, but not him.

"See," Seth said, "guys like you think small. You're not looking at the big picture. Here you are young, energetic, alive, but no sense of the future, no sense of what it means to be proactive. See? And yet, you're one of the best shooters in the goddamn shop." Doug was slipping off the stool to go to the john. He stopped. "Ahhhh! Now *that* got your attention!" Seth said. "I got my eye on you buddy. Was it the Bellwick Cage wreck? Not much of a story, there, total throwaway, but man, you were on it! That's what I mean! You didn't ask, 'this a good story?' You gave it the ol' hustle anyway." Seth signaled the bartender. "There'll be spilled milk. Always is. But, you, my friend, are going to land on your feet. Give it another couple weeks. Is same as before okay?"

* * * * *

TEN YEARS. TEN YEARS it had been since Vern Balstad had inherited the company, taking charge without ceremony, preamble, mentor, solace, or advice—without, in short, any real preparation at all. It hadn't been right.

The old man was a demon to the very end, Vern thought, as he sat at his office window. Everybody knew that. The ancient bastard had clutched at power with the last greedy ounce of his being, even at seventy-five, when it was all too obvious his brain was cutting in and out like shortwave from the *Titanic*. There was no father-son chat at the end, no sage advice, just me, me, me.

Vern grabbed some tobacco, stuffed it in his pipe, lit up and took a puff. No competition from DVRs or Internet, in the day. No, the old man had had it blessedly simple. And yet, he had gotten all the praise for supposedly making WEE-TV what it is today! It was pitiful.

Well, there would be redress.

TV stations were still a prestige property particularly among the big hedge funds that had started consolidating ownership of local stations. They no doubt figured they'd eventually make a killing selling the TV frequencies to cell phone companies, but meanwhile there was money to be had running lean and raising ad rates.

". . . Vern?" squawked the obsolete intercom. Vern bit the pipe and growled. The damn two-way speaker was a Radio Shack antique. Yet another stumbling block left by the old bastard!

"They're here? Let them in, Flo!"

". . ."

"What?"

The intercom snapped angrily but indecipherably.

"Goddamn it, Flo! Let the fu—well, just let them in!"

That box was a booby trap, a bitter and vindictive ploy. Now, Flo opened the door a crack. "Mr. Kleizer is here to see you, sir," she said. There was a silence as tall, white-haired Foster Kleizer and three nondescript underlings padded into Vern's office. *Goddamn*, Vern thought, *Kleizer's brought a fucking entourage!* It was no doubt the New York way. There were only three chairs in Vern's office, not counting his own and normally that was not a problem since, as a policy, Vern enjoyed letting staffers stand.

But protocol was different here.

"Foster! Wonderful! Hi ya!" Vern pressed the intercom. "Flo, bring in another chair, would you?

". . ."

"Oh, just a minute! Please, be seated won't you? That is, all but one . . . it'll be just a minute, here, as she . . ."

Vern pressed the key again. "Flo?"

"Hellfire, Vern," Foster said slowly, "let's just . . ."

Vern waved a preemptive hand. "Don't even think it, Foster," he said. He darted to the door and opened it fast enough to afford an element of surprise. Flo seemed to be on the phone. "Very well," he said, loudly, "I'll do it myself." He pushed the copies of *Advertising Age* off the extra chair by Flo's files, and, failing to catch her eye, dragged the upholstered chair across the threshold and onto his exquisite Persian carpet. He smiled at Foster Kleizer as he closed the door. "That was certainly more trouble than it's worth! Well, Foster, who are these wonderful people!"

By modern standards, Vern's office was a broom closet and yet he had done wonders with color and texture to evoke a refined elegance. And odd as it might seem, Vern felt sentimental about the space. His dad, Vern Senior, had sat at this very desk. The great patriarch was still there in spirit, one could say. His portrait stared down owl-eyed from the wall. The painting seemed to change with the light: sometimes somehow appearing to cast a sarcastic smirk on Vern's day-to-day decision-making though, of course, the old man had been dead these many years.

"This is Marissa, this is Theo, and here's young Josh," said Foster Kleizer. "Afraid I threw you a curve ball."

"Oh, no, no, no," said Vern.

"Great. You appreciate the imperative."

"Well, yes. I certainly do."

"Marissa brought her fine-tooth comb. She's talked to Chet. She'll crunch numbers through the weekend, if need be."

"Well—"

"Josh and Theo will want to roam the halls, get a feel, so to say. The water cooler perspective."

"Well, but first lunch," said Vern, emptying and refilling his pipe. "WEE-TV has a long and proud heritage in the upper Midwest. I can help Marsha, and Josh and—everybody—get a balanced impression of . . . plus, there's the video . . ."

"Marissa. Yes, and we'll want to see that tomorrow," said Foster Kleizer. "You'll have time around 11:00, Marissa?"

"Yes, Foster."

Foster smiled at Vern. "I wonder if you could have Flo order sandwiches. Pretty old hat for the guys, reading the tea leaves, but a punishing schedule nonetheless. A whole lotta paperwork."

Vern didn't have PTSD. And yet, Foster seemed to be triggering a sort of traumatic flashback. Vern could practically smell Vern Senior's stale breath. Sure, if you're going to sink money into an operation, go ahead and kick the tires, sleep on it. But Vern hadn't expected Kleizer Equity Corporation to launch the Spanish Inquisition, yet here it was.

"Everything's on the up and up, Foster. Double-digit profit bump last year. And like I say we got morale through the roof, bar none."

"Kids," said Foster Kleizer, "you heard the man! Get to work, and he and I'll dine someplace?"

"Yes indeed, Foster!"

They *were* kids. They practically trotted out the door and nobody but Kleizer had bothered to sit down.

* * * * *

Sometimes Doug Pepper liked to stop and smell the roses. This was literally impossible in the newsroom though because it was the basement. Still, TVs played like in the gym, except the sound was turned down, and there were no subtitles. When big news broke, somebody turned up all the channels at once. It was distracting and not that great. But Doug was usually on the street then anyway.

Still, now that Doug and Seth were buddies, Doug was loosening up a little, hanging around in the newsroom at the start of his shift to shoot the shit. A new dawn was breaking for Doug, and he owed it all to Seth Pedersen and their drinks at Felice. It paid to be a Good Samaritan. It paid to lend an ear to a friend.

"What's on tap, cap?" Doug said, balancing his butt on the edge of Seth's desk.

"Oh, hey, Doug! Haven't looked. Pretty full day. You play your cards right you could be off, 8:30 or 9:00."

"Sweet!"

"Now watch all hell break lose!"

"I'd be on it!"

"Accounting called down about those sunglasses?"

"Why? Is that a problem?"

"How you'd break them again?" said Seth. "You sat on them?"

"Yeah. Forgot and left them on the seat while shooting something, and—"

"I did you a favor and told them to forget it. You know better than that, especially now. That hedge fund's minions have upstairs in a tizzy. $300—what were they, prescription?"

"Givenchy."

"Even so."

"That's okay, Seth. I appreciate everything you've done. We can't win 'em all. I'll be in the car if you need me."

"Hey, bonehead!"

Doug Pepper stopped centimeters short of Tammy Bailey's huge knockers. True, there were worse things to careen into than a pair of billowy tits, but Doug was hands-off at work. "Snipe!" he said, to the lovely girl, "You're in the flight path! And 'scuse me? 'Bonehead' you say? He's just right over there."

Doug pointed at Seth, who no doubt would've laughed, but was on the phone.

"Don't be funny. Not Seth. You know *you're* the bonehead!"

Doug rubbed his scalp. Tammy's vaguely upturned lips suggested a smile. But it wasn't one. "See," Doug said, "if this is about you and me last night, then you're just being silly."

"For your information it isn't the first time you've pulled that trick. And I'm sick and tired of getting used and abused by people like you, Doug. And you're the worst one of all! You're so lame!"

Tammy's hands were on her hips and her head tilted up. She was as close as a girl that size could be to getting in your face.

"Now, now. Look, Snipe, try to see things normally," Doug said. "You're just a friend, not a girlfriend. What was I supposed to do? Ignore my feelings? Is that what you want? You had a great enough time! I'm not blind. I introduced you. They bought you drinks. You didn't need me around.

"I didn't know what happened and you left me alone."

"You drove your car! It's not like you had to catch a bus, or some shit! Jesus!"

"And then you didn't answer your phone."

"It wasn't opportune."

"I must have called you five times."

"Yeah. I think you did."

"See? I don't trust you anymore. And you're a bonehead. Catch me ever going anyplace with you again. You can just forget it!"

Tammy was little, but stacked. She was okay—though immature and prone to misjudging the realities in any grown-up situation. Here in the basement, she worked with scripts and looked busy. People liked her. She was somewhat sexy, too, in a vulnerable, eager-to-please little girl way.

"Look, Tammy, I'm sorry if I hurt your feelings, but circumstances were way beyond my control."

"No they weren't. I saw you on the dance floor. That was lewd, crude, and unimaginable, with that . . . that *bimbo*."

It was a dim memory, but it made Doug smile. Yes, it had been a good night. One of many for which some of the credit, at least, had to lay with Felice's DJ supreme, Sammy-D.

Bill and Ruby, Doug noticed, were craning their necks now from inside their glass cage and unless his blue dot starting blinking soon they'd be gunning for him.

"Tammy, look, this is not the time or place for this discussion," Doug said, in a soft but firm voice. "You must have some unresolved abandonment thing. If a boy leaves you in a bar, with no fault of his own, then what we have to wonder is if maybe you're overly emotional or having a breakdown or other—"

"WHAT!" Tammy shouted. Seth, over at his desk, covered his mouthpiece and looked up. Some people stopped typing on their screens. This was not the Tammy who puppy-dogged around the newsroom!

"Okay, now—"

Tammy jammed a sharp red fingernail into Doug's chest. It hurt. "No, it's not 'okay,'" she said. He put out his hands, fingers spread, motioning to keep it down. "You and your bimbo are no concern of mine, Mr. Doug. But you respect my person or you take the consequences. And from now on you are nothing but a jerk in my book. So just don't you even look at me because I have been disappointed too many times."

The words Tammy used were different than her usual nicey-nice lingo. Doug sensed that the entire room was listening. The odds were against him and something was different. A swift calculation in Doug's mind proved beyond a shadow of a doubt that Tammy Bailey had been talking to Tanya Thorpe. This, then, was pretty much a typical Tanya-type ambush coming out of a sweet little girl. There was no way to win because, sadly, this was not a court of law.

"Tammy, I'm sorry to say this, but it's me, not you, who is broken-hearted by this mess. I tried, through no fault of my own, to do the right thing. And look what's happened. A real SNAFU. I can only hope time will rectify the odds, and someday we'll be friends free of undue influence."

It was an okay speech, filled with sincerity and real emotion. As such, Doug had used normal volume and anybody listening had to know that every word came from the heart with others to blame. Doug turned away and walked from the room. It would have been best to go upstairs to the street and drive away. Instead, he mistakenly went into the backroom.

In a sense, he had yet to leave the scene, because he was still stuck in the basement. He slipped into the gear room and closed the door. The gear room was windowless with shelves, piled with broken equipment and obsolete crap like he was asked to use everyday. It had been constructed to fit behind the edit bays. It was isolated and relaxing. Doug sat on the workbench.

Last night's festivities were hard to recall. Details were scarce. The girl, Betsy, had a great tongue. Betsy? No. Not that. Yet, his memory wanted to say Betty Boop. Being possibly Chinese, Doug acknowledged, she might, in all liklihood, call herself any crazy thing.

There was a stuffed crow on top of the lockers that had once been real. The lockers were padlocked. The dirty little secret was Doug's Sony X-70 was crummier than the others. He lacked a wireless frequency-lock. This overt discrimination was one reason he'd begun using his iPhone to cover the news. His skill more than compensated for any slight drop in video quality. The upshot was no one could say he was ripping-off the company in any real or detectable way.

Doug spotted his old Post-it between the tits of the bosomy "Jugs" calendar babe, though now the gal sported a handlebar moustache. Doug'd written months ago. He took the note down and read it. *"All right why the hell don't I have a frequency-lock just because of nights? You guys have one! The least you could do is loan! Signed, Doug P."*

It'd probably served its purpose, though nobody had said "boo."

Chapter 3

Bonnie Lee Thayer, director of Public Relations, and a veteran of plenty of WEE-TV's staff meetings, smiled to herself. She looked at her colleagues sprawled, as they were, wherever there was room. Middle-aged men, as a rule, seemed ungainly, their inevitable failure to maintain the sleek elegance of youth on hilarious display. Poor Chet Florey was floundering on the carpet like a carp. Bob Tratcher, too proud to sit on Vern Balstad's floor, leaned against the wall, his belly straining the buttons of his dress shirt.

Still, she was touched, in spite of herself, by the homeliness of the scene. These were her coworkers, stripped of pretension, and dignity, though thanks to their unshakable pride, utterly without shame.

Bonnie Lee eased her tired old frame onto the soft arm of the huge leather easy chair that Stephen Cooney, WEE-TV's hard-charging sales manager had commandeered. Forget chivalry. Cooney barely moved. Nor did he offer acknowledgement of her presence. Cooney was a man incapable of offering a lady the one good chair.

Today was the big day. The presentation would be in the conference room, thank God. This strategy session, such as it was, felt more like a criminal enterprise with all-and-sundry crammed cheek-by-jowl in Vern's miniscule office.

Youth culture, proliferating entertainment options, shifting tastes, should've prompted action years ago. Bonnie'd told Vern just that—endlessly.

But Vern was just not his father. Look at him. He should be coaching high school football somewhere in west Texas where false bravado was appreciated.

Bonnie Lee was never gladder than today about all that Apple money piling up in her stock portfolio. She was a woman of independent means.

"Look at that tie!" she said, to Stephen Cooney, grabbing his necktie and holding it high like a noose.

"What? You've never seen a blue tie?" Cooney pulled it back and smoothed it.

"Sure. On a baby bonnet!" Bonnie Lee said.

She could play the game. This place was a 1950s time warp. But she liked that.

She made herself comfortable, adjusting her black woolen pants and resting herself against the cushioned back of the chair. Bonnie wore her hair tied back. She wore a dark vest of green brocade with gold trim that went well with her black trousers. It was a smart look. She could afford it.

"Move over, you big pig," she said to Stephen.

In the corner, writhing painfully, gray old Chet Florey was slowly adjusting his sagging self to make the floor comfortable. She liked him, the Nervous Nelly. Remarkably, he had a wife. And three loving kids. Chet would be gone if the deal with Kleizer closed. Did he know? There was nothing she could do about it, anyway. Hell, she'd be gone too.

*****

DOUG PEPPER WAS A MAN of action. He knew he couldn't hide in the gear room all day. For one thing, his all-important blue dot was missing in action. Bill and Ruby were sure to mark him AWOL. Probably the unrelenting bastards had already alerted Seth Peterson.

Doug left the tiny room and moved through the dim half-light of the glass-walled edit bays.

From here in the shadows, the entire newsroom was on panoramic display. There was Tanya Thorpe! She should be out on a story, Doug thought. She was tall and slinky and made quite a pair alongside curvy little Tammy whom she appeared to be lecturing. They were standing in the middle of Doug Pepper's path to the stairs. He could bluff his way to the stairway. If, for example, he had something he could carry, something big and noticeable, people would surely understand he was on an errand and in no manner shirking responsibilities.

Batteries!

Doug had no time to enjoy his brilliant tactical insight. A sudden barrage, an explosion of sound, shattered the peace. The noise, unexplainable, was loud, persistent machine-gun-like and triggered a nasty shot of adrenaline. Doug steadied himself and turned to the plate glass behind him and saw Cat Barnum's grinning teeth.

The fool should be editing. Doug raced through the sliding door and into the room.

"Look, here," Doug growled, grabbing Cat by the lapels of his shirt. Cat was quite big. Muscular. It was a fact easily overlooked. The man spent his days in the shadows hunched over edit screens. "Cat. I've seen you in here. You leave early . . . no harm done. Let me just . . . sorry about your shirt. Should, you know, reshape somehow." Doug didn't try to help smooth the wrinkles. Cat seemed wary of additional physical contact. "How come you were pounding like that? Give somebody a heart attack! Could have been dangerous because unexpected. Jeezis!"

"You're a very jumpy guy," said Cat in a soft voice, shaking his head. "You know, it's just not good to be so . . . also, what's with you and Tammy? Truth is, she's a damn fine little lady. She had you going. Epic!"

God, Doug thought. Tammy goes ballistic and the whole newsroom knows! Cat sat back down at his screen and typed something.

"Nothing could be further from the truth, Cat," Doug said. "That little girl isn't even on my microscope. I was down here for batteries. Even the new ones are dead this time. A bad batch."

"Yeah?" said Cat. "Check this out. The Phantom Scripter. It's on YouTube. Seventy thousand hits, I see. Wow!"

"You should be out shooting," Doug said. "Big guy like you doesn't need to be squirreled away in a room all day."

"Yeah. It's ready. Take a look."

The Phantom Scripter was a person unknown who had recently played a joke on the anchorman, Jack Roberts. By changing the teleprompter, the Phantom Scripter tricked Jack into saying pretty stupid, embarrassing shit.

"I thought that was over."

"Not at all. The Phantom's unstoppable," said Cat. "Look!"

The screen showed a picnic cookout in sunny Langston Park. There were tight shots of food, steaks and buns. Doug heard Jack Roberts's voice. "The public filet show had everybody smacking their lips," he said. "Yes, sir, filet show. A show of filets! It's not everyday our viewers can watch experts fellate such big, smooth, mouthwatering slabs of meat . . ."

Cat Barnum started laughing midsentence which made it hard to hear. "It's practically Shakespearean," he said.

"It doesn't make sense!" said Doug.

"Oh? Okay, my bad. Let's do it again. Take two!"

"It's not that well shot," said Doug, as he watched.

Cat froze the picture on a plate of steak. "Doug, are you playing with me?" he said. "'Filet show?' Fellatio? Cock sucking? The Phantom Scripter is getting braver and braver. Jack Roberts, on the other hand, is an idiot. It trended on Twitter, too. In the Cities."

"That's . . . oh, yeah," Doug said. He thought about it. "Ha! Cock sucking, yeah. Yeah!"

"That's really something, getting the words just right, like that," said Cat, letting the rest of the video play. "That's not easy to do!"

"Yeah, cuz that's what fellatio means," Doug said. He laughed at the idea of the famous anchor saying that in public on a public show on television. He slid the edit room door shut. He was sensitive sometimes about a high-pitched component to his laugh, which could become embarrassing at times. "Filet show! Fellatio!"

"Those phony Cambodian villages, though," Cat said, in a somber tone. "That was crass. I don't buy that kind of shit."

Doug didn't know what he was talking about. Who cared.

"That's just crazy to say that about cock sucking out loud on TV! Who would do that? Was Jack, like, embarrassed to death? Did he say, 'Folks, I'm sorry for saying cock sucking? Oooops, I just said it again!'"

"Take your time. Breathe deep. Sit down," Cat said.

"Whoooo!"

"You have a mercurial personality, Doug. Pretty awesome!"

"What Cambodian villages?" said Doug, wiping his eyes.

"A bunch of them. Sexist shit. Sexual innuendo but not the funny kind, because demeaning."

"Oh, yeah. Yeah! I remember! That's right! Funny!"

"Only to some."

The mood in Cat's edit room cooled down pretty suddenly. Blacks were often touchy for reasons unknown. The Phantom Scripter was either funny or he wasn't, Doug thought. So you were in for a penny, in for a pound, no matter what, like they said back in Eveleth. Doug slipped out the sliding door and scoped the newsroom. Tammy was still pretending to work on something, holding some papers, and sucking up to Tanya Thorpe. It was no good without batteries. He popped back in on Cat.

"I gotta get back to work," said Cat.

"I know. Great. Do you suppose you could run in and get me some batteries, Cat? The big Anton Bauers?"

"What the hell are you talking about? Get your own!"

"But that's where I can't!" said Doug. "There's reasons why that's an impossibility! Help a guy out!"

"No," said Cat. "Take some responsibility. Christ!"

"If that's the way it has to be," Doug said, in a low voice meant only for he himself to hear. "Will do." He was close enough to the glass to see his own reflection. Every chiseled feature of Doug's face was highlighted in a dramatic way. "Looks like we'll have to do it my way," Doug said. He liked his tone and hoped Cat had heard him. "Will do."

"'Anton Bauer,' you ever think that's probably a real guy?" Cat said.

"What? No. I did not." Doug adjusted his hair in his reflection.

"I mean, the guy who makes the batteries. That's his name. 'Anton Bauer.' You know, Doctor Scholls was a real doctor. He had a lot of historic importance. Most people aren't aware. In school at roll call: 'Anton Bauer?' 'Here!' And all the time he's thinking up batteries. Unbeknownst."

"Who . . ."

"Kleenex, Band-Aid, that's a whole different ball game," said Cat.

"It's weird to even think that bullshit."

"I wonder, you know. What about the old names? Hamilton-Beach, Procter-Silex, Remington-Rand. These are facts from another era, like it or not."

"Okay," said Doug.

The bright lights of the newsroom could be a sobering sight to a person who didn't watch his step. You could imagine it was like a stage where everybody else was the audience sitting around and watching every step a person made every single moment of the livelong day. The whole world was maybe like that. You had to read between the lines and be watchful since everyone was watching you.

For instance, Doug sometimes saw Cat Barnum at the Chute nightclub. That was no big deal. He himself went. However, Cat danced with *men*. You could add two and two about that: The Chute was a gay bar and Cat always danced with the same white guy. It didn't take a genius. Cat here was pretty much a known homo. That was a pretty safe bet.

Mostly, who cared, except with Doug now in the same room for an extended period, with hardly anything but accent lights to see by, you had to wonder. You had to, that is, except that Doug liked nothing but gals, so no worries.

"Crosley," Cat said, in a low voice. "Ingersoll. Bell and Howell. You ever think about it, those had to be people too. Wife-and-kids. Petty squabbles, love and hate, hectic home life. You name it. Now they're on eBay. Such is life."

"You're too cooped up, is what," said Doug, as outside the newsroom activities dragged on.

"Consider this, Doug Pepper," said Cat. "You provide the raw material of a broadcast. But I hone it, and refine it down to a coherent state required by the WEE-TV audience. You need to have a congenial environment for it to happen. Like this is."

Doug's cell chirped. "Shit!" It was Seth Pederson.

"The desk? That's the trouble with those things, they work," said Cat. "Another reason I don't shoot."

Doug was gone without bothering to slide the door shut.

Chapter 4

Some really big shit was coming down.

Bob Tratcher, WEE-TV News director, was on needles and pins as he stood in Vern Balstad's office. Bob wanted to check the time. But, naturally, the minute he looked at his watch, Vern Balstad would misinterpret and interrupt the meeting and say something snarky, sure as shit, right in front of everybody. Bob rubbed the crystal of his watch with his right index finger and looked out the window toward the pigeons sailing across the street. The minutes ticked away to the beat of his Rolex.

Steve Cooney sat in one of three chairs in Vern's little office. Leave it to him to get the luxury accommodations. Steve had brought *Excavator Wars*, a cheap little reality series featuring hydraulic shovels, to the Twin Cities. Souped-up Caterpillar excavators, and Kobelcos, and Komatsus, from Japan, competed for supremacy in an arena that was really a Louisiana swamp. They'd swing at each other like mechanical dinosaurs until one capsized or fell apart. The show made big money for the station. The viewers loved it. Cooney deserved a chair if anybody did, even with old Bonnie Lee Thayer perched on the armrest.

Tubby Chet Flory shifted his butt. He was the CFO and he knew how to say "yes." That was it.

Bob Tratcher rubbed his naked forearm. He glanced at the blue babe with the forked tail. Sometimes he wished he could get that tattoo changed. It was a little sick, when you thought about it. That tail made her part animal any way you looked at it.

"Got some place to be, Bob? We keeping you from something?"

"No, sir, Vernie! Not at all! Got me a little smut on the crystal of my watch, here." Bob rubbed his watch face with his thumb. Goddamn Vern never missed a chance to carp. Bob dropped his arms to his sides and grinned, feeling stupid.

"Jesus," Vern Balstad said, and rolled his eyes.

Things had been very different in the National Guard, naturally, where Bob was a first sergeant and Vern was nothing but a weak-ass private. Bob loved the Army and mostly he loved being a recruiter. Bob would offer some farm boy, say, "Tank Maintenance" and watch his freckled face light up. Sadly, those assignments were provisional, as the contract the kid would sign clearly stated. And that new recruit, like as not, was headed for the no-frills infantry, any way you cut it.

"Well, I think we can get started," Vern said, at last.

Bonnie Lee had waddled in a good fifteen minutes ago. There'd been no Earthly reason for this endless wait, Bob Tratcher thought, except that Vern needed an audience as he lit his fucking pipe. He lit it now—slowly, of course. "You are the lucky few," Vern said, slowly, "in as much as right now what I'm gonna show is hush-hush. Foster Kleizer and his herd of sheep think they'll be first to get a peek. But, oh no. That's where they're way off base. Because they're not seeing anything 'til tomorrow a.m.!"

Vern's dinky office swirled with a haze of blue pipe smoke. Bonnie Lee coughed daintily. Bob leaned against the bookcase. He hadn't seen the new news promo yet though you'd think as news director he'd have had a preview long before this. Vern never asked him anything. So be it. Bob knew he was mainly a cheerleader anyway. It was okay. Vern came through with the gig just when that recruiting brouhaha was heating up, and saved Bob's butt.

There was only the one TV in Vern's office. It was an antique, a floor model, complete with cathode-ray.

"Okay, now," Vern said. He punched the remote and there was a shifting of bodies as everyone maneuvered to see the screen. "Give it a second," he said.

On screen, a helicopter, with WEE-TV in huge red letters dropped into view and landed. The two new reporters—Greta and Bud—jumped out smiling.

Next came a scene in the WEE-TV newsroom showing Greta and Bud smiling and looking important. They were talking, but all you could hear was a jingle.

"This is the crew that knows what's news,
This is the news crew that brings it to you,
These are the journalists who know what to do,
WEE stays on top of the news,
WEE stays on top of the news,
WEE stays on top of the news!"

Next a handsome new logo spun around. "Do you ever wonder what's happening when the cameras aren't looking? So does WEE!"

That was it.

"That's a sweet thirty seconds," said Vern.

Everybody cheered. Bob Tratcher opened his mouth to join but he didn't make a sound. Something was wrong here, he thought, possibly the grammar.

* * * * *

"Well, well, well," said Bonnie Lee Thayer. "That's quite a production, I must say. Any special reason I wasn't consulted?"

Vern emptied his pipe and cleared his throat. "Not at all, Bonnie Lee," he said. "Other than the utmost secrecy. You'll be brought up to speed before the roll out. But in a nutshell the Kleizer deal commands quite a little spiff if the numbers jump prior to closing. Heinrich Schermer and Associates counseled circumspection, of course. My hands were tied."

"Who?"

"The investment banker."

"Oh. Sure."

"Glad you approve."

"I'm . . . *ecstatic,* Vern," said Bonnie Lee.

"The helicopter and the news vans and the rest of that ENG are a real bonanza for everyone on the management team, Vern," said Steve Cooney, beaming. "As I said yesterday."

"Thanks, Steve," said Vern. "There's the kind of enthusiasm I like to see!"

"Well, you got it on this end!" said Steve.

The Schermer people had warned Vern there'd be some splashback when he rolled out the tweaks. Always a glum group, his senior staff now looked as grim as the day Vern Senior died, not a single person thinking about the future, but instead mooning and moping about the past. Vern would've fired the lot of them way-back-when, if, that is, the old man had given him half a clue how to run the goddamn place.

"Chet," said Vern, "don't be a stump on a bump, let's have a little feedback here!" Chet Flory was drifting toward horizontal on the carpet. He'd have been asleep in no time without Vern to rattle his cage. Vern had blindsided the poor old fart, of course, having failed to consult Chet on the relevant financials. Obviously, with Schermer on board, there'd been no need.

"Uh, well, Vernie. There's a whole lot there. Quite a little bit I'm not fully familiar with," said Chester Flory. "Our logo on the 'copter gets me puzzled. Does it mean ownership? If so, you've got a massive expenditure in house. I'll need to think about that. The insurance alone . . . the exposure . . . well, I'd have appreciated a heads up."

"An 'A' for the day, Chet," said Vern. "Schermer said we needed an asset. Something fungible. Not the elevator you insisted we go whole-hog on, and for why? That's a below-the-line item, see, really indistinguishable from the building itself in valuational terms, which, as opposed to a full-scale remodel, is unrecoupable, doesn't do squat on resale. See?"

"Well, *safety*, Vern. I just wish we'd talked. A canny tax strategy would have . . ."

"I've been real busy, Chet, not that you've noticed," said Vern, digging with his pipe for the last of the tobacco. Once again, Flo had missed the mark and the humidor was all but empty. He sprayed the bowl with his butane torch and the smoke curled around his nostrils with a pleasant sting. "I don't really have the time anymore to lead this company by the hand!"

"A helicopter has a certain promotability, of course," said Bonnie Lee, breaking the silence. "Though as a tool for news reporting I'm afraid they come up short in most cities. That's been my experience."

"Wasn't that the era of pre-motorized flight, you and the Wright boys, BLT?" Vern said, with a hearty chuckle. He glanced at Alva Avery of HR, who'd arrived early enough to find a chair. There had been rumblings of trouble. Vern's hearty good humor had been misconstrued on occasion by persons who so far had chosen to remain anonymous. "I'm just real disappointed is all, on a real human level, in performance, and notwithstanding any implications of . . . any other kind."

Not cuz of you, Steve," Vern said, quickly. "You've been doing bang-up in every way, shape, or form. Top drawer."

Vern had informed Steve of most of the particulars weeks ago. A solid rainmaker like that required deep schmoozing. Steve's latest coup was *"Snackers,"* an hour-long syndicated filler that featured five dot-com geniuses who'd lost their shirts in the downturn but were trying to run a restaurant and make their fortunes back. The gag was they all had shitty personalities on account of them being clueless nerds. They insulted suppliers, and they dissed their best customers, and each other, like little Larry Davids, only worse, and didn't even get it.

Plus, it was Steve Cooney who came up with the new Channel 3 News motto: *"What happens when the cameras aren't looking!"* which he probably stole from some reality show or other.

"Before Steve," said Vern, "we were running CBN all night just to make ends meet." Vern smiled a friendly smile at his sales manager. "Steve saw *Snackers* coming before anybody! And he made sure we had it locked down. He got Tony Robbins and Lawn Lion, too. And you know what, he's going to help us knock ol' uptight Hal Parsons on his ass! We whip Channel Five, ladies and gentlemen, and we'll be up to our asses in bonus checks when the Kleizer deal closes, believe-you-me! Right, Steve?"

"Thanks, Vern. If I may add my two cents?"

Vern nodded warily. Steve had pulled out his phone and had been blatantly texting, or maybe playing *Words With Friends*, and that raised a question or two in its own right. "I'd just like to second the motion, here, Vern," said Steve. "I like it, what you've shown us. I'm fired up. We got the ball. I know we're all going to run with it!"

Vern smiled through his teeth. He waited but there were no more comments. "Good. Okay. Thanks, Steve. You heard him. He's saying what I pretty much already said. So, good! Let's get to it. We're a ship on a bounding main. Bounding along. Just like, it's, see . . . you got to give it the old heave-ho! All hands to the pump! Ring out those golden eggs for once! Now, get outa here!"

Chapter 5

"DO YOU STILL LIKE HIM?" said Tammy Bailey.

Tammy and Tanya were standing side by side and paging through the Riverside Development plan without taking any of it in. Tammy still had Doug Pepper's rude behavior on her mind. The poor little girl had been very, very hurt by Doug's thoughtless treatment, though it was a week ago. Well, she was a little trooper, anyway, thought Tanya. She'd grow from it.

"I think he still likes you," Tammy said, as she smoothed the big fold-out map of the Riverside shoreline, which neither of them cared about at all.

"Shush, honey, we're working," said Tanya. "Anyway, he'll hear you. He's talking to Seth right this minute!"

"He is?"

"Don't look up! He's spending less and less time in his car. And suddenly he and Seth are best pals. He gets in and parks his big butt on Seth's desk first thing. Every day. It's a pattern."

"He should be on a story."

"I'd almost say he's figured out how to kiss ass, but he doesn't have the discipline. Or the imagination. Don't look up!" Tanya kept her head down. "He's looking this way."

"I think he's a stalker. Anyway, he isn't a good man."

"Oh, Tammy. He hurt your feelings. He isn't a bad person. Just thoughtless, self-centered, boring."

Tammy giggled. Tanya joined her. They both needed a good laugh. The last few weeks had been very hard.

Tanya had said nothing about her feelings to Tammy but she was terrified by the big changes occurring in the newsroom. None of the new hires, for instance, made any sense. The place was headed toward fluff. That was obvious. Unless, of course, she was just overreacting. Maybe things would turn out fine, because Seth, for one, wouldn't let anything bad happen.

"Why does somebody behave like Doug, Tanya?"

"Well, Tammy, I can't give you an answer. What I can say is Doug Pepper is a very angry person."

"Angry! But Doug never gets mad at anybody, except when he's pretending! He's always smiling! That's the only good thing about him!"

"Keep your voice down. Of course he smiles. That's because he's so afraid. He can never show his true feelings unless he feels very comfortable with you. Then, look out!"

"Oh!"

"You see? It's such a sad irony, Tammy. As soon as he really likes you, bam! He's hateful!"

"But you said he isn't a bad person."

"Oh, honey. He isn't. Don't think that. He's just like so many of them, a big kid in a grown man's body. He's actually a scared little boy in many ways. Truly. But I'm no mommy."

"Well, he sounds terrible."

Greta B. Jones, looking windblown and confident, had just come in with photographer Red Bertram. Well, Greta at least had every reason for confidence. Vern Balstad himself had hired her, so it was said, straight out of Orlando, without even checking with Bob Tratcher, who was in the newsroom less and less these days. Greta had short blond hair, a narrow face and red, red lipstick highlighting a toothy smile. She was actually pretty in an aggressive, wolfish sort of way. And she seemed to fit the profile of the new WEE-TV reporting style, having made her name working undercover in a Minnie Mouse suit. The occasion was Disney World's "gay day." She fired up the Christian-right fringe and bam! She was an instant star in central Florida.

"Don't look now!" said Tammy. Doug Pepper sped by so close Tanya could smell him. "Must be a fire someplace, huh?" said Tammy, watching Doug gallop up the stairs. "But he does look good in those tight shirts."

"He's too old for you. You said it yourself. Way too old."

"I don't mean for *me*, silly!" said Tammy.

But Tanya wasn't listening anymore. Suddenly there was a tension in the newsroom. Something was up. Seth ran his long fingers through his thinning hair, a nervous tic that meant breaking news. Tanya's heart raced. It looked like Red and Doug were the only available shooters but that would be okay. She'd handle either one.

Bud Vanderpein, that other reporter newbie, scooted up to Seth's desk and stopped, interrupting Seth just when he needed to concentrate. Bud was a show-boater and no serious journalist. Seth's shoulders were hunched and his forehead was shiny. Bud Vanderpein's head, just inches away, bobbed up and down like a star athlete getting the touchdown play from the coach. Tanya felt the blood drain from her face.

A fraction of a second later Bud was out the door and up the stairs.

The air seemed to go out of the cramped basement. Seth walked to the bank of monitors and turned them all on. Oh, this was going to be a big one.

Tammy watched Tanya, but stayed quiet. Tanya forced herself to look at the big map she was supposed to be studying. It was colorful. There would be lots of shops, here on the west side of the Mississippi, just south of the Hennepin Avenue Bridge. This was Councilman Del Hammer's project wasn't it? He was such a funny little man, a preposterous gadfly. She should call him. Maybe she'd get an exclusive. For a moment she caught Tammy's eye and it was almost too much. She couldn't really pretend this was fine. She wiped her eyes but it was no good. "Excuse me," she said. She ran down the hall to the ladies' lounge, an artifact almost unchanged from the ancient days when the WEE-TV building was really a theater. Tanya let herself understand that she would no longer be the reporter with the plum assignments, gathering the news in short order, writing clear, concise copy and delivering a live report with calm authority. She looked in the mirror and watched the tears come.

Tammy came into the bathroom and stood beside Tanya. "That should be you," she said. "Instead of Bud, I mean."

Tanya grabbed Tammy and held her close. Maybe there was something she could have done. Maybe she was too assertive. Maybe she had crossed an invisible line and sealed her fate. The new WEE-TV promos used the phrase, "What happens when the camera isn't looking!" It was on billboards and buses. The very concept was absurd. If the camera wasn't on, then you didn't have TV. But the public was buying it, and the ratings were crawling upward.

"It's quite a dangerous time, Tammy," Tanya said. "Because I just don't know where I am anymore."

Chapter 6

Bud Vanderpein had floored it. He was passing everything on the freeway. It was Doug's job to drive, of course. A reporter behind the wheel was an unwelcome, unexpected shift in the scheme of things, in Doug's view. Bud should be staring uselessly out the passenger-side window and maybe searching the dial for Freddie Mercury.

"*And another one down, and another one down . . .*" Doug sang to himself, as he watched another ramp fly by. The tune wasn't coming to him. He turned on the radio, which was playing "Stairway to Heaven." "There's cops through here, you know," he told Bud.

"I'm concentrating, Doug."

"That's good. Concentrate on not hitting that Nationwide. You're doing fucking eighty."

Doug examined his backpack. He shook his head. It was the same snarl of mic cords and connectors and crap. At this speed they'd be at the airport before he untangled shit.

"Captain Max, he does this live shit all the time, right?" said Doug.

"*I* do it all the time," Bud said.

"Oh. Then you're familiar with the hook-up."

"That a question? Obviously."

Doug breathed a sigh of relief. The smug bastard probably set up live shots from the helicopter in his sleep. Doug hadn't ever done it and consequently didn't have a thought about how to make things work. Seth's little lecture on the subject, though it was less than an hour ago, hadn't sunk in at all.

"Great. I'm a little new at this, Bud. So it's just XLR jack into female plug on the onboard mixer, then."

"Yup."

"Great. And we got a guy on Rosehaven's water tower? Throwing beer bottles and shit?"

"You know as much as I do," said Bud.

"How'd he even get enough beer up there, I wonder. That's got to be tough-going up a ladder."

"Like I say, I'm driving now."

Doug repeated Bud's snarky remark in a mocking manner, but only in his head. Then, "Real sorry you can't answer a simple question while driving too fast."

"If we don't get there while the guy is still on the tower we don't have shit, Doug," said Bud. "I'm guessing every cop and his uncle Harry is talking him down. Trying to. Pretty soon, the guy'll listen to reason. That's the odds we're up against here. So let's shut the fuck up and do our jobs. That sound like a plan?"

Whoa! Doug felt a sudden, exhilarating rush of excitement! Here was his long-missing, much-lamented nickel stash hidden at the very, very bottom of his pack! Doug fished out the fat bag of leaf from under the tightly snarled-up mess. Oh, wow! As god was his witness he could not remember putting it here! And now he was holding this jumbo baggy of premium quality Zombie Triple-Threat! A gentle squeeze proved it was as fresh as that day in the park. That stuff wasn't cheap, either. You had to wonder how a serious person could forget something important and just go on with their life as though everything was cool. But all that was water under the bridge and maybe he was meant to find it only at a certain time when it mattered most.

The cords were still fucking tangled incomprehensively but now Doug had a little perspective. Maybe the stash was like fate saying, "Hey, Doug, don't forget we're on your side!"

Doug re-secured the weed deep under all the crap, which was actually a great place to hide it. Many a night tooling around and around just to keep Bill and Ruby happy he could have used a little herb when the cupboard was bare.

"What was that you were saying?" said Doug.

"What?" said Bud.

"Did you ever realize our poor human understanding fails to realize the forces for good that lie hidden in wait for the chance to pop up and lend a helping hand on a rainy day and you'd never even know except it's there when you need it?" said Doug.

"Jesus," said Bud.

"Yeah, Him or any of them."

You could invent a game, Doug thought. "Loop the Loop," call it, and you'd be on the clock with lots of tangled cords and you had to get them straight, though sometimes it was impossible.

Bud took the ramp into St. Paul, and they crawled through downtown. They made up some time on the bridge, and then followed the side road along the Mississippi to Holman Field. The gate was open and suddenly there was the 'copter, all shiny on its platform. Captain Max was climbing up the side of it, messing with something. He dropped back down, and the blade dipped toward him and started to turn in a lazy way. Max waved at Doug and Bud. They parked and came out of the car to unpack.

The chopper wasn't all that big. It was a Bell Jet Ranger but not the twin turbo. Doug had smoothed out a couple cords and was pretty sure they'd work.

"Give me that shit," said Bud. He took Doug's pack.

Doug helped him pull cords, and he surreptitiously took out his baggie of grass and slipped it in his jacket. "Need to tap a kidney, chief," Doug said, throwing a thumb toward the waiting room, which was only an empty space with a couple of chairs but had a john with a lock.

Inside, he rolled a quick one and smoked as much as he could without undue delay. He saved the butt and glanced out the window. His timing was perfect. He folded the baggie and stepped back out into the breezy glare. He slipped on his dark glasses and gave Captain Max a high sign. "A good day!" he said.

"We're going live, Doug. Don't mess up," Bud said, in an unnecessarily defeatist tone.

Doug refused to take it personally. "You just watch your own self," he said. He had flown in the helicopter once, when a barn blew up in Shakopee and then something had happened and they'd missed the shot for some reason.

If Bud had connected things right Doug wasn't going to be much more than a passenger on this flight. The camera would just ride his shoulder, which would be cool.

Doug buckled into the back seat and looked at the pavement. The helmets had intercoms and Captain Max joked. Doug clicked on and said, "No shit!" in a humorous way and everybody laughed.

The blades began spinning and the thing started shaking but no one freaked. Doug remembered you had to trust professionals and that included pilots. They had the most to lose if things flew apart because guess who got blamed. The camera tugged at Doug's arm, and he noticed the asphalt speeding by and then the chain-link fence was underneath and the river and suddenly part of downtown St. Paul was flowing below them and everything seemed fine. He Instagrammed a couple shots on his phone.

St. Paul was flat. They were headed west over trees and houses and businesses and lakes. Some lakes were completely surrounded by houses. If you didn't happen to live on that lake there'd be no chance you'd know it was there.

Someday, Doug thought, he'd like to do a story about that. Sometimes people airbrushed off the lakes so they were secret and got sold in black markets to rich fuckers. It was pretty insidious. He thought about bringing Bud in as a partner.

"You connected up?" said Bud.

"Huh?"

"We're not getting bars. What's going on, Doug?"

"Oh!" Doug flipped a switch and sure enough color bars bloomed on the screen.

"We're in Rosehaven," said Captain Max. "Right now."

"Give me a count, Bud," said Doug.

"One, two, three, four."

"And I'm reading you loud and clear. How about the station?"

"We're cool," said a voice over the intercom. This was no different than any other live shot only a whole lot sexier. Doug glanced out the window and thought he saw a little bar he'd been to just off the parkway, though he wasn't sure.

"Heads up, everybody, there's the crazy!" said Captain Max. The water tower was green and faded and looked like a giant mushroom. They were far enough away to see all the cars and people underneath. Doug felt butterflies. He wasn't used to this. There would be a whole lot of people watching and who knew what they'd be thinking. People were very unpredictable. Take a look at this poor sap. The helicopter was maybe a couple hundred feet from the tower now, and the guy on top was sitting on a blanket with his shirt off.

"Like a day at the beach," said Captain Max.

"How far away are you, chopper one?" said a voice on the radio.

"Oh, god! It's Tratcher!" said Bud.

"Why's he on?" Doug said.

"We're breaking into Ellen, is why," said Bud.

"'Chopper one'?" said Captain Max, in a humorous tone. "Somebody tell him we only have one chopper. This is the bird," Max said on the radio, "Looks like we're about ready up here. What's our mark?"

"Uh. About five minutes," Bob Tratcher said. "Next break."

"Sounds good. You guys ready?"

"Nobody said we were breaking into Ellen," Doug said.

"Look it," said Bud. "How about you aim the camera and let Max and me take the lead on this. Okay? You just aim. And no problems."

"No. Sure. No."

"Doug," said Captain Max, "sorry if this got thrown at you. We're going to approach the tower, and Bud will unclip if it's safe. Bud'll be free to join our friend on his blanket and, assuming the kid's conscious, we'll get a talking head. Thought you'd been briefed."

"All you need to know, Doug," Bud said, "is stay wide. Max, we thought Red was doing this but his camera's down. Which is why . . . this."

"Gotcha!"

"I don't know, guys," Doug said. "Seems like this is a little chancy. So far off the ground and all."

"Maybe you didn't notice this harness I was putting on? Do your part and we'll be fine," said Bud.

Doug stuck his camera out the window, and the station said the picture was fine. The chopper tipped abruptly and the engine roared. "Gaining a little altitude here, fellas," said Max.

"No worries."

Captain Max came around the tower again. "That's our man," said Bud. "Taking a little breather."

"Guess he's out of bottles," Doug said.

The kid was skin and bones, Doug thought. He must have been a real climber, though. But he was all spread-eagled now. The station started feeding programming through the headset. Doug heard about Cialis.

"Ready?" said Bud.

"Sure thing," said Doug. "I'm a go, Max." Doug was starting to sweat through his shirt. He licked his lip.

"Coming to you in ninety," said Bob Tratcher.

"Max," said Bud, "when I let myself down, and tell you, you pull back until you see the tower in frame and just hang there. I'll do my song and dance with what's-his-name and then we're out. You come back and I'll clip on and we're free. Maybe we give our boy a lift if he doesn't smell like shit. Mike test, Doug?"

The needle was banging in the red.

The commercials ended and there was "News Bulletin!" on the little monitor.

"The following is an exclusive W-E-E Television News Presentation. The Minneapolis suburb of Rosehaven is the scene of a dramatic standoff between police and twenty-four-year-old Randy Nadler, who is camped atop the municipal water tower. Mr. Nadler had been in contact with police via cell phone, but that communication has ceased for now. Police say they're unclear on what Mr. Nadler's demands, if any, might be."

"Steady, steady," said Tratcher, even though Doug was rock solid and it should have been obvious to everybody.

"These pictures are from the WEE-TV Sky-High-Eye, now on the scene." Ned the noon anchor was talking. It must be his big chance, Doug thought, getting on this late in the afternoon. "As you can see Mr. Nadler appears to be somewhat under the weather, just now, lying in an apparently collapsed state on top of the tower. But earlier today he was shouting and tossing beer bottles into the parking lot below the tower. Our Bud Vanderpein is in the Sky-High-Eye, which is providing our live picture. What's happening, Bud?"

The chopper tipped toward the tower but Doug stayed with the scene. There was the blanket and the half-naked guy on his back. Doug pulled wide to show most of the top of the water tower and then zoomed in again.

"Yes, Ned," said Bud, "as you can see we are within yards of the tower right now. From here, I'd say Mr. Nadler may be disoriented at the moment. That's a question we should be able to answer shortly. For the record, his protest, if that's what it is, began some four hours ago when he climbed 200 feet up the Rosehaven water tower here, which is situated adjoining the Rainbow Foods parking lot, and is protected, though obviously not well enough, by a Cyclone fence topped with barbed wire."

Captain Max brought the Jet Ranger closer and closer to the tower. A gust dropped the ship a couple feet and scared the hell out of Doug but he held the camera steady anyway. Bud didn't miss a beat.

"Weather's a little choppy up here, Ned, but let me explain what's about to transpire. Captain Max is maneuvering into position so that I can step onto the tower, unhook from my safety harness, and then have what we hope will be an intimate and revealing talk with Mr. Randy Nadler."

The helicopter calmed down. Doug could barely hear it now and its jumpiness subsided. He stayed wide on the tower until his instincts told him to get a shot of Bud and so he slowly panned off the tower and focused on the chopper doorway where Bud was unclipping the harness and stepping down onto the tower. It was a perfect shot. You could see Bud and even some buildings in the background.

"Now, Ned, some of our viewers may be surprised at our interest in Mr. Nadler and his story. But before we dismiss him as simply part of the crackpot fringe, let's hear his side unfiltered by anything but our live microphone. It's news that's fast, fresh and focused!

"I'm now standing on the tower, as you can see, and as the chopper pulls away, we'll just see what Mr. Nadler has to say."

The chopper moved back slightly, and Doug adjusted so that Bud and the whole tower were visible. Bud stopped talking after grunting down from the door. The silence stretched for a considerable amount of time. There was Bud in the viewfinder. There was Randy Nadler's towel and blanket and backpack. There were some antenna-things for cell phones. But Bud was alone on the tower.

Doug zoomed in on Bud. Bud's mouth opened but no words came out. You couldn't hear it but he might have said, "Fuck" if you read his lips.

Chapter 7

"CHOPPER TOPPLES TOWER SITTER," said the *Minneapolis Star Tribune*. The *St. Paul Pioneer Press Dispatch* had a similar banner headline. "MAN DIES IN FALL: WEE-TV COPTER BLAMED."

Both papers used the same picture. Randy Nadler's high school yearbook. In the *Strib* another little picture, from the TV, had Bud with his mouth open. "Stranded above it all," the caption said. It sounded snarky.

Doug sat at home with the papers. Somebody must have liked the story. It went on for pages in both papers. The *Star Trib* even gave the tower a half-page shot. Some arrows showed Randy Nadler's fatal path from the top down to the fence he hit.

Doug watched TV and played a CD but he couldn't concentrate.

There was a book *WEE-TV Personnel Directory*. He fished it out from a drawer. It even had the new people in it.

Here was, "Thorpe, Tanya." "Jones, Greta B."

"Hello?" Doug said. "Is this Greta?"

Some sorrowful hillbilly song was playing in the background. "Yes," she said. "This isn't Doug Pepper, is it?"

"Hi," he said, with a catch in his throat. "'Scuse me."

"Oh, brother, are you calling the wrong person," said Greta.

"Hmmmm?"

"Like I say, this isn't going to work. I'm going to hang up."

"Oh, no! I . . ."

Such flat-out rudeness was unexpected. In a way, though, it fit. Weeks ago, when Greta was new, they'd had a drink. Doug took her home and things got steamy—sort of a "welcome wagon" thing—because she probably needed a little consolation for being new. To be fair, Doug remembered, it got a little out of hand and pretty perverted counting some bites, fluids dripping all over, complaints from the neighbors. Nothing to be proud of.

They'd been pretty shy around each other since, though that shouldn't really hinder friendship in its deeper sense, especially in a time of need. Yet here it was: Greta maybe had unresolved issues, Doug thought.

"Greta . . ."

"Look, I'm very sorry about what happened to you, but I'm not willing to have a discussion with an individual who's been so destructive to the company."

Doug laughed at how stupid that sounded though his humor made him want to bash her head in.

"This is not about anything else, Doug," Greta said. "We're two ships that passed in the night. It was fun while it lasted, but I'm a big girl now, who makes her own decisions and moves on. So just get that out of your mind. I'm not willing to have this discussion."

It was possible, after all, that she was crazy as a bat, Doug thought. "Well, you're a real piece of work," he said, and hung up before she could. Maybe she was a drinker.

It was dark out now and under the window an old lady he'd seen before made her way along the sidewalk like a cripple. It shouldn't be allowed, he thought, for someone that messed up to be out alone.

He could call Cat Barnum. There he was. "Barnum, Cat." That would be fraught with consequences. He was plain and simple a homo, and a known one, at that.

He dialed Thorpe, Tanya, a number, which he almost remembered except a few digits. She answered on the first ring. "I didn't know if it was you at first," he finally said, "or a message. Then it turns out it's you! Like, live! Ha, ha! Hi! Hello!"

"Doug," Tanya said, after considerable quiet.

"Yeah," he said, and his eye twitched.

"Channel 3's a leaky ship, wouldn't you say?" she said, in a casual tone, as if she was already halfway through the conversation.

"I don't know. 'Leaky ship'?"

"C'mon, Doug," Tanya said. "Vern, Bob, Bonnie Lee, Chet Flory? Don't pretend you're unaware."

"I don't know those higher-ups."

"Don't act like a child. Take some responsibility!"

Doug's life lacked compassion and warmth, he could see. Here was a good example. Tanya was busy suddenly attacking him, and all he'd done is dial her up to maybe shed a tear over that guy Nadler, and, sure, maybe she could say it wasn't his fault what happened, and he was as much a victim as anybody, which he was.

"All I'd like is a little talk," Doug said. "Just two people who maybe had a little something once, but it's all water under the bridge. You know? Nothing's left but a little bit of caring for each other. And a sympathetic ear."

"Doug, I'm probably not the person."

"But there's nobody else, I don't think," Doug said.

"Doug," Tanya said, "we talked. Do you remember? We talked and talked."

It was really true. He didn't have anybody. He should have put somebody aside for a rainy day but didn't think of it.

"Oh. Okay," he said.

"Christ! Don't say it like that!"

"What?"

"You're begging! Christ!"

"I'm not. For what?"

"Yes you certainly are. Like a hangdog dog. Like, 'I'm so sad, toss me some scraps, I'm so sad.' Is exactly what you sound like! Exactly. Brother! This is so . . ."

It was always like this with her. One minute she was on his case. The next minute, she was on his case in a different way. "All I wanted was to maybe have a drink and know how you are," Doug said. "I can't help being a little sorrowful about this, if that's what you're implicating."

"Look. We agreed. We keep our distance. No problem."

"Yeah. I see. Sure. I'm getting that from . . ."

"Because I'm not your mommy, Doug. And I'm certainly not your therapist. And I think you need one. And, yeah, I'm on your side, okay? The station's out for ratings and so it pulled this cockamamie stunt, which went all to shit and is using you for a scapegoat. It's obvious. Sure. It's why I picked up when I saw you."

"Yes."

"See? That's your problem! One minute you're Mr. Macho. You turn around and you're suddenly all passive and nicey-nice sort of like a normal person but not really. Who needs it!"

"But just a drink okay. Someplace loud enough you won't notice if I'm whatever!"

"Tell you what: you promise to shut-up, and, maybe. But you drive. And I mean you're the *designated* driver. I'm drinking like a fish if we do this."

"Okay."

"Because I got a lot to forget!"

* * * * *

THE BLACK DUCK WAS A PIT. But it was loud. Doug knew his bars. That was clear. Tanya let Doug lead her through the crowd.

"I'm a man who flunked out of the school of hard knocks and I'm living my life on the rocks . . ."

She recognized the oldie by Chuckie Bigelow. She'd been a whole lot younger when that came out.

"What's so funny?" Doug Pepper said.

"How the mind works," she said.

"You been here before?"

"Nope."

"That's good. I thought you were a nice girl."

"You thought I was a good fuck."

"God you're a hard ass!" Doug shook his head.

Tanya laughed. Somehow they'd freed up enough to talk this way. They were both pretty uptight as a pair, she thought. Maybe they were meant to be friends instead. It was possible.

"You remember how you used to read *Cosmo* at the newsstand?" Tanya said.

"No! I don't even know what that is."

"At the grocery. Every time we went. You stuck your face in *Cosmo*!"

"No way! It's a fag rag!"

"Hah! You do know! And it's a women's magazine, you idiot! It was endearing I always used to think! You had a little bit of sensitivity under that hyper-masculinity."

"Now the truth comes out! You think I'm a closet case."

But she could see he was pleased. The beers flowed and Tanya matched Doug glass for glass. She remembered he always liked chocolate milk because he said it was healthy. Here was a man with a lot of red flags but somehow he was more appealing than not. But you had to set your boundaries. She let the music roll over her.

"I want to say, Doug, I think you're a real professional. When Nadler fell, you didn't lose your shit. You kept thinking. I mean, I watched the way you handled the camera. It was obvious things had gone to hell in a hand basket. But you had nerves of steel, man."

Doug looked a little bleak. He signaled the waitress. He acted like he hadn't heard, but her voice could penetrate the blare of the Wurlitzer, she was sure of that. Doug was just Doug, she thought. She smiled and waited for the beer.

"Word is Bud's going to be charged with something," Tanya said. "Max too. All he did was keep the thing in the air. But that's the FAA for you. They've got to throw the book at somebody to look like they're doing their job."

"That kid died in a real ugly way," Doug said, and he poured a glass from the fresh pitcher. He was glassy-eyed. She topped off her own beer and saluted him. If she was playing Florence Nightingale tonight, she didn't really care.

Tanya sipped her beer and then had another glass. She was getting dreamy, and the amber bubbles racing up the sides of the Wurlitzer were so bright and happy. They were like the Christmas tree lights that bubbled in their little glass tubes. She didn't suppose they made them anymore.

"Did you know Bud Vanerpein did nothing but features in Denver?" she said. "He wasn't hard news at all. *Candid Camera*-type shit. Ghastly."

"*Candid Camera*? It's an old TV show."

"He wired ATM machines so he could talk to the customers and tried to get them to go double or nothing on their withdrawals. Gambling!"

"Wow! Did they go for it?"

"That's not really the point, Doug. It's bad journalism. It's shit. It's playing to the masses. It's venal, and stupid, and it's what Vern Balstad evidently wants to usher in at Double-E."

"Hmmm. Okay. I get that. Sure."

Maybe Doug wasn't a journalist, thought Tanya. But, really, he didn't need to be—not if his heart was in the right place.

"Doesn't seem right to blame him for the chopper, though," Doug said.

"You can rest easy, though."

"Doesn't mean I feel too good."

"But you did your job."

Doug nodded and poured himself another glass. "I've never been a liar," Doug said, out of nowhere. "No matter what. I never lie. Never did."

Tanya let it pass. She was not in a confrontational mood and bygones were bygones. Chuckie Bigalow was getting a workout on the jukebox with another self-pity anthem.

"*Friendless, growing older, with no understanding shoulder I can cry on, I spent a long time looking for the milk of human kindness but it's all gone . . .*"

"Somebody in here must be feeling real sorry for themself," Tanya said.

"Well, it isn't me. I didn't play that," Doug said. He was wasted.

"You wouldn't lie about that would you? Because you never do."

"What?" Doug said. "It's different now."

"What's different, Doug?"

How many pitchers had it been? Tanya couldn't remember if the waitress had been by. As it was there were two, but empty. No. There had been plenty. Lots of others. For sure.

"Truth."

"What?"

"Truth's different."

"Truth? 'Different' you say?"

"Yeah. Sadder, some way."

Oh, fuck. She was such a sucker for that kind of way-out talk. It sounded sensitive. Open hearted. But with Doug there was a good chance it was nothing but mindless prattle. It was the kind of thing that sold her on him the first time: poetic off-kilter talk that was kind of sweet and naïve and vulnerable and what-have-you.

Maybe he was really innocent and unaware. Either way it worked to his advantage when he talked like he was. So he was one seductive bastard who had to be watched.

Goddamn, thought Tanya, it really was a kind of paradox. Let's allow that Doug Pepper was a sensitive man. Okay? In the harsh light of dawn that added up to a big, overgrown baby. That much was true. That was Doug. Big, dumb and helpless. And angry.

The bright lights of the Black Duck warmed. The glare disappeared. Maybe her eyes adjusted. She saw herself as a little girl in the big house in Clinton, Connecticut, not too far from the Sound. She had flannel jammies. She'd snuggle in bed listening to trucks growling all night along the highway a mile away. Four-thirty and faceless men went to New York City. Or Miami. She'd never lost the feeling of romance she'd felt conjuring nighttime worlds of mercury-vapor lamps and mystery in the dark beyond her bedroom. She'd fall asleep cuddled in her warm blanket telling herself stories . . .

The waitress had forgotten them. Doug Pepper seemed to be asleep. "Those fucking reality shows," he said. Tanya didn't know what he meant. He gave her a loopy grin. "'Scuse me," he said, and pushed himself up from the table.

Chapter 8

BONNIE LEE THAYER was missing in action when she should be pouring oil on troubled waters. Vern Balstad stood at his office window. That woman could see what was happening as well as he could. If he had to tell her what to do, then he might as well do it himself. What *that* might be, though, was a big fat question.

The sun was boiling down on the street. Little glitters in the cement made the sidewalk sparkle. Vern watched a pair of tanned girls mince along Ninth, their little butts doing that thing in their short shorts. They had on skimpy teenager tops, which barely hid some sizeable boobies. He put his head against the glass but they turned at LaSalle and that was it. Now the street was empty. There was the Metro. You wouldn't want to be out there. He adjusted himself and sat back down to do some work.

Flo actually had good boobs. Perhaps that was why he had failed to make good on a plan to fire her ass. With HR hiring, any change would be a huge gamble. The intercom squawked.

"What is it?"

". . . Pepper, Vern."

"Let him in."

What was Flo? Forty? Fifty? She had one of those faces. Plus, with make up, there was no telling. Even Bonnie Lee looked good when she remembered to do herself up. Theresa, down at the switchboard, though, now there was a gal! She didn't need Clinique or any of those brands he himself had taken to using for professional reasons. He wondered if she could type or if secretarial work would damage those long fingernails.

They didn't have enough blacks anyway. He'd see what Alva Avery had to say. The door opened. Vern sized up the kid standing there. He was unfamiliar, but run of the mill, the kind Bob Tratcher always hired. The paper hadn't even run his picture or Vern would've recognized him.

This Pepper was dressed more for bowling. Did you bowl in shorts? His t-shirt advertised a comic book. It was a fucking insult, this Pepper coming in like that, and him a photographer for WEE-TV!

"You get that free with your comics?" Vern said.

"Huh? No! We did a live shot at the premier. Just bumps and a voice over, it turned out. Because of that flood on the Cannon."

"Must of shrunk."

"Huh? Oh, no! I've been bulking up pretty good there, sir. That's all right."

Vern was starting to see why there was a disaster in his newsroom on Bob Tratcher's watch. The fool hired fools like this. A muscle-bound dumb bunny in a "t" that hawked comics on company time! Vern lit his pipe and sat back. Doug Pepper rocked back and forth in high-tops. Very hip.

Vern picked up the HR folder. There wasn't a lot in here, just an application. Smudgy. He sucked in the cherry tobacco and let it out through his nose for the pleasant burning feel of it.

"Says here you like, 'carving.' That right?"

"What? No sir! They must—maybe, canoeing?"

"Learn to print. Who cares. You're from what, there, Eveleth?"

"Yes. That's what it says there. Eveleth."

Vern looked up from the paper and studied Pepper. It was a little hard to tell from his tone, but the chances were this idiot was trying to be smart. "Oh, I can read, Pepper," he said. "Trouble is, you can't write."

Doug Pepper shrugged in a noncommittal way, a little smile on his face. He was a smart guy, all right. A dime a dozen.

"You can't write," Vern continued, "and you can't shoot worth shit. Whoa! Guess that knocked the smirk off your face! Another damned upstate food-stamp baby!" Vern was getting a little hot. He'd spilled his pipe but he poured coffee on the embers and they didn't hurt the blotter. He wasn't worried about Pepper. He could take him if he had to. He punched the DVD player and turned on the Magnavox. "Now, let's see if you can tell me," Vern said, calmer now, "what in hell is news about Bud Vanderpein's fat face? All hell is breaking loose around here and you stay on his fat face. Don't think I don't know what's happening!" Vern's voice rose slightly but he kept his feelings in check. "Pay attention now. I wouldn't want you to miss it like you did the first time. See, the chopper moves out from the tower so you can get a shot of what's happening on the ground! And what might that be? Well, it's a guy that hit the blacktop at ninety miles an hour, is what! Better than that, he's half and half because of that fence. But what do you do? You zoom in on that prick on the tower! Even the pilot knew what to do. And he's a rental! And somebody mops up the asphalt and there's nothing left to shoot!"

Vern's breath wheezed and caught in his throat. "The best equipment, Pepper, and a great story made for the bird! How can you fuck it up? No way except the obvious! Use you!"

Vern forced himself to shut up and breath. He took his time and counted awhile. Buzzing little bees. "Bob Tratcher says you're a deadbeat," he finally said. Doug Pepper had turned red. His face seemed to have puffed up, like some sea creature.

"Mr. Balstad," Doug said, "that moment was made for the close-up! Bud, the tragic awareness dawning on his face? Are you kidding? Perfect! You could see the pain—"

"Jump back, you dumb motherfucker!" Vern shouted. He bit his tongue until he tasted blood. "I don't care about Bud Vanderpein's fat face! Nobody cares about his fat face! You get the hell out!"

With Pepper gone, Vern popped an Elavil. He imagined bees buzzing in a summer meadow. What kind of flowers? Think. Poppies and hollyhocks. Yes. The smell. Breathe. He listened to them buzz, buzz, buzz. Pretty soon, his pulse was down, and he felt better. A heart attack was around the corner. He knew better than to get worked up.

Chapter 9

THE MANY BITTER YEARS had yet to fade from memory. Vern Balstad cast a wary eye at the painting of his old man. The image looked back at him with a kind of aggressive disdain Vern hadn't noticed before.

"Flo!"

"What?" said Florence, her voice crackling over the machine.

"Call downstairs right this minute and tell Tratcher that this Pepper is out!"

"Doug Pepper?"

"You're damn skippy! What other Pepper?"

"Fired?"

"That's what 'out' means, Flo!"

"'Fired' means fired, Vern."

Everybody was a smartass now. Alva Avery in HR would earn his keep the next few weeks. Downsizing was in full swing. Flo had just joined the ranks. Again.

* * * * *

LE PEEP HAD A SOLID lunch crowd. Cat Barnum and Tanya Thorpe sat and watched the room thin out. She played with the congealing syrup and remains of a short stack. Le Peep was a refuge from the drama.

"A lot of blood on the floor," Cat said.

"It was just so quick."

"Efficient. I expected Pepper to go. But the others?"

"Somebody said it's a ten-percent reduction. I'll be goddamned if I'm going to let that place turn into a tabloid," Tanya said. "I should have said something."

"Still could," said Cat. "Yo! Tammy!"

Tammy Bailey came in. She was puffy-eyed and weepy. "This is a terrible week," she said, as she sat down.

"Poor kid," said Tanya. She put a hand on Tammy's arm.

Cat wiped his mouth on a napkin. "Prepare to wait if you want to order, Tammy. Not a waiter in sight."

"She knows that."

"I don't want anything."

"This place does great," said Cat, looking at the unbussed tables. "Money people. Bankers, investment types."

"How would you know that?"

"I run in those circles," said Cat.

"Whatever," Tanya said. "We've got to get you something to eat, Tammy honey!"

"I'm not hungry," said Tammy. But she grabbed a fork and gobbled the remains of Tanya's buckwheat cakes.

"She's gonna live," said Cat.

"Yes, she is. Good girl!" Tanya squeezed Tammy's arm. "What's funny?"

"You," said Cat.

"Have you heard one of the Roving Eyes is gone?" said Tanya.

"Yeah? For real? I thought that was a rumor."

"It is, but it's true, too. The paper had it."

A fleet of satellite trucks, called, "Roving Eyes," were part of the new WEE-TV. They were pricey. Each one had full editing facilities on board and a sophisticated microwave system. Vern Balstad bought the fleet to broadcast football and basketball games, Tanya thought, not for news.

"Somebody stole a Roving Eye van?"

"Apparently, Tammy."

"Let me show you guys something," said Cat. He took out his smart phone and held it up. "This's all ready on line!"

"Oh no! The Phantom Scripter again?" said Tammy.

Jack Roberts was looking at the camera with a deep frown. He said, ". . . when flattened to road pizza by a light-blue-and-tan pickup truck . . ."

"Oh, God! How does that stuff get on the air?" said Tanya.

"First off, try hiring an anchor with the smarts not to spout whatever's on the prompter," said Cat.

"Maybe it's a ghost!"

Tammy and Tanya laughed in spite of themselves.

But it wasn't funny somebody had died in a particularly horrible hit-and-run incident, Tanya thought. To call the mangled body "road pizza" was intolerable. The Phantom Scripter was a symptom, Tanya believed, of the sickness that had invaded WEE-TV. But how did the Phantom do it? How did the copy get into the computer system?

"But Bob Tratcher didn't freak?" said Tammy.

"No," said Tanya. "He thought it was good copy."

* * * * *

DOUG PEPPER DREAMED it was snowing. There was so much snow that he couldn't see a thing. The snow didn't scare him. He swam through the flakes like a fish in the air. By willing it, he flew left and right, and up and down. He was moving at lightning speed and he loved it. The flakes pelted him but they were like cotton, and he didn't feel cold at all. Instead, he sailed through the whiteness faster and faster. He wanted something, and he heard a voice calling, but he sped past the sound not catching the words. He could go on forever. He tumbled head over heels, diving, flipping backwards, through the total darkness, for the fun of it. This was no dream, but it was a dream. He saw fir trees lit by the moon. He saw a rolling black ocean with white caps and spray. He woke up.

He was on his sofa. His watch said 9:30. He went to the faucet, and through the window he saw it was raining hard, silver cascades coursed down from the streetlights. He got a glass and gulped a full glass. Up and down the street all the shades were closed. Were they afraid of peeping toms? Who cared about their stupid lives? Yosemite Sam was waiting on the kitchen table. He still held a couple inches of expensive scotch. Doug downed it. Hmmmm! It cleared his sinuses. He poured some more.

Overhead, some loose pipe or gutter was banging as it drained the roof. He knew where the problem was, too. He could fix it as easily now as later. But he stayed in the chair.

It was unexpectedly rotten, getting fired. For no reason, either. Yosemite Sam would have shot somebody. Using his rootin'-tootin' six-shooter! It was a good plan. He took Sam and the bottle and headed for the stairs. He got to the front door of the building and shouldered it open. His car was up the street a block or so. He smiled at Sam and poured another shot and then another. Fortified, he got to his car. His windshield steamed up and he sat there as the blower worked and he put Sam and the bottle between his legs.

Vern Balstad had called him a "food-stamp baby." Mr. Balstad seemed to have a problem with his hometown, Eveleth. It wasn't fair to judge a whole town by one person who used to get food stamps. Doug took some time comprehending and then he drove downtown, looking both ways, and braking a lot.

* * * * *

THE BANKS OF THE MISSISSIPPI were very muddy below Lake Street. Doug stood in the parking lot and contemplated the slope, which was shiny with ivy leaves and little waterfalls glistening in the moonlight. The Roving Eye van was top-heavy, he could see. The satellite dish on the roof threw the vehicle out of balance.

Doug poured a couple inches into his Yosemite Sam glass and sipped in contemplation. Somewhere a dog barked. Mist lowered from the trees. The river sparkled and the currents swirled back and forth.

"Sam, you and me and Jake will have to jump," Doug said. He sat back behind the wheel and drove off the asphalt and nudged the van forward until it angled down toward the water. He waited a couple seconds and stomped the accelerator. The river rushed toward him while the engine roared, and then Doug jumped with Sam and the bottle. He landed on his knees in the mud and saw the huge van hit the water with a splash.

The Roving Eye floated primly into a patch of moonlight. It began to spin, perfectly upright. Doug toasted it with a drink. The Roving Eye tipped to the right as if in response and then dove leaving only a few bubbles and the flat surface of the Mississippi.

"Fuck you, Vern!" Doug said. He could see his breath. He walked to a pizza place and ate a slice and called a cab.

Chapter 10

"YOU KNOW, YOU LOOK LIKE SHIT," Cat Barnum said, through the glass door. Doug Pepper had come down from his apartment in his boxers. He stood in the foyer of the rundown building, looking to Cat like a beached carp. Doug's eyes were puffy. His skin was gray. His mouth was slack. No, Doug didn't look very pretty, Cat thought.

"What the hell are you doing here?" Doug said.

"Open up, damn it! I can see your dick!" It was almost true. "Next time wear pants. Christ!"

"Go home, Cat! It's . . . whatever time it is."

"Let me in, or I'll call the cops! And I think you know why!"

Doug opened up. "What the hell do you mean?" he said.

"Let's continue this in private, shall we?" Cat said.

Pepper's ratty sofa might have spent time on a sidewalk. A nice robot statue and a cheap lamp sat on a stack of magazines. The one Cat could see was "RX Parent." There was only the one room. Cat opened the refrigerator.

"What do you eat? Beer?"

"Stay out of there!"

"It looks like a lab experiment."

Doug didn't answer. He was on the sofa asleep.

He was really puffy, Cat thought, but young enough to retain the appeal he'd need to play the charismatic loser. Cat felt a pang of admiration tinged with a kind of sympathy as he contemplated the prone body. Doug was totally unaware of his own appeal, but he was strong enough and self-centered enough to carry the weight. Yep! Doug Pepper needed no more than a gentle nudge, Cat was sure. He watched the muscular chest rise and fall. Doug would definitely play on YouTube.

* * * * *

"WHAT THE HELL ARE YOU doing here?" Doug said. Cat tensed. He'd put Doug in a calming headlock if necessary.

"You're a mean drunk. You know that?" Cat said.

Doug showed his teeth but didn't say anything.

They were both on the sofa and Cat must have fallen asleep. It was sunny. The lethargy that made Doug seem almost mellow last night was gone. Cat casually slid off the sofa and into a modified wrestling crouch, just in case.

"Let's take a hard look, Doug."

"I didn't invite you. Get out."

"Your name is mud. You've got no job. Looking around, you're behind on the housework. Is it your fault? No! Everybody thinks you got a raw deal, Doug! You're a goddamn scapegoat! But Doug! Listen to me! Don't be blind to the upside!"

"I'm sick of you blowing smoke up my ass, Cat. Get the hell out and leave me alone."

"You got silverfish. Did you know that? Creepy buggers."

"Better than ants. Besides, where?"

"I saw tons. Earlier. They're a night animal."

"Who says?"

"Silverfish are nocturnal."

"I'm up nights. I'd have seen."

"It doesn't matter. The point is you're a friendless, empty shell."

"Wow!"

"But you're also a celebrity. Or will be. And you've got support!"

"I'm a victim. But I've got me."

Cat laughed. "Did you steal that Roving Eye? If so you're more perp than victim, compadre. That's what the cops'll say. Though nobody's judging anyone."

"I don't know about stealing nothing."

"I'm saying 'hypothetically.'" Cat said. "Like, this is the plan: you drive to out-of-the-way places all over the US with this hundred thousand dollar production studio on wheels only we camouflage it as a laundry truck or something. And you do stories from interesting places about interesting people but, see, you're still on the run! Plus, as a real fugitive you're Robin Hood, too, an honest-to-god headline-generating felon, man! You can't buy cooler credentials! You do great cool stories for the Internet! Bingo! You're a hot item!"

"I don't agree with that nonsense," Doug said. "Because I happened to have got fired. Plus, what if there's no van? "

"Hypothetically, there's a van, Doug."

"There's no TV job. And what's more there's no van. No van, at all, Cat. What if it was underwater in a river somewhere? Also, I've got a headache."

Chapter 11

Greta B. Jones reported from Doug's Franklyn Avenue apartment. It looked worse on TV, Cat thought. "They should have lit it," he said. "You can't tell what's what."

Greta B. Jones sounded pretty good. She had a low voice and seemed concerned about Pepper's suspected involvement in the Roving Eye van theft, now getting maximum attention from TV, radio, and newspapers. "The million dollar value of the missing van is in sharp contrast to the squalid quarters occupied by Doug Pepper," Greta said. "The apartment's management company provided us entry and WEE-TV News has learned Pepper was behind in his rent. He has not been seen here for days. Police consider him a prime suspect in the disappearance of the van and say he had a motive. WEE-TV executives have not commented but there are those who viewed Pepper as an irresponsible and mediocre employee!"

"Whoa!" said Cat.

"She does have her claws out," James said.

"You should have seen what she wrote for the six o'clock. She wanted to say his bathroom mirror was streaked, and towels were on the floor. A hatchet job."

"You edited that?" James said.

"I do video, James. Not content. But I made Greta tone it down."

"Not enough."

"Do you do Greta B. Jones's hair, James?"

"Shhhh!" James said. "I'm trying to hear this!"

"If you do, you could charm her, buddy! Who knows what we'd learn!" Cat mussed the younger man's hair roughhouse fashion and then loaned him his lemonade as a peace offering. "Just a sip. You had yours."

Greta and Doug's little affairlet had been common knowledge, and Cat had made sure James was in the loop. So her report was like the juicy second act of an insider melodrama and Cat and James watched fascinated.

"Some who visited him here," Greta intoned, "knew Doug Pepper as a sad, reclusive person, contemptuous of authority, not able to get along with others even when they tried to help. He was uncommunicative even to those who made every possible effort!"

"Ha ha ha ha ha ha!" laughed Cat.

"She's really mean," said James.

"Clues to his whereabouts are everywhere but they are mute and pointless—left to be examined by the police who must make what sense they can of this troubled man's troubled, troubled life."

"That's right, honey," Cat said, "pour it on!"

"Where's your detachment, Cat?"

"What?"

"I thought good journalism was 'detachment.' You're getting too much pleasure from this."

The camera cut to an object on the floor, as Greta said, "On Doug Pepper's floor, a used hairspray. Since he was well known for a pretty boy image, we ask: 'Was it abandoned by Doug Pepper at the moment of escape?' We hope soon to have the answers. This is Greta B. Jones, WEE-Three News, in South Minneapolis."

"Well, I hope you're proud of yourself," said James, in a not unfriendly tone. "I see that you are."

Cat knew better than to confess such a thing. James had, in Cat's view, a moralistic streak. But, as it happened, he was *very* proud. "I don't think Greta could have helped us any more if she'd put a gun to Balstad's head," he said, patting James's knee.

"You know," said James, "you're meddling in people's lives."

"Yep."

"I won't go to jail for this, but you might. You're implicated in some very dicey shit here."

"When costs outweigh benefits, we stop," Cat said. "Hey! I said a sip!"

James handed him the empty glass, smiling. "Thanks."

"Did you notice Greta ignored her own little romance with the fugitive?"

"I didn't notice anything. This is your deal, not mine."

"Aw, honey, admit it. You were transfixed. Plus, you love it. But she should have acknowledged her relationship with Doug. That was unethical."

"The pot has officially called the kettle black," said James.

"Don't bring race into this!" Cat said, grabbing James, and aiming for a joke that somehow veered off toward stupid.

James giggled anyway. "Okay, let's use a more PC metaphor. Let's see, uh, 'your skin, my jizz?' Let's find out . . ." James grabbed Cat and nuzzled his neck. Usually that was enough for some Olympic gymnastics. But, for the moment, Cat was distracted.

"I wonder how she got into Doug's apartment," Cat said, gently holding James at bay. "He gave her a key, do you suppose?"

"No, I don't suppose. She just said the manager let her in. And this is getting out of hand!"

"C'mon, honey!" Cat hugged James hard. "Imagine we're at the top of the grade and the roller coaster is about to free fall! You've earned it! Mr. *Phantom Scripter!*"

"We're not in it for thrills, remember?" James said. "This is social commentary. Or was."

"Yes, yes! We're on the same page, darling! We're making a statement. I know that! But you and I know how to have fun! We've always been that way! C'mon! Let's see a smile. A little one? Please?" Cat took James's face in his hands and brought him close, rubbing their lips together. His tongue traced James's mouth. "A smile like this!"

James laughed and shook his head.

"Okay, okay!"

"That's better! Much better!"

"But just remember though," James said, "hacking is a criminal offense."

"Steve Jobs could have taken lessons from you, baby boy."

Cat remembered with perfect joy James's first hack. The WEE-TV Venus Server flashed, "greetings," as James entered the network, for the first time. At the "login" dialogue, James typed, "guest," and the Venus let him in! For a password, James typed, "C-A-B-A-L."

"How'd you know the password?" said Cat, as the next menu appeared.

"It's a default. CyberKinetics ships everything that way. Any IT security geek worth his salt would change it the minute he unpacked the box. It's a stupid, unforgiveable lapse. A Venus this sophisticated is 100-thousand bucks. At least."

"Lucky us."

"Takes two seconds. Venus has great virus protection and redundancy and all kinds of safeguards against hackers but it's worthless because WEE-TV didn't change 'CABAL.'"

The Venus system proceeded to roll out the red carpet. The whole station was on that network. James immediately made himself systems manager because nobody else had bothered. He wandered through the station's records, reading personnel files, rewriting scripts, checking budgets perusing expenditures. James was wasting his talent doing people's hair, Cat thought. He probably knew more about WEE-TV than Vern Balstad. And James was a great writer too!

"James, " said Cat, "maybe the Phantom Scripter makes a comeback. Huh? Stir the pot?"

"Nope."

"Dude! Yes! You're the modern Shakespeare!"

"There's enough going on."

"All except your only misstep, those 'Cambodian Villages,' which was gross."

James smiled. "A little mild sexism's too much, huh? Hacking's a felony. The FBI, FTC and FCC'll each take a bite of us, cutting us up like a hog on a spit if this ever comes to light. But *you* think 'Bangh Mi Twaht' was a bridge too far? Wow."

"'Cause it's gross, is why," said Cat.

"Care for a whiskey?"

"Sure."

* * * * *

DOUG BARELY KNEW YouTube from AOL. You could put videos on both, he thought, and look at yourself. Beyond that, except for Instagram, his mind was a blank on so-called "social media." He hadn't visited MySpace since he was a kid, and without his own computer Facebook was pointless. And so what? But now he had a cool new iPhone and laptop, courtesy of Cat Barnum.

And, funnily enough, Doug was living in a brand new camper van in Cat's driveway. Minnehaha Creek was only a block away, and the house was huge and Doug walked in any time he wanted to use the kitchen or take a shit or hang out. Of course, Cat and James were there. But Doug kept things professional and neither guy tried any funny business.

The new van had a foldout desk and a comfortable bed, and an original Terry Mollfrey sea serpent mural on the side panel. There was a pirate ship, too, and a moon that lit up the scene. Doug was ready for the road but Cat kept pestering him about uploading and strong passwords and Vine and Facebook as if he were in guerilla TV boot camp.

Tonight, though, was different. Doug was nervous. He was at an apartment building near Menomonie, Wisconsin. It was Cat's idea of a final exam. "St. Clair Arms" was big and unwelcoming and stretched for blocks. There wasn't a single light on.

"You go to a fire you shoot the fire, no questions asked," Cat had said. "It's way too easy! I want you in the driver's seat. I want to see what you got as a producer."

Doug was up to it. He pulled out a compressed-air siren from A-Boy, and his phone.

He held the phone at arm's length and aimed it at himself. "I've got a couple air horns in a bag here," he said. "They make a whole lot of noise. Which isn't very welcome at this time of night. Namely, uh, 2:00 a.m., Central Daylight."

He turned the phone around to face the building and the camera did pretty well through the dirty windshield. "You feel like a crook sneaking up on a place like this with everybody asleep and shit, which is what we're doing, you know. Because we're not breaking in or anything, well, except for the tape I put on the side door so as it won't lock. But I mean, this is an alert for their own good, you could say. Okay?"

Doug got out of the van and started walking, the phone camera setting the scene. "There's a lot of livability in a place like this because it's real nice. I don't know how much you can see the dark. Most of the places have washer and dryers and lots of amenities." He went in the side door. He saw the red fire alarm lever and pulled it. "This is probably better," he said. A clanging bell split his eardrums. "Shit!" He ran through the hallways pressing the air horn siren just in case anyone could have missed the fire alarm.

Chapter 12

Vern Balstad sat at the traffic light. The light changed, but he took a second to refill his pipe bowl and tamp it down. The car behind him honked and finally pulled around him. Vern fished out his lighter, the one with the "Big Red One" insignia etched on its side. He'd never been in the First Infantry, which was where the insignia came from, but as a former member of the National Guard, he supported its goals. Vern lit up and continued home.

On SiriusXM a station played something with violins. Vern recognized "Danke Schoen," a Wayne Newton classic, though in general, Vern's knowledge of the highbrow was minimal.

Leaving Excelsior Boulevard he moved through the leafy streets of Edina. Successful people lived here. His home was lovely too and of no mean stature. And yet, Vern couldn't help noticing the more stately mansions on his route. Sculpted lions guarded one driveway. Another place was painted pink and had arched windows on the second and third floors. A couple of huge estates were all but invisible behind huge iron gates and a jungle of trees. This was old money, inherited money. Vern was not invited to their parties.

Vern passed the McGee compound. It had turrets. Mel McGee owned the Medical Arts Building, downtown, which was full of doctors of various kinds. The rents piled up. People, of course, naturally got sick. Their teeth rotted. Mel got his cut.

Vern had no such luck and, by contrast, had to beg merchants to buy ads for a few bucks. What was worse, the cash dried up at the first sign of an economic downturn.

Vern pulled into his driveway. The Scottish hedge scraped his car's lacquered finish and Vern cringed. The Hispanics never did their job.

Vern checked for scratches but couldn't see a thing. Sprinklers hissed below the rockery. He couldn't see them. There was only the expanse of lawn and the huge firs beyond. The place was really too big. He would sell it soon, but not just yet. There was still a chance Bunny would come back.

He remembered her body throbbing and bobbing as he licked between her legs like a dog. She was only twenty-two but very mature, and he himself had the body of a much younger man. She loved to hear about the early days and how hard it was to make it in TV. Then she left for some kid in mail order.

Sometimes he and Flo got a little something going after a few drinks at the Marquette. But she was elderly as hell and soon to be downsized. Mostly his sex life was just plain shit.

Vern hummed a little song as he walked up the flagstone steps. "Danke schoen, darling don't explain . . . ta da da da da da danke schoen . . . la la la." He was getting more into music, these days. Possibly it was because he was older now. It took maturity to get a handle on what Mozart and them were trying to say.

Inside, the place was stoney quiet. Vern took a couple straight shots, no ice. His voice, he had noticed, had a special resonance in the marble expanse of the foyer. "Danke schoen, ya . . . ya . . . yah!" Bunny had had cameras installed all over the house. You could watch them on your laptop if you knew how to do it. Vern studied the opaque glass dome in the ceiling. It was no bigger than his fist.

Maybe Bunny peeked in from time to time. The thought kept him hoofing it around the living room now and singing at the top of his lungs though he was actually wrung out from a rough week and would have liked to sit down.

Slowly, Vern let go of the day, tossing aside his suit coat and tie.

Then, the big leather chair embraced him and he sank into the cushions. He picked up the paper Rosario had left with the cold cuts. Page one made him smile. The theft of the Roving Eye van was still a big deal.

The *Star-Tribune* as a rule ignored WEE-TV except to blast it in John Carman's "On The Air" column. But now things were changing. Maybe Bonnie Lee was making headway. Plus, Greta B. Jones was a real bird dog, and Vern had personally assigned her to investigate any and every aspect of Doug Pepper.

"WEE-TV THEFT STUMPS HULPA. FBI CONSULTS. STATION INVESTIGATES ITSELF," read the *Star-Trib* headlines.

No, sir, you couldn't buy publicity like this. This was branding at its best. Vern noticed he was quoted in the second paragraph: "'The Roving Eye is the greatest TV breakthrough of the decade,' Mr. Balstad said."

Vern laughed out loud. Give the media a disaster, and they gave you page one! Vern was not certain he was a genius. Surely, that would be for history to decide. But his brilliance at least was, at this stage, beyond any doubt. A month ago it was the idiot on the water tower. A real fuck up. But Vern had learned from that misfire. This time, when opportunity knocked, he pounced!

Vern drowsed through the evening in the big chair. The Glenfidich was to his taste. He'd have preferred it with ice but with no immediate need to urinate, he didn't see any point in wrestling out of the chair and visiting the fridge. *Snackers* was on. The syndicated show was a big hit with males twenty to thirty. The show was a cash cow. But Vern had seen this episode. He wandered the dial.

He watched a Tony Robbins infomercial and felt inspired. He needed to keep a pen handy next time and write that shit down.

He turned the channel and a giant "3," glowing like a fireball, tumbled across the screen. It was news time! There were a bunch of shots of reporters, and then the Sky High Eye landed on a roof somewhere. Next there was a crane shot of the Roving Eye van. They'd used a Steadicam a lot too. The audio was partly a female orgasm mixed with the rewritten news theme. The whole opening, short as it was, cost a hell of a lot but it was great! You'd have to have the willpower of Patton to change the channel with *that* mash-up on the air.

Now Jack, the anchorman, spoke up.

"Water, water everywhere!" Jack said. "And for our farmers, that means soggy fields too mucky to plant!"

"Fuck!" Vern shouted. "Who gives a shit?"

He switched to Channel Five hoping Hal Parsons's third-rate operation was showing boring farm shit too. Funny. You could spend a fortune upgrading the graphics and gear and all, Vern thought. But the result? News. No matter what, it was the same shitty news night after night.

Channel Five was showing crap, Vern could see, which was a relief. Tim somebody was anchoring. He had a picture of some guy over his shoulder.

"Channel Five does not condone the actions of desperadoes," Tim said, "but we believe that you, the audience, deserve to understand the motivations of a man allegedly behind the headline-making heist in the Twin Cities of a state-of-the-art high tech news gathering vehicle owned by a competing television station. It was a brazen assault on the very foundation of the public's right to know.

"Yesterday, Channel Five received—by snail mail—a flash drive. It had surprising contents. We have verified the video on the drive as coming from Mr. Doug Pepper, the Channel Three videographer suspected of stealing a mobile television studio—a so-called Roving-Eye van—valued at nearly a million dollars. WISK-TV General Manager, Hal Parsons, has carefully reviewed Mr. Pepper's communication. In Mr. Parsons's opinion, and that of our news department, the words of this possibly deranged man, Douglas M. Pepper, may be of vital importance to our audience."

Vern froze in his chair. At last he recognized the toothy smile in the photo behind the two-bit anchor. It was that thug Pepper!

"Here is WISK-TV General Manager Hal Parsons."

"Jesus Christ!" said Vern, out loud.

Hal Parsons sat at a desk with his hands folded in front of him. The camera moved in closer. The lighting on his smooth and chubby face made him look a little like a Sunday school saint complete with a halo-like shimmering glow behind him. Hal started to talk, showing his obviously capped rock-star teeth.

"In releasing this communiqué from a purported criminal," Hal Parsons said, "we do not, of course, endorse or condone wrongdoing no matter how justified it may appear to those who engage in such behavior. Neither WISK-TV, nor its employees, nor its sponsors, assume any liability real or implied that may result from the actions of Mr. Douglas Pepper, or from person, or persons who may prove to have aided him in any documented criminal activity.

"And yet, we here at Channel Five firmly believe this man reflects something in our culture we simply cannot ignore. Our children, our neighbors' children, children yet unborn, will most certainly face temptations like this Doug Pepper. We as a community, as parents, in learning about this apparent fugitive, may come to identify the frayed bonds we all must struggle with to build a stronger nation."

The camera kept moving around Hal Parsons like a pacing cat. Behind him there seemed to be an arched window, as if he were in a church or a castle of some sort.

"Ladies and gentleman, let us watch, and it is our deepest hope, learn."

Vern bit hard on the first joint of his middle finger. He tasted blood.

Now, the screen showed a dark night. It was grainy video. It looked shitty as hell. There were lights and parked cars and it was very shaky and the lights streaked across the screen.

"I'm not saying which town I'm in," said a voice. "Just 'cause of the cops. They're going to figure it out anyway, but . . ."

He didn't even bother to finish his sentence. Vern knew right away who it was. It was that bastard, talking in his high, goody-goodyish Northern Minnesota twang.

"You wouldn't believe how easy it is to break into this place. I don't see how these people sleep at night, knowing you can probably get robbed at the drop of a hat from people breaking in real easy. It's just a shame."

Suddenly there was a shrill sound like an air raid siren, and then a loud bell rang and rang, and you could see Pepper's fist. He was running through hallways banging on doors. Vern's fingers dug into the leather armrests and left marks that scarred the finish and, he was to learn much later, never went away.

"Everybody thinks we're having a disaster," Pepper said, "so, look, here they come, out of the building!" A lot of people were leaving the building. Some pulled suitcases. A guy carried a small flat screen, which looked like it was too heavy for him. People wore bathrobes, and housedresses and boxer shorts.

Suddenly there was a fire truck.

Chapter 13

A TEENAGER WAS ON CAMERA. "I thought I smelled smoke even before I heard the alarm," the kid said, "so I started knockin' on doors. Up and down the halls, and that. I told them to just don't get scared and panic, and all. Stayin' calm is how you get out, see. I did what I could."

Doug Pepper's voice said, "What bull! I pulled the fire alarm myself. So what's he talking about? It's plain bull. So, he's a liar, sorry to say!"

Then Doug Pepper's story was over! It had happened so quick! But now, Vern Balstad told himself, it was gone.

WISK-TV's address came on the screen and the anchor said something about "public service" but Vern shut it off. He had some pills Bunny had left behind that had helped him a little before and now he downed some. Vern stared straight ahead at the black blank screen.

He remembered he needed to sell WEE-TV. The plan was to monetize his investment and get on with life free from crap. The key, of course, was to close the sale with Foster Kleizer. But Vern saw with sudden clarity that he had an even higher priority now. He had to get this Doug Pepper first. He had to crush Doug Pepper like a Dixie Cup in a dumpster. He had to because it was really important if he did it. There wasn't any other way to make life worth living.

* * * * *

ONCE UPON A TIME, the WEE-TV building was a theater. Probably, that was in the 1930s and 1940s. When Vern Balstad Senior bought the building, he built three floors of offices and a studio out into the cavernous space that was the theater auditorium.

A window still looked out from the third floor onto that darkness in which the orchestra pit and the stage remained hidden. They were artifacts of history preserved by accident and likely to be revealed only at such time as the building itself met the wrecking ball.

Down a newsroom hallway, in the basement, once the theater's sprawling ladies' lounge, a door led only to a cinder block wall, constructed, seemingly, as a barrier to the unused theater space. In those narrow confines, between sheet rock and cinder block, were faded stage sets, parts of some unknown mechanism, and stacks of film cans containing old news stories. Now, with no film projectors in the building, the old stories couldn't be watched.

Tanya Thorpe had never seen the film cans, but television news was once again undergoing change, and now it was she who risked being consigned to the irrelevant. The two top stations in the Twin Cities, including hers, had reduced journalism to a shameful marketing war, one the viewers seemed to embrace. Her talents were no longer in demand. But she was still on the Channel 3 team. As such, she was still relentless.

She mostly covered press conferences now. Greta B. Jones was getting the lead stories. Not because she was any good, mind you, but because Vern Balstad himself had intervened and made sure she got them.

Tanya and videographer Ron Stellges were at the Minnetonka Roadways' vast construction site. Like the Riverside Project, Minnetonka was a Delbert Hammer deal. Of course, that meant big budget trouble. Tanya had long ago spotted City Councilman Del as a small-time con man. But he usually flew under the radar. Since her demotion at Channel Three, Tanya had discovered she was more or less on his level. She was penny ante too. But that was Del's bad luck. She had gone over every document on Minnetonka she could find, teasing out hints of double-dealing. Naturally, they were plentiful.

Tanya stood near the backhoe Del Hammer had commandeered as a podium. He was answering a question from some kid at *Space*, the Minneapolis alt-weekly. Del was giving a typical non-answer of course and Tanya smirked. She was all about specifics. She was journalistic flypaper.

"So how much, Del?" she said. "You've got a price tag on the overpass? Can you give me a figure on this?"

Councilman Hammer nodded.

"Thanks, Tanya. As I just said, this represents a lot of good people saying 'yes' instead of 'no' and we're just grateful. You, me, everyone here, we have a real stake in what we send to Washington and St. Paul and some of that money needs to come back. That's what's really cool about this project, Tanya. With this overpass, every citizen in this community is getting a little something back. It's been a real pleasure working with our good mister Mayor Sagenbush, and with Congressman LeValle who—there he is—Congressman!—are creating what is a real fine legacy for the people . . ."

"I just wonder whether my figures are correct, Councilman," said Tanya, leafing through her ringed notebook. "The project cost is seven million dollars, the allocation is five." She shrugged. "Are you actually two million dollars short? Or, more properly, over budget? Either way, who's going to make up the difference—and when?"

Delbert Hammer smiled. He folded his hands in front of him. "Well now, you, as I say, you're getting into the details there—"

"Hard to see two million as a 'detail,' Councilman," said Tanya, interrupting. "In any case, this budget is from your office. Is Minnesota facing a huge shortfall because of this project?"

It was a dance. Tanya was leading.

"Budgeting anticipates future monies . . ."

"Would that be next year's budget, Councilman? There can be no certainty there. Can there? Given our legislature, that's a little problematic, isn't it? At best?"

"We pay our bills, Tanya."

"The taxpayer certainly does, yes," said Tanya. "Though prudence, it seems, would suggest a contract signed, sealed and delivered in advance, would it not? With provisions to protect against overages like this?"

"I thought Vern Balstad taught you people better manners over there at Three. I guess I was wrong. I say again, we pay our bills, Tanya."

If there was a veiled threat in his mention of Mr. Balstad, Tanya wasn't intimidated. She was encouraged.

"But that's just my point, Councilman. You started this project with two million dollars less than required to complete it. Would that have to do with investments you've made along the right-of-way? Those'll pay off I imagine?"

Poor Del. He seemed to think Tanya hadn't heard him. "Vern Balstad is a very good friend," he said. "And Tanya, I'm going to tell you just once more what I just said and I'd advise you to listen very, very carefully." He made a show of enunciating slowly, as if to a slow-witted child. "I don't have those details, so I really can't comment any more at this time!"

"Well, Councilman Hammer," Tanya said with a shrug, "the figures aren't really in question. The appropriation simply falls short of the successful bid, which you would have had to have known, of course—"

"Cut the comedy, sister!" said Councilman Hammer, his voice rising to a squeak.

"Beg pardon?" Tanya said, her heart racing with the thrill of conquest.

"I don't have to justify myself to you! You just turn around and march your little butt back to where you came from and forget it, missy! I answered you a dozen times but you're going to harp and complain and bitch! Well, shut the fuck up!"

"Did he just call me a bitch?" Tanya asked Ron, quietly. She really wasn't sure. It was a stunning and unexpected reaction from the little man.

Later, his uncivil retort bleeped out, was broadcast on every newscast in town. And you could read his lips.

Tanya took no great delight in the drama, now that it was over, though she was pleased the public had the facts. She'd shed a little light on the bureaucracy.

That afternoon, she and Tammy Bailey watched the tape.

"That was really mean," Tammy said. "You shouldn't have done that."

Tammy Bailey seemed leaner, these days, more mature, more serious. It was as though she had shed her baby fat in the crucible of the

WEE-TV unfolding tragedy and become, in a matter of weeks, the woman she was meant to be.

"Tammy, I know it sometimes seems harsh. But these politicians will manipulate you and distort the facts until hell freezes over unless you are as direct as you can be. My loyalty has to be with the viewers. Cordiality is fine, but it's secondary. People trust me to bring them the facts and Del was anything but honest. Now they know he's a fraud and they're stuck with the bill."

"I don't think he was lying to you, Tanya," Tammy said.

Tanya studied her young friend's face. Tammy didn't seem mad; nor was she accusing Tanya of anything. But Tanya was suddenly, unaccountably embarrassed.

"Well, all I can say is I had to get the facts out of him somehow!"

"But you didn't. You got him mad. You could have called and let him know what you wanted. Then maybe he could have answered. That's what the public really wants to know, it's about the money. Isn't it?"

Tanya didn't answer. The world was changing, and she was losing it. It was almost like every dirty thing she had ever done, or thought about doing, was piled on her doorstep and she suddenly had to deal with each one right now. And she had no friends to help her through.

Take Tammy. Tanya used to rely on her for support. Now she was an accuser.

No, she couldn't blame Tammy. They seemed to have switched places, though. Tammy was the mature one. Tanya was the child. She couldn't look at Tammy. Tanya went back to her desk and sat down. Tammy watched her go. Did Tammy know she was a fraud? Tanya wondered. Well, she herself knew. All her talk about journalism and ethics was a lie. She should have quit weeks ago instead of abusing a half-assed city council member just to prove she still deserved to be a reporter.

Tanya logged on to Greta B. Jones's Facebook page for no good reason. There was Greta and her Audi. This time, they were someplace on the North Shore with Lake Superior in the background. Greta's Florida boyfriend, Mike, was smiling, with his shirt off. It was like picking at a scab, checking in on Greta like this.

If Tanya were to quit, what would happen to her Camry, the one with AM-FM, but no GPS? And forget about the pretty living room set from Sears. All Tanya's hopes and plans would end if she didn't have a salary. The future had turned on her like a snake. Even Doug Pepper, ass that he was, was out there somewhere trying to make a statement.

Tanya took a sick day and Tammy didn't call to see how she was. Tanya watched TV. Somebody was rebuilding a house to a young couple's specifications. The pair was absolutely ecstatic. It was now past three. Tammy would be getting busy after three and definitely wouldn't call. Tanya tuned to Discovery and watched a *Shark Week* rehash, with plenty of blood.

Doug Pepper, Tanya thought, was a pretty, dirty, Iron Ranger— northern Minnesota trailer trash. But that was a turn-on. They used to drive out to the country, she and Doug. He'd complain about his job and then they'd fuck. But now she wished she hadn't been so superior and self-righteous and maybe listened sometimes instead. But, there it is, as he would say.

Doug said other things, too, about wanting to be good at what he did. The specifics eluded her. He had this curly hair on his chest and she used to play with it as he jabbered on and on. He was pretty much an idiot. They'd pull off to the side of a country road and fuck in the corn. Minnesota farms were great for sex even at noon. She could scream and scream as he hammered her, and the rustling corn sucked up the sound like it was rain.

Men didn't dominate the world. Not if they were like Doug Pepper. She'd had the upper hand the whole way through. Where was Doug now?

Tanya'd been married to her job, anyway, and she'd felt good about it. She'd planned to sink into a private life sometime later when she'd achieved the journalistic honors to which she was entitled and won the admiration and love of a worthy man. But right now Pepper was evidently out somewhere on the road fighting for something, and she was watching a two-minute spot for Dove Soap.

Around four, Tanya changed her mind and went to work. Seth Petersen had assigned Tammy a breaking story, and she was glowing with pride. Tanya knew better than to disrupt the girl's concentration. Still, she was heartsick, and strangely desperate to connect with the young woman. "You're busy," Tanya said.

"I don't care, the fire was sort of already out, but it was good," said Tammy, waving her script in the air. She smiled as if she were not on deadline. "Cat edits fast. How come you look that way?"

Unaccountably, Tanya began to cry.

"Oh, Tanya! Come on! We need to go to the ladies room!

Chapter 14

Bud Vanderpein saw Tanya Thorpe crying her eyes out about something. Tammy Bailey was right there behaving like a mother hen. Bud ignored the histrionics and continued prepping a story. As for why high-strung ol' Tanya Thorpe was crying? Bud wasn't plugged in enough to know.

There was definitely a divide in the newsroom between the "Balstad team" and everybody else, Bud thought. It'd all work itself out eventually, of course. The old guard—Tanya, Doug Pepper, and others—would make peace with itself, *and the new realities and the revised pecking order* would sink in. That was the beauty of it. And Bud was on the winning side.

Sure, it was irritating to see Tanya Thorpe still swanning around the newsroom like a prima donna. She was just an egotistical type-A bitch, Bud thought. It was sad, really, to see her going down that way.

Some of the old timers, even Seth Peterson, still blamed Bud for the water tower incident, even though he was as much a victim of it as anyone. Ever since, Bud thought, Seth had avoided assigning him the "hard news" stories that were the one reliable gauge of prestige in this newsroom. Bud was getting a steady diet of fluffy features these days.

Well, he was a feature guy anyway—witness his well-received "Minnetonka Mansions" story last week. It was as successful as anything he'd done in Denver.

He studied the map in front of him. The trick was to pick the right chopper route. People never guessed what they were about to see. That's what made his stories exciting. That's what kept the good people glued to their screens.

It was he alone who would reveal the gleaming castles the rich called "homes." They were unimaginably huge and sometimes hidden only a few hundred yards off insignificant side roads that the unaware masses traveled along every day!

From the air these architectural wonders were breathtaking. They were true monuments to excess for the wealthiest one percent. Of course, he never put it that way on the air. He tone was one of admiration—tinged, of course, with subtle irony. His basic presentation might be an aerial rebirth of the old *Lifestyles of the Rich and Famous*. The ridicule was between the lines.

Denver viewers had lapped it up. What the fuck—everybody was a voyeur at heart!

The Minnetonka thing had gone very well, but a measure of caution was wise. So far, no rich bastard had complained to Balstad. In Denver, some people went ballistic when he took the helicopter up those canyons and revealed the feudal homesteads hidden there! Take Evergreen! Those guys were assholes!

Some people had called their lawyers even before the newspaper article about his exposes. Vern's job offer had saved him. In consequence he now diluted his mockery with a whole lot of awe and respect.

To Bud's surprise, Vern Balstad hadn't been as chummy as he'd seemed in those first meetings. None of the WEE-TV newbies offered a whole lot socially. That Greta Jones, for example, was a pill. Bud was finding himself very much alone these days. But that was okay too.

Bud studied the zip codes. He found Sunfish Lake on the map. According to the demographics, the people in that burb had more money than God. They were almost as rich as Long Lake folks. Great. He didn't know if there were estates out there, but Captain Max would help with that. And Bud would break journalistic boundaries once again—only this time, respectfully, of course. There was no sense pissing people off and killing the goose that laid the proverbial golden eggs.

Bud grabbed a legal pad and tapped it with his pen, beginning to consider tactics. From Holman Field, he could drop down on Sun Fish and then maybe circle Apple Valley. Who knew what was out there in the Valley? There might be investment banker castles. A careful aerial survey might reveal a hidden amusement park built for the entertainment of a single rich kid! Bud had never defined himself by his job. He was independent, resourceful, even without this high-paying TV gig.

But this was fun!

"Think of anything! Quick!" Cat Barnum said, interrupting Bud's thoughts. Bud looked up from his legal pad. The big black man was still talking. Bud didn't know what he was saying.

"What do you want?" Bud said.

Cat waved his hands in the air. "Tornados and floods," Cat said, "and other important things on the news catch the eye, right? But the commercials are usually just as good! Agreed? But why is that?"

"What? Cat?" said Bud, as politely as possible, "Don't you have something to edit?" Someone had said that Cat Barnum lived with a male hairdresser. He wore garnets and rubies on his fingers—though naturally the rings might be cut glass for all Bud knew.

"I'm saying," said Cat, "we think we've got a handle on excitement but the commercials do it better almost always. I'm not hearing an argument out of you. You know exactly what I'm talking about." Cat pointed a long, narrow index finger at Bud.

"That's not really my thing, Cat, I'm not much of a speculator. That's something I don't know about." Bud cleared his throat. "Right now, though, Cat, I'm a little busy?"

"Hey, no prob!"

Seth Peterson put his hand on Cat Barnum's shoulder. "Excuse me, Cat. Sorry to barge in but, Bud, can I talk to you? Bud, Tanya seems to have disappeared, and I've got a breaking story here. I'm going to have to send you."

Bud noted the language choice: *have to*.

"Sure, Seth, what's up?"

"There's a fire—looks like a big one—on East Franklin. This is most likely a live shot. We got nothing else—just FYI. Red's all ready geared up and waiting."

"Red!"

"I'm with you there, man," said Cat, under his breath.

"Yeah. He's all ready in the car. I'm pretty sure he's—he'll pull around up top. You can go right up."

"Hey!" Cat said, shooting Bud with an index finger gun. "We should get together sometime!"

Bud almost laughed at the thought. He grabbed his reporter's notebook and raced up the stairs.

* * * * *

THE BOARDING HOUSE was an 1890s kind of place. It was burning like a pile of orange crates.

Bud watched the fire trucks from behind the police tape. East Franklin was a bad part of Minneapolis, high crime rate, no jobs. The fire would clear half a city block, or so. Maybe that was a good thing. On the other hand, there were plenty of vacant lots already with nothing on them but ruined foundations. Indians from reservations around the Midwest lived here. They didn't have any money. East Franklin remained a wasteland.

The hoses shot a relentless stream into the smoke but it didn't seem to slow the fire. Bud imagined a battlefield. He said to himself, "This is a battle between the fire department and the anarchy of flame . . ."

He wrote "battle," and "anarchy of flame," on his notepad.

Red Bertram had gone somewhere, following the other photographers, and was not in sight. But a fire was by the numbers, anyway. There would be no official comment until the excitement died down. The small crowd of bystanders held no interest for Bud.

Who were these shabby people? Bud imagined them gloating as their neighbors' lives went straight to hell.

Rain, a few drops at a time, began to fall, and the temperature dropped. The rain should have helped slow the blaze. Wind blew the cloud of smoke and steam onto the street.

Bud's sinuses hurt. He couldn't see. He remembered his jacket was still at his desk.

Suddenly the roof flared into flame. There was a tiny explosion and sparks showered the street as the roof started to cave.

The TV station broadcast trucks arrived. There was the Roving Eye. Shit! Seth was planning a live shot! Bud listened to the confusion—the hum of the big hook-and-ladder water pumps, and the squawk of emergency radios, and the shouts of the firemen. This was no great story. But the rooftop flames looked great. Any producer would love this as long as the fire held out. Maybe going live would be fine.

The Roving Eye Van's telescoping microwave pole began to rise above the roof of the van. The wide dish-style antenna turned on its axis and aimed at the IDS Tower downtown. Bud looked at his watch. It was 5:20. He'd be on the air in less than an hour.

* * * * *

"Hey Freddy, Freddy, Freddy. Testing. Testing!"

"Yeah, Bob. We got ya!"

"Good deal."

Bob Tratcher was wearing his wireless headset. He was still in his office, but he would soon move out among the troops. Tanya Thorpe and Greta B. Jones were standing there expectantly, and the rest of the staff was gravitating toward the TV sets. It was time for the six o'clock newscast.

The headset put Bob in direct contact with master control. He could have gone up to the studio but here the staff was all around him to witness his new take-charge attitude.

Bob felt like he was on stage, sitting at the edge of Seth's desk, just below the row of TVs. Bob crossed his arms. He said nothing, not yet. Like a military officer, a news director needed to intervene in a broadcast only rarely. Generally, he just let his underlings maintain the flow.

The oddly bouncy new news theme started. The flaming three whooshed by, and, suddenly, there were pictures of two dilapidated houses on fire.

"Flames destroy the homes of Minneapolis residents! That story tops the Six O'clock Report!"

Bob stroked the multi-colored gal on his forearm in nervous anticipation. Sadly, the bosomy chic had started to smudge a bit. Perhaps it was the weight he'd gained.

Ned Storm, the anchor, was on screen for a couple seconds and then the direction cut right back to the fire.

"Since one-thirty this afternoon a fire has raged at the 1600 block of Chicago Avenue South. Firemen have been fighting the blaze for over four hours. On the scene with them is WEE-Three's Bud Vanderpein. Bud! What's the latest on the fire?"

The live picture showed Bud. Behind him smoke poured from a three-story structure. Smoke or steam swirled around the fire trucks and momentarily enveloped Bud. "Whoa, well, Ned," said Bud, slowly, "at least seventeen families and indigents occupied this apartment house and neighboring structures until this afternoon. Now, sad to say, they have been evicted by the ravenous flames, the hungry flames, uh, only too happy to get their ... uh ... to destroy the buildings with their flickering tongues."

Tratcher shook his head. "Jesus Christ!" he said, to no one in particular. "You writing *War in Peace* or doing the news, for Christ's sake?" A couple people stifled a giggle.

"Get the camera off Bud!" Tratcher shouted into the headset. "Flames! Gimmee flames!"

Smoke was everywhere, and the boarding house had begun to turn black as the paint blistered.

"Well," said Bud, "the fire's still going. Though it's kind of hard to see that. The fire department doesn't seem to be able to get at it. Oh! Look at that thing go! There's lots of smoke. But that's ... that's to be expected."

Suddenly, the lower floors of the structure were engulfed in flames, flaring like a bonfire. Bob Tratcher lit up. "Keep him on it!" he shouted. "Dump that farm thing! We're staying with this!"

Almost on cue, a spray of water from a fire hose doused the flames. Suddenly there was even more smoke than before. Tratcher drummed his fingers on the desk. "Okay," he said to whoever was listening on the headset, "let's wrap. We'll take the picture as a bump at the break."

Bud was still talking. His voice was higher pitched now and seemed to have developed a tremor.

"I imagine, uh, well, think of all the living things, you know, dead now, in there. I mean killed. Pets—real dogs, cats. But, of course, that's not the important thing. There were all those lives, all those people, I mean, left homeless—not dead! Kids, mothers . . . they're not dead. Not the people. They're fine. Uh . . . not *fine* per se, but in a manner of speaking . . . most of them taken away we know not where yet."

"Fuuuuck!" said Bob Tratcher. "Fade to black!"

The newscast ended without further input from Bob. The crowd around the TVs dispersed. Bob sat alone. Vern Balstad had hired Bud Vanderpein without saying "Boo!" about it until it was a done deal. The kid was obviously a weak sister who couldn't do a simple live shot without getting tangled up in his words. And who would get the blame for signing this nitwit?

* * * * *

RED BERTRAM SNARLED at Bud Vanderpein the moment he signed off the air. "That was pure shit, buddy boy," Red said.

Red was Red, but this time, Bud knew, he was right. Bud had demonstrated embarrassingly sloppy thinking on a nothing fire story. It was like being naked in front of the audience. No fig leaf, just his balls hanging out to give everyone a big laugh.

Bud told Red he'd ride back in the Roving Eye but instead he walked along the sidewalk toward downtown. He needed time to collect his thoughts and become confident, no-nonsense Bud Vanderpein once again.

The producer for the ten o'clock show called to tell Bud not to worry about voicing a report on the fire. They planned to do it as a reader. That should have cheered him up, but not today. To Bud, it seemed his shitty performance had polluted the story. He half expected to be fired.

Finally, Bud entered the WEE-TV building. It was nearly empty now, and he walked slowly down the stairs to the newsroom. He sat at his desk and picked up the map he'd been using to plan his flight over Sun Fish Lake. He didn't lift his eyes from it though the markings danced before his eyes and made no sense at all.

Bud slipped on his coat and left. The station's upstairs hallway was empty, and to avoid the foolish old man who handled the switchboard at night, he let himself out back by the loading dock.

It had been raining. Neon restaurant signs and bright store windows colored the street. The air was biting even though it was midsummer. Wishing he had a cap, Bud hunched his shoulders and moved along the sidewalk.

There was a movement in the shadows and Bud stopped short. "Hey stranger!" said a voice. It was some kid. He was hardly more than a shadow in the half-light. His body language suggested some sort of come-on. The boy lit a smoke. He couldn't have been more than sixteen. Bud felt a crazy physical rush. But he walked away fast. He didn't turn around even when he was two blocks away. He turned the corner and there was the bus stop.

The bus came, and Bud got on. He didn't understand how someone could sell his body. Maybe it was indifference that let someone be that intimate with a stranger.

The rain pelted him with bullet-sized drops from the bus to his place. Inside, he shook his coat and hung it on the closet door. He put on some coffee and plopped in a chair. It was getting windy and the branches were waving outside the window.

The figure Bud called, "the old lady of Lyndale Avenue," shuffled up the sidewalk's slight incline. She was a familiar sight at all hours though mostly at night and Bud felt a little sorry for her though she obviously didn't have to be out in this weather. He watched her disappear and then he watched the wet sidewalk.

He took an Ambien and went to sleep.

Chapter 15

It was early in the morning. Doug Pepper was naked, taking a pee, watching the sun come up. He took a deep breath. The air was fresh and dampish and getting warmer—and the light was perfect. From here, he could see forever. A couple miles off, a silo or a metal barn reflected the sun. Mostly there was corn—corn and corn and more corn—and a few trees. It was a perfect spot. Doug himself was lost in the green fields and pretty much invisible.

He checked Facebook and added a couple selfies and put a butterfly on Instagram. Social media was cool. He poured cereal into his mouth 'til he couldn't even chew and put it on Vine. Doug hadn't had a lot of friends but a check of his newsfeed showed that was changing.

Of course, he didn't dare show a whole lot of landscape in his photos. Nebraska didn't have much scenery, anyway, but show the wrong house or a certain tree and—wham!—the feds would swarm down and it'd all be over for Doug. He mostly posted himself in tank tops leaning against something or sometimes with his shirt off. Either way he got lots of comments on his pecs.

He was safe from cops, he thought. But, on the bad side, stories weren't showing up. Cat Barnum—the one person Doug talked to—bitched and bitched about content.

"Great you're arms and shoulders are pumped," Cat said. "But no more posts about your work out."

"Why?"

"Nobody cares, Doug."

"Don't tell that to Stacey B. Or a whole lot of others!"

"You've got just one guy to please, Doug. That's Hal Parsons. Not some bimbo in Denver or wherever. Next time you need to photograph your deltoids think about Hal Parsons. Think about how much he cares. You're not a movie star Doug. You're a ratings gimmick. Without the numbers you're nothing. And neither am I!"

"It's not just her, dude! Lots of people want to see a built guy like me running along some country road and, like, training. It was lit great also."

"Hal fucking Parsons trashed the video, Doug. He dumped it. You keep this up, you kill the franchise."

Doug had done a dumpster raid, looking at trash, to see what average people were all about. But it didn't turn out to be too interesting. It was mostly crap in there: spaghetti sauce, Cheerios boxes, diet aids and other garbage shit. Next, he did an obstacle course with his iPhone set-up in multiple spots. He did some of it in slo-mo, too, though that part was fake, with him just pretending to run while barely moving. Even with all the effort though Hal Parsons had been completely thumbs down about it.

"If we don't start racking up airtime at Channel Five, like, right now, you might as well get a job in Topeka and stop burning through my cash," Cat said.

"Want me to interview a corn cob?" said Doug. "Because that's all there is out here!"

Doug and Cat hadn't talked since. Doug put a handful of cornflakes in his mouth and chewed slowly. The map said there was a town up the road though you couldn't prove it by looking out at the corn.

Doug packed up and rifled through his dirty laundry for a shirt and pants and bumped through the corn and back to the road.

* * * * *

VERN BALSTAD GOT UP from his desk and watched the street below. All his life, he'd been struggling. But what he got for his trouble was more trouble.

There was nobody on Ninth. A delivery truck was parked up on La Salle. Suddenly he felt a little surge of anticipation and sat back at his desk. He'd bookmarked, "Busty Babes On-Line," primarily because they got their hair pulled while they got off. It was an unexpected turn-on and tension reliever, and Vern knew he needed a little of each just now.

Someone knocked softly at Vern's office door. He looked at his day calendar. Fuck! He took a minute. There was that knock again. "Come in!" He put a smile on.

"Mr. Balstad?" Greta B. Jones opened the door slowly and minced timidly into the room. Her soft voice was musical. She ran her long fingers over her forehead brushing back a little wisp of hair. She smiled, nervously. Greta closed her eyes and then opened them again in a kind of pleading way while looking directly at Vern. He'd seen that look before but since Greta was a newsroom gal, and thus morally not available for any kind of hootchie-coo, it was a no go.

"Sit down, sit down," Vern said, edgily.

"Thank you." Greta laughed at something private and sat in the chair in front of the desk. From the navel down Greta B. Jones seemed built for stability in high wind. But her face was a delicate mix of button nose and high cheekbones. Her breasts, Vern noticed with some agitation, had an adolescent heft.

"We've been watching you Greta," said Vern, leaning back in his chair. "Good, solid, in-depth work. Top Drawer."

"Thank you," said Greta. She wriggled in her seat.

"So it behooves us to make better use of your talents. And it's just damned good luck that we have something that will really challenge you."

"Oh! That's exciting!"

"Yessir."

Vern picked up a stack of maps from his desk. He unfolded the first one, and then the next.

With the fourth map, his desk was fully covered. Vern moved from behind his desk and continued unfolding maps. These he placed on the floor. He spread them on the carpet in an orderly way, their edges not quite touching. Finally, with all the maps spread, Vern stepped daintily between them and returned to his chair and smiled at Greta.

"This here is most of the United States of America!" he said, spreading his arms.

"Well, yes, I see," said Greta, leaning forward as though to get a better view. "A lot of maps, too!" She gave a little laugh.

"Yessss. A lot of maps," said Vern, crossing his arms. "But why do you suppose so many maps, Greta?"

"Well, Mr. Balstad, you just unfolded them, in a very orderly way."

Vern fought down an urge to imitate her in mocking fashion. His social coach, Dr. Jules, had warned Vern that such teasing inhibited flow and often boomeranged with unpleasant consequences. The doctor said Vern's belittling may very likely have cost him his marriage to Bunny. The court proceedings, though by no means complete, were putting his very house at risk. Vern softened.

"Yes?" he said, coaxingly, "But we're journalists here?"

"Yes?" Greta said.

"He's out there!" Vern shouted. He stood up and stamped on a map. "That prick is out there somewhere. Maybe out on some bayou." He kicked at Louisiana with his toe. "Could be he's still out on the plains—but I doubt it. Maybe out West! Since he looks like a ski bum, maybe he's somewhere skiing, or hiding out if there's no snow." He ground his heel into Colorado. "The damned bastard! Using my gear, too! Expensive shit! Maybe it's Oregon. Could be Canada! Some little town . . ."

Vern opened his arms suddenly and turned a three-sixty twisting paper underfoot. "You just don't know! Coulda gone to Connecticut, for Chrissake! Yeah but no, probably. Not there! Bet the cocksucker went west."

Greta's smile froze on her pretty face. Her eyes drifted to the middle distance. Her fingers drummed on the arms of her chair.

"Am I keeping you from something?" Vern said.

"What? No! No, Vern."

"Not working on a big story?"

"No, I . . ."

"That's good," he said. "Because there isn't any story bigger than this. Look at all those roads. All those little towns! God knows how many! It's a big country. The thing is, if I send you out there into this great big country of ours, America the Beautiful, and what not, looking for that damned bastard, that's what I want to *hear*! I want you to blow out the chaff! It'll take some digging. We'll help you with information we get here at this end. But finding that bastard out there in the wild blue yonder—that's your bailiwick! Go to those towns! Look around, leaving no stone unturned! Learn the people. Learn this land we call the USA! Don't let a single clue escape! You stay on top of this, and we'll nab Pepper in a heartbeat! Keep updating his whereabouts every single day and we'll be fine!"

Vern stopped talking. He'd gotten a little hot under the collar. He wished he could remember what he'd said. As it was, he couldn't recall, just now, and more than likely it was lost, though it'd been pretty good.

Greta B. Jones was fluttering her hands at him in a girlish way.

"But Vern, won't this be a problem? I mean, logistically? We uh . . . *don't know where he is.*"

"I'll worry about that," Vern snapped. "You take care of what you're good at, and don't go sticking your nose anywhere else." He smiled, picked up his pipe and lit it. "All you gotta do is edit and email a story a day. Hal Parsons thinks he's got an exclusive running Pepper's YouTube shit. Well, you and me, we'll do him one better, with your no-holds-barred, hard-as-nails reports from the frontlines! But that means, good shit! No namby-pamby crap!"

"But Vern," said Greta, "what if I'm in Texas and he turns up in Washington, D.C.? By the time I fly out, it'd all be over!"

"First off," said Vern, "you're driving. Gotta have you on the ground matching Doug Pepper mile for mile. We're going to give Hal Parsons a little promotional tit for tat here. See how he likes it! Some days maybe you do a little something on people's lives ruined by Pepper. Good stuff! Plus you're going to have Red Bertram. He's been a videographer twenty-thirty years. An old newshound like that knows the ropes if there's problems."

Greta paled and put a hand on her chest. "But Red can't shoot! He's a terrible cameraman," she said. "I can't rely on somebody like that—an incompetent!"

"See that he isn't!" Vern said. "Who's the boss here, anyway!" A map drifted off his desk and Vern stomped it into the garbage can. "Let's try to figure out our position here. Let's worry about ourselves. Ask if we can do the job before we worry about others! We on the same page?"

"Yes, I am, Vern," said Greta. "I am! Certainly I want to do a good job. It's just that . . ."

"We're not going to send you out with no ammo, honey. You're going to have all the support you need, logistical or otherwise. If you're in Texas, it's because we're goddamned sure Pepper's in Texas. You'll be on his tail before you know it." Vern sat on the edge of his desk and looked down at Greta. "I'm not going to let this thing fuck up. If that's too much for you to handle, then you'd better say so, and I'll get somebody who cares a little bit about doing a good job and cooperating a little bit."

Vern crossed his arms.

"I'm enthused, Vern," said Greta, quickly, "make no mistake about that. Forgive me if I seemed out of sorts but—"

"Good," said Vern, picking up the phone. "I'll arrange to get you guys a travel van. You leave first thing tomorrow. I wish I could give you a Roving Eye to go live, now and then. But they're too small to sleep in."

Chapter 16

The blue dot on Doug's phone moved along the map toward "Bleeker." He passed a sign, "Welcome to Bleeker, Pop 677," but there wasn't anything in sight but corn, corn, and more corn.

"You see any town around here?" Doug said, holding his phone at arms length. "No. Which is because the city limits sign's a lie. I bet the Chamber of Commerce put it up for taxes! Maybe we should get to the bottom of this."

Doug held the phone out the window to shoot corn but he was too late. There were buildings in view now, and the cornfields came to an abrupt end. Doug slowed as he approached the little, dead main street, which appeared to be all there was of Bleeker.

Nobody was around. He saw cars on the curb and he drove past a vacant furniture store and went another block and parked. He got out and stretched with phone in hand.

"I'm not saying the name of this place," Doug said. "Just forget that. In case you're a cop, you'd love it if I spilled the beans, but no way."

Someday, Doug thought, he'd probably get caught and put away, maybe for a long time. But at least his reports would live on, on Facebook and You Tube. And it was entirely possible they might last forever.

"Look at this store. Here's a place that sells wigs! Yeah! Unbelievable, because why! Wigs! I'm not lying! That's got to be crazy Right? In a town this little? Because who cares? And nobody around? But okay. Maybe, like, if you're a bald lady, or love doing drag or whatnot. But let's take a look, though, inside."

Doug opened the door to the dusty shop and a little bell announced his entry.

"God, good thing there's no Wal-Mart around," Doug said in a whisper, "otherwise this place would at least have to clean up. Yuck! Which I'm not sure if you can see or not. Which Wal-Mart probably has wigs, also." Doug panned a row of Styrofoam heads in the window display each sporting long tresses. "Don't know how you get all these cobwebs unless a hive of spiders. Also, quite a few dead bugs, we see. Who needs the Discovery Channel, ha ha! Anybody here?" There didn't seem to be a clerk on the sales floor. "Except could be I could use a wig for disguise. Being wanted and on the run, so to speak."

The place smelled moldy. A TV or a radio was on in the back. He shut off the phone and listened. There was no sound but the broadcast. Some of the Styrofoam heads were bald. There were lots of empty shelves. The place was weird and depressing. "Hey!" Doug said, and waited. Lousy service, he thought. No wonder business is bad.

A plaid curtain blocked the way to the back. It moved a bit but it was only air coming through from someplace.

"You're back!" a man said.

"Yes. But not for long."

"Then, you're not staying?"

"Oh, I'm *staying* all right," said the woman. She was really upset.

"But . . ."

"Can't you see?" the woman said. "I'm dying!"

Doug didn't know for sure, but it sounded like *The Guiding Light*, which was always pretty good.

"Dying! When?"

"'When?' you ask? I'm not a crystal ball reader, Tom. If I were perhaps I could tell if you have even an ounce of empathy or concern! Which I doubt!"

"Oh, I do!" said Tom. "I'm so sorry!"

"'Sorry'? About what?"

"Well, you dying . . ."

"I'm dying, but I'm not dead. Don't count your chickens before they're hatched, for God's sake!"

"Please, darling! You're my wife!"

"Yes," said the woman. "But not for long!"

A powerful chord blotted out any more that might have been said and then there was a commercial. Doug had put the iPhone on the counter and turned on the video and made a show of looking at his watch and drumming his fingers on the counter.

"May I help you?"

"Whoa! I didn't see you . . ." Someone came through the blanket. He was old and had teary eyes. "You okay, sir?" Doug said.

"Some wrenching experiences caught me in . . . uh . . . at a—never mind. I can't talk about it now." The man dabbed at his eyes with a Kleenex. "A wig then?"

"Oh? Well, a wig," Doug said. "Yes, I can imagine, if the right color . . ."

"Our inventory is depleted," said the man. "Very few models, just now. Good quality merchandise. You can see that yourself."

"Yes," said Doug.

"Sales are cyclical. Been a long lull. That's the gist of it."

Doug grabbed his phone from the counter and got shots as unobtrusively as he could.

"One of those new phones?" said the man. "If you're looking to buy this place I could let it go cheap. I don't own the building, but the inventory, the store name, the client base. All yours. 'Wig Barn.' Franchise opportunity for the right man. That's where the money is. It'd be yours very economical."

"That'd be pretty impossible, sir," said Doug. "My assets are tied up in legal difficulty."

"Reason I wonder, is your out-of-state plates," said the old man. "Nice rig, too. Got me wondering."

"Yeah. No."

"Then why might you be photographing my interior, if I may ask?"

"I just shut if off," Doug said. He held out the iPhone, the screen black, for inspection.

"Because I think I know who you are now and my apologies," the old man said. He walked back of the counter and lifted a box into view. He set in front of Doug. "Looky here!" He removed the lid and shoveled magazines onto the counter.

They were 1950s men's magazines, with covers featuring babes in bikinis, some in danger from grizzlies or wolf packs or other wildlife. A half-naked woman was ensnared in octopus tentacles, and a guy with scuba tanks was rescuing her with a knife.

"Ya shoulda said something but I knew who you were anyways."

"This isn't . . ."

"Ahhh, don't be scared!" The old man's corded neck muscles tensed. "I was scared of gals. Now I phones 'em up and talks to 'em easy as pie. And sometimes I just breathes."

"Mister, this isn't at all what I'm into," Doug said.

"Well, they're mint," said the man. "Spicy as you'd want —em, too, there's—"

"Even if I was into girlie mags, you think I'd just stroll in here? A wig store? Anyway, this stuff is tame!" Doug leafed through a copy. "You've got entirely the wrong idea, sir."

"Say! By God! It's no wonder! Oh, no, now!" He put his hands to his head. "I want to formally apologize! I was momentarily undone by that TV. But now I know exactly who you are!" The old man jabbed his finger playfully at Doug and lowered his voice in a conspiratorial way. "You're the Simmons boy! Didn't recognize you without the hat! That and that swell new rig! Really something!"

"Hat or not, what are we talking about?" said Doug.

"Well . . . that depends. You interested or not?"

"Oh, I'm interested. I'm sure as hell interested!"

"Now you're talking! Okay, then. 'Buck' is it?"

"Buck Simmons?"

The old man nodded. "Okay, then. The deal stands. You get a cut. Depends on what we get for the ring, though. But it is one jumbo diamond. That's for damn sure. Pop paid through the nose."

"Okay. But what d'you need me for?"

The old man looked at Doug. "Just what the hell might you mean by that? You know exactly why, cuz my mama's down there. So don't be cute."

"Okay," Doug said. His mind was racing. The journalism part of news was tough. "I'm naturally going to need a little more information here."

"What're you talking about? I run the backhoe. Then, after, you and me run up to Denver and that guy of yours gets us a good price. It's what you said. And after which you get your cut, like I told you. What's so goddamned awful mysterious about that?"

"No. Except that we gotta have the exact location of your mama."

"She's up on the hill like always, Buck. Goddamnit! I don't think that's going to change. Christ almighty! Did I make the right choice here or no?"

"Sure you did. Of course you did. And that's why the backhoe, then."

The old man stared at Doug. "You stupid?"

"No, sir, just mulling things clear. You got me to fence the merchandise, as you said. I wait here in a hotel, you bring down the ring . . ."

"Hold on there, hoss! You ever work a backhoe digging up a burial? A back-breaking job. Shovel work. Then the lifting. I'm not a young man. Were you listening at all or were you drinking yourself stupid, you and that that pretty gal at the Salt Lick. She turned your head too much."

"Well, sure I heard you. But we, the both of us, were a little worse off than usual that night. No denying it."

"Sure, Buck. Sure," said the old man. "No harm taken. But I gotta know can I count on your support here. I'll be fair. I can promise you that."

Doug knew enough law to imagine there was another felony in all this, unless maybe the old man convinced a jury this ring was an heirloom, and thereby defused the prosecution. But Doug needed a YouTube quick. "Do you mind if I go out to my rig for some medicine?"

"Sure. No, go ahead!" the old man said. "We don't need to do it tonight though the weather's good."

There was a poster on a phone pole near the van. "Bleeker Crawdad Daze!" It was a ragged piece of cardboard and might have been up there a year, though the dates mentioned happened to be right now. A crawdad in a top hat stood in boiling water with a big smile and a saltshaker in his claw. It was probably a stupid festival, but easy to photograph and put on YouTube. If Doug did that, Hal Parsons and Cat Barnum were sure to whine about another worthless story. But grave robbing, if that's what the old man was getting at, was a nasty addition to Doug's mounting list of serious crimes.

Doug called Cat.

"How could you *not* do this?" said Cat. "Don't you have any sense of social media at all? You're falling way down on the job out there! Not just that stupid dumpster-dive story, which Hal Parsons didn't even run. Where're your Tweets? Where's the drama? It's not just YouTube, either. You need BuzzFeed, Gawker, Mashable."

"Well, I can't just post . . ."

"Get newsworthy! Hear me? *Newsworthy*. We need national! We need viral! But I can't do it! It's totally up to you!"

Doug sat in the van and watched a squirrel chasing around the trunk of a tree. It was going in circles for no reason. Doug Pepper could relate. He wanted to be a newsman because of Truth, not because Hal Parsons needed ratings for his fucking TV station. On the other hand, he was in deep shit, stealing a van and drowning it. He needed help. Cat was it. His only half-assed friend.

And Cat was right: to have a voice you had to get attention and the more the better. Someday he'd probably go to jail, yeah. But he'd go as Robin Hood.

Doug looked across the street at the wig store. He'd been unsuspecting when he walked in there. The world was worse than he thought. So far, the only Truth he'd run across was sordid shit. Where was the uplift?

Doug got up from the park bench and peeled the faded crawdad poster off the telephone pole.

* * * * *

"YOUR PAL, PEPPER, sent us a goddamn eight-minute story about eating crawdads! On a thirty-minute show with a twenty-two minute window," said Hal Parsons. "We used thirty seconds because it was kind of gross. But I don't have to tell you that eight-minute shit's a no go! Maybe if Jesus comes back and blood boils in the veins of the damned! Otherwise, no go!"

"Very graphic, Hal, thanks," said Cat. The sky was clear, and the sun shone brilliantly through the trees. Cat would have preferred no crows. Sighting along his thumb, he fired at a few with his index finger. "Look. You have my personal guarantee Doug Pepper's working on something very, very big. It'll blow the lid off the culture wars in a way I don't think anybody is prepared for, Hal. Believe me."

"Oh, for Christ's sake, Cat. Don't fool the fool! Cut the bullshit. Right now I'm not seeing a whole lot of percentage in this fiasco, frankly."

"Don't talk like that, Hal. You'll lose my respect. You read the papers. You've got the best tie-in a smart guy like you could ever hope for, Internet, multi-media, print. Plus—and I know you don't care about this—you're tweaking the fuck out of Vern Balstad. Yes?"

"Whatever," said Hal Parsons. "But mind what I said."

"You just kick the promotion department in the butt and make sure they're ready when WISK-TV's a viral sensation! You'll be dancing your lard ass in the street!"

Cat set the phone down and stretched lazily. Life by Minnehaha Creek was almost pastoral, about the equivalent of living on the Canadian border, not that he ever had. The Canadian border was just too far from the action. Cat couldn't have been happier than he was living here in Edina. True Doug Pepper, his star player, was turning out to be something of a self-righteous, unimaginative dunce. But good management was all about contingencies. There were no real red flags. The boy took direction, after all. Yes, he was a whiner, but probably solid.

Cat smiled to himself. *I am such a dilettante, a dabbler.* But no, that wasn't right. Cat was more of a scientist, he thought. The Minneapolis and St. Paul television market was his laboratory.

He gathered up sections of the *Wall Street Journal* and walked outside. In a few minutes, James would be home. One of the downsides of living with a hairdresser was that Saturdays were shot. James, bless his heart, was too fucking fair-minded to schedule himself off weekends despite Cat's endless pleading.

In the *Journal*, *Snackers* was the subject of a feature story on page three. The reality show ratings phenomenon was tangled in lawsuits because the youthful stars had double-crossed the syndicators, turning the show into an infomercial for a chain of restaurants called, "Snackers." Advertisers and stations were pissed and screaming for "make-goods."

WEE-TV had to be hurting since *Snackers* was Vern's biggest show, Cat thought. The station needed revenue and *Snackers* was the cash cow. Too bad it was self-destructing.

Cat was a little disappointed in himself. Instead of worrying about his colleagues' suffering he felt good. *Snackers* demise would drive Balstad crazier and heap still more pressure on the Channel Three newsroom.

A door slammed in the front of the house. James was home. Cat felt a familiar thrill. He knew what people said—"Cat's a steamroller, and James is his doormat."

Well, Cat saw their point. He was overbearing. He could suck the air out of a room. But James was no doormat. James had all the power in the relationship. Cat had given James his heart, certainly an inadequate payment given his need. His heart was irretrievable. It belonged to James. Even death, Cat knew, couldn't change that.

Cat and James sat long into the evening drinking Scotch. The crows had gone to bed and there was nothing but the creaking of crickets.

"James, did you ever read *Mommie Dearest?*"

"That thing about what a bitch Joan Crawford was to her kids? No."

"What about the book by William Saroyan's kid?"

"Who? No. Who?"

"Well, there's plenty, anyway. You've got exposes of Peter Sellers and Bette Davis and Bing Crosby and Walt Disney and David Geffen and Bob Dylan and Justin Bieber."

"So?"

"And they all have relatives, I guarantee you that."

"Probably. Want a snack, honey?"

"Don't interrupt!" Cat said. "*Celebrity Love Stakes*! You heard it here first. Mark Burnett, look out! Or maybe he buys in! You get Chelsea Clinton or someone telling her story. The audience weighs in on who had it worst. What about Denzel Washington's kids?"

"He has great kids."

"Let's wait and hear what they have to say, shall we?"

James shrugged. "I think I'll thaw scallops."

"Fettuccini! Make fettuccini! They go together."

But James was already inside.

Chapter 17

"I'm not crooked, I just want what's mine," said the old man, whose name was Barney Folger.

"Yeah. No kidding," said Doug.

"Way you disappeared there for a few days, I thought you were weaseling out on the deal."

"Barney, you got shafted. Paying for all your mom's home care, and then that ring goes into the ground on her finger. It just isn't right. I couldn't let you down."

"You're telling me."

"I'm not sure I should take a cut even. I know it's our deal, but it doesn't seem right, somehow."

"Well, you've got a point. 'Course, I'd feel I owe you."

"Well, sure. I see. Have you ever heard of *The Real Housewives of Beverly Hills*?"

"I've seen it some."

"Well, what if we tried to do a reality show on your situation. Sort of a heart-wrenching tale of you struggling to make ends meet and driven to desperation. That'd be a way to pay me back, some way. Telling your story, I mean."

"The wigs don't bring in much, it's true. Lord knows I've been denied my rights. But embarrassing me on TV? Family matters? No. That's something I don't believe I could do."

"Barney, something I know about you is you don't live in the past. Am I right? You're a man who stands up for himself. Come hell or high water, there's Barney standing up. You're not ashamed are you?"

"No."

"Well, then by rights, it's a matter of choice. Putting your trials and tribulations out there would be up to you. You get on TV, well, reality shows make a lot of money."

"How much would I get?"

"Hard to say. We'd have to start small. For example, I'd take a few pictures. See how it goes."

"I ain't got nobody anyways."

"All the more reason."

"But you'll still dig?"

"What? Oh! Sure! I'm the shovel man, you operate the backhoe. I take some pictures. We see what happens."

"Okay, then. But I don't put a lot of stock in TV. Never have."

"Point taken. But I've got connections."

* * * * *

A WINDING GRAVEL ROAD led up the hill to the cemetery. The moon was already up, and there was a glow over the cornfields, which rolled in a greenish-gray haze out to the horizon. It was peaceful and quiet when Doug stopped the van. White stones covered the hilltop. There were plenty of people up here.

Doug tested his little infrared camera as the light faded from the sky. It worked fine.

"See how that does?" Doug said, showing Barney the viewfinder. "Bright as day!"

"But everything looks green," Barney said.

"Well, that's the infrared."

"Okay. The hoe's up there."

Barney disappeared into the dark.

Doug put on a jacket and stood around because there was nothing to do. The backhoe had a little headlight, and it bumped along between the stones toward the van and then stopped. The headlight lit up one particular stone and Doug felt a creeping chill come up his back. The little machine roared to life again and scooped up dirt. Doug zipped up his jacket and sat on a stump. Then he remembered he was supposed to take pictures. He took a few shots of the backhoe, and then moved around to get coverage. Finally, he had to show the gravestone itself and the widening pit around it. The stone said "Emma Daymire Folger." When she died she was eighty-nine. She was about to resurface in the light of the moon.

Barney shut down. "Don't you think you ought to dig?" he said. "The bucket can't do close work."

"Sure, okay." Doug pocketed the camera and jumped into the hole and stuck his shovel blade into the fresh dirt. "Out in Ketcham, Idaho, one time, I saw the grave of Ernest Hemingway."

"Yeah?" said Barney. "Don't worry if you scratch the finish on that casket. They don't last anyways."

"The writer? Me and this gal skied Sun Valley. Here's this big chunk of rock and she goes, here's a great man lying here."

"You better speed 'er up," said Barney. "Nights are short."

"Yeah. That was some book. *Old Man and*—what—*the Sea*, which we had in class."

"Dawn breaks," said Barney, "and there's nothing to look at around here but this hill. At which time there'd be questions, me doing work and nobody dead, if you see what I mean. And you got to fill in, too."

Doug jammed a shovel in the gravelly dirt. It felt good to get a workout in. He dug until he was sore. He didn't make much progress.

"Makes you wonder just what's waiting under the ground around here," said Barney, gesturing his arm at the graves. "Could be *heirlooms*. You never know unless you look." His eyes were shiny ovals.

Doug's shovel struck something hard.

"Heads up, Barney!"

It wasn't any six feet down. But the box—with the old lady inside—was right there under Doug's feet.

"Maybe it's time we trade places, Barn. It's your mom, and all."

"No sir, that's not the deal. I'm not getting in that hole."

Doug climbed out to get a flashlight and thought of driving off, just heading back down the road on the way to wherever. But he marched back and climbed down again and cleared away the rock and dirt and loosened the lid of the expensive coffin. There wasn't any point in getting video, he thought. Nobody would want to watch this. He sure didn't.

"There's two lids on this thing, Barney!"

"What's that mean?"

"Looks like you got a set of hinges you can open for just her face there."

"Well, it's a Slumber-Rest."

"Okay."

"I'd have said no, but railroad insurance kicked-in."

"Yeah. Okay. I'm opening the bottom."

He pried the lid loose and lifted. There were rags and bones but nothing else. Barney peaked over the rim.

"No ring, Barn." Doug scanned with the flashlight.

"Goddamn," Barney Folger said. "So that's the deal. What the hell! She could of pawned the thing. Might have. Said she did."

"She said she pawned it, Barn? The ring? Why are we doing this if she pawned it?"

Barney shrugged. "No reason. I never believed a word she said."

"Well, didn't you look before she went in the ground?"

"No they only opened her face. Couldn't see shit except, naturally, her."

"Christ!" Doug forced the lid down. "Family reunion's over."

"Yeah. But, then again, who knows what we got elsewhere?"

"Huh?"

Barney turned on the radio hanging in the cab of the backhoe. The low, tremulous twang of a sad housewife's country song blotted out the crickets and the light night wind. The gal had been driven to her wit's end.

"Pretty," Barney said. "You know, I been silently calculating. The files got wet, up at the grave office. But could be there's some 370 folks resting in peace up here. You can't help but wonder."

"Don't say it Barn. You're gonna disappoint me."

"Some of these old boys are rich too. Back and forth to New York, and then Florida in the cold. Just loved to talk about it, too, every one of 'em. This and that, and what they done, and all that, and blah blah blah. One of them, of course, 'Pink' Martin, had a whole pool in his living room to swim in. Which they filled in with dirt, later, on account of upkeep. What a pisser if there's a Patek-Phillipe, with four season movement, just waiting under old Pink's slab, because they never seen it since, so guess what. It could be right here. A clear and easy thirty-thousand. A damn heirloom! Thirty-thousand. Easy."

"Yeah."

Doug wondered what Cat would say. Cat would say thumbs up or maybe not. There was maybe an *Antique Road Show* kind of thing going on. Each dig could be a big surprise with plenty of excitement. You'd have to pick the good ones, but Barney seemed to have a handle on that. Could be a little bit of Monty Hall and "doors number one, two, or three." Or maybe Barn was just an old nut case. There he was on the backhoe playing some sad song.

Barney looked like he was dreaming of getting rich and leaving this graveyard and the backhoe and the wigs behind and maybe heading for Las Vegas. It was a sad and twisted world. Doug didn't want anything to do with it.

He climbed out of the grave and dusted himself off as best he could and headed to the van without saying goodbye. He looked back from the road as he was winding down the slope and old Barn was still contemplating the graves in the moonlight.

Anyway, Doug thought. Relatives would probably sue if they tried to do a show. This was a litigious time.

Chapter 18

BOB TRATCHER WAS NERVOUS. Network reporter Harrelson Fogarty was in town. The network sent celebrities like Harrelson in now and then to wow the local affiliates. Most of the time, it was no big deal if they showed up.

But Harrelson wanted to interview the news director at Channel Three. That was maybe a bad sign.

Bob sat in his office. Harrelson Fogarty was still upstairs with Vern Balstad talking about who-knew-what. The minutes ticked by. There was no way to prep for a Harrelson Fogarty interview. The kid specialized in the gotcha moment. Bob'd seen him on TV. Harrelson Fogarty played nice at first and then—bammo!—he'd ambush some unsuspecting gun runner or mob boss with the exact right turn of phrase and sit and wait for an answer.

Bob Tratcher folded his hands. He would have done his nails but it was too late. Harrelson Fogarty was sure to walk in the minute he brought out the clipper. Bob picked up the top paper from the stack he'd just made on his desk and looked at it as if he was interested. It was important to make a good impression the moment Harrelson arrived in the newsroom. The place ought to have been a lot quieter, Bob thought. Somebody just outside his office was laughing. A bunch of staff was lounging by the desk in front of the televisions. It was obvious foolishness going on, though the words were muffled and everybody was talking at the same time.

"Ahhhhhhhaaaaa!"

Tanya Thorpe! To Bob, she sounded like a hyena in Africa! Bob tried to calm his nerves. He let out a little growl. He could hear his teeth grinding. He knew it hurt the porcelain and the dentist had warned him.

"Worse than that other one—the rabbits, and—whatever!" Tanya Thorpe again, talking nonsense.

"No! Cats! Cat poachers!" Cat Barnum? The black? Bob strained to hear the exact conversation.

"Well, whatever. It's still a lie!"

"Go ahead! Hire actors! Get a good script and go for it!"

Hee hee, ho ho and ha ha. Everybody was laughing, laughing instead of working. Bob turned over some official document. He wrote down Tanya Thorpe, and then the black guy. He listened hard. There were plenty of people out there. They were in deep shit.

They had to know Bob was in his office, he thought. Right? His door was open a crack, and the light was on. He coughed, and cleared his throat. He did it again, louder.

"Get this! Kenwood Heights—there's a flourishing trade in pedigree cat skins—Angoras and, you know, Egyptians. Produce it like a movie with exclusive interviews with *trappers*! Except we get great actors! We shoot in one of those ravines in Kenwood, big mansions in the background! Christ! Every cat owner in the fucking neighborhood's gonna freak! How're they gonna save their poor little Fifi from turning into trim on a gown from Paris, France!"

That got whoops of laughter.

Bob needed more names. He had the two but Cat was talking nonstop. He shifted his chair. A solution might be to peek out. He weighed the risks. He shut off his light.

"Bullshit! Bullshit!" Tanya laughed.

"Okay, I've got one!" It was Stellges. Bob wrote him down.

"Yeah, yeah."

"Have a camera guy out in morning rush hour every day—get a shitload of bleary-eyed commuters through their windshields and run 'em every night! Throw them on with some music. Maybe slo-mo it! You ever see a lady doing lipstick in her mirror? There's through-the-roof numbers, right there!"

"I'd keep that one quiet! If Tratcher hears that, he'll do it!"

That got the biggest laugh of all.

Tratcher lunged from his chair. Before he knew it, he was in front of those idiots. They quieted fast. Tratcher could hear his own breathing. Nobody was laughing now.

"I'm warning you! I'm warning you . . . !"

Tanya Thorpe shook her head. "Bob," she said, calmly, "we're joking."

Bob's head was hot. He couldn't think of any words.

"There's still room for fun, isn't there?" Tanya said. "Even with everything we've faced? We really *do* take our jobs *seriously*, you know. The last few weeks have been hard on everybody. I guess that's why we've needed to let off a little steam, Bob. You know?"

Tanya gave him a confident smile. Tammy Bailey stood next to her. She had the same kind of look on her face. *Holier than thou.* "We *do* care," Tanya said. "And you do too. You've suffered just as much as any of us. More, maybe. You should loosen up too, huh?"

All of them were looking at Bob with frank sympathy on their unlined faces. There was even a trace of a smirk here and there. Oh, they thought they knew it all, Bob could see. He'd played into their hands and now he was a clown, standing there like a dope for entertainment purposes. The smug bastards.

There was no way out except to up the ante. They were laughing at the wrong guy.

"I'm watching you, goddamn it! I know what's going on behind my back! You," Bob jabbed a stubby index finger at the spoiled U of M graduates and interns and newsroom lifer hacks. "You wanna stay in my newsroom, you show serious commitment! Or get the fuck out now!"

He wiped his forehead and took a breath. There was no back talk. His hands shook.

"You think this is *Saturday Night Live*, you got another think coming." Bob stopped for dramatic effect. He shouted, "You here for laughs, get out! Don't come back, you bastards!"

Stellges turned to Tammy Bailey and winked. It was an appalling display. The naked indifference, the smug superiority revealed how Bob amused his underlings when they should be scared shitless. Bob leapt at the longhaired fucker. His hands closed around Stellges's throat.

Suddenly, a dreamlike apparition, Vern Balstad was there.

Time slowed to a crawl. Vern had an unreadable expression on his face. His hands were folded in front of him like a nun. Bob watched Vern's hands. The tips of his fingers touched, then pulled apart, then touched again.

Harrelson Fogarty—*the* Harrelson Fogarty, the network's evening news star—stood next to Vern. Bob had never seen Fogarty except on TV. He was little, with little hands, little feet, and lots of hair, which maybe gave him some size on TV. Fogarty looked older on TV, too, talking to Martin Gillis and Lois Feng, by satellite from all the who-knows-wheres across the country. Sometimes he showed up in Europe. Sometimes he was in China. He'd made a fortune shoveling shit on unsuspecting suckers who'd violated the law and then got caught.

Bob dropped his hands to his sides and pulled himself together and smiled. In his embarrassment Bob wasn't sure he looked as friendly as he should greeting a VIP as big a Harrelson Fogarty.

"Howdy," he said, at last, wobbling his head back and forth to show he meant no harm. "Howdy, howdy. Nice suit."

"His name?" Fogarty said to Balstad in a monotone.

Vern looked blank.

"Never mind. I'll wait until your news director gets here."

"He *is* the news director," Vern Balstad said in a whisper. "It's Bob, uh, Tratcher. There." Harrelson Fogarty pulled out a reporter's notebook. He got out a pen.

"Bob," Vern said, "Harrelson Fogarty is here. He's going to talk to you about the complications of having, uhhh, this Pepper on the loose stealing our van, of which we're pretty sure. Because who else. I talked to him. Now he wants you."

Bob couldn't think. "Okay," he said, in a happy, sing-songy tone. Harrelson Fogarty followed him past the people and back into his office. Vern didn't come in. In a daze, Bob sat down at his desk.

Fogarty made a show of dusting off the chair in front of Bob's desk with a handkerchief though it was clean. He hiked his pant legs and sat down.

"Do you know," Fogarty said slowly, in his deep, phony voice, "that Vern's office looks like the situation room in the Pentagon?"

"Hmmm mmmm," Bob said, shaking his head and striving for an earnest tone of voice.

"A bureaucratic nightmare, the Pentagon," said Fogarty. "'Tension-fills-the-room,' you could say." He opened his notebook slowly. "I wrote something about Vern, this morning, Bob. As I observe, inevitably, words come. So I wrote them down." With a flourish, he lifted the notebook in his right hand so that the page faced Tratcher. Bob tried, but he couldn't make out what was printed in ballpoint there. "Paranoid provincial clown," Harrelson Fogarty recited. "Those words, Bob, they came to me. I wrote them here."

Bob Tratcher's face was hot.

"It's not my question to you, Bob," Fogarty said, chuckling. "No, not at all."

"Coffee, sir?" Bob said. His face reddened. He was unsure how to address a network reporter of high stature.

The only sound in the room came from the nearly unintelligible murmur of a little television on Bob's desk that had a broken volume knob. Bob fought a nearly uncontrollable urge to watch the screen. His loyalty to *My Cup Runneth Over*, was an accident. The dialogue leaked through every day, and somehow it must have just penetrated into his life.

"Catchy," said Harrelson Fogarty.

"What?"

Fogarty raised a finger in time with the *Cup* theme song that was playing because something emotional was happening. "Compelling and tuneful. But if I can take you away from that?"

Bob made a show of turning down the sound though of course his effort had no effect whatsoever. "Broken," he said, bobbing his head with a grin.

"So what does it all mean, Bob?" Harrelson Fogarty said. "Is the media in danger of becoming the story?"

"Just how would you mean that, Mr. Harrison—Harrelson? Mr. Fogarty . . . ?" Bob said, casually, crossing his arms to show he was at ease.

"This Pepper steals one of your vans, the newspapers pounce, make it a big story. Day after day, headlines on top of headlines. So Pepper, using your equipment, mind you, becomes a celebrity of sorts, at which time your competitor Channel Five, gets involved. And WISK-TV, playing off your misfortune, capitalizes on Pepper's notoriety by featuring him on the air. At which point they become number one. Am I missing anything?"

"Well, temporarily," said Bob, shifting uncomfortably.

"Yes, yes! 'Temporarily'! Because WEE-TV must now wrest the prize from it's competitor and recapture viewers! But, how?

"Well, what's good for the goose is good for the gander. Is it not? So Channel Three simply builds on the Pepper phenomenon with its own coverage." Harrelson Fogarty looked down at his notepad. "You send this Greta B. Jones to search for Pepper. It all makes a kind of sense, doesn't it?"

"Well, she hasn't left yet," said Bob, relaxing, now that he saw Harrelson Fogarty was on board with the plan. "We're awful proud of her."

"Vern mentioned 'branding,'" said Harrelson Fogarty.

"What? Oh! I see, like commercials! For a moment, you know!" Bob flourished an imaginary branding iron. "Fssst!" He gave a barking laugh. "She's not that bad!"

"I'm speaking of promoting your station, Bob. Advertising by any means possible?" Fogarty seemed lost in thought. "It seems somehow masturbatory, doesn't it? Even incestuous, perhaps? A little like your soap opera, there?"

"Well, no, Harrison," Bob said, managing a smile, "not at all. *Cup* is a lot more for adults, per se."

"Oh?"

"Oh, yes. Like Edie. She has her problems, but who doesn't? She's on the brink of happiness with a much younger man."

Harrelson Fogarty flipped a page in his notepad and wrote things down.

Chapter 19

Tanya Thorpe chewed her sandwich resentfully. Finally, she pushed the spongy mess back into its shrink-wrap and tossed it in the waste can. It landed with a hollow thump.

She couldn't get Bob Tratcher out of her head, the way he walked, red faced and sweating, into his office with Harrelson Fogarty nipping at his heels. The image made her sick.

If Bob was scared, he had a right to be. Unless the ratings spiked, real quick, he was out on his ass. He was such a dumpy, slow-witted man, Tanya thought. But good-hearted.

It was nearly 1:30. If she hurried she could step out for a chocolate yogurt.

"Tanya, know what, you've got lovely hair," said Cat Barnum, appearing out of nowhere.

"Wow! You scared the fuck out of me!" said Tanya. "Stick to business."

"Get over yourself, doll. Learn to take a compliment. Your hair looks very nice." Cat took a finger and moved a strand off her forehead.

"Horsepucky!" Tanya said.

"'Horsepucky'? We're back to second grade?"

"Okay. Horseshit."

"Hmmmm. You're upset."

"Sorry. Common courtesy is hard to muster these days," said Tanya.

"No kidding. You and Mr. Bob Tratcher both," Cat said, in a low voice.

"Yeah. The poor sod . . ."

Tanya felt a tap on her shoulder. "It's a day of surprises," said Seth Peterson, with a grin. "First, Harrelson Fogarty in the WEE-TV newsroom, now, Vern Balstad invites you to his office."

"Lovely hair," Cat said again. "Go in and see James. He can do something for you. Friend-discount applies!"

"You leave my mop to me and my blow dryer," Tanya told Cat. She turned her attention to Seth. "What does Vern want with me?"

"From the looks of things, he's probably looking for a news director." Seth raised his eyebrows comically.

* * * * *

GRETA HAD LOST TRACK of time. She and Red Bertram were on the road. The days blurred into one long, ugly ordeal. Oh sure, they'd seen antelope running across endless, unfenced prairie. And one morning some comical tiny gray birds had tried to steal Greta's half-eaten Minute Mart sandwich.

But Red didn't bathe.

Maybe the camp showers were too drafty and short on warm water. Maybe he just liked filth. But his putrid odor was increasingly impossible for Greta to endure.

She had a terrible headache. How blunted could his olfactory organs be, after all? But Red was the type to hold a grudge. Greta knew better than to try talking it out.

Journalism often required sacrifice. Look at the female reporters in the Middle East and South America who suffered hardships without end. But night after night Greta slept with only a sheet separating her from Red. She gobbled junk food because there was no time for a real meal. She took abuse from Mr. Balstad every day. She didn't complain. She paid her dues.

"One time, I seen these two ciggies," Red said, glancing briefly at the road, as he wandered back and forth over the yellow line. "You'd of thought they wouldn't roll like that. But there they was both of 'em side by side on the sidewalk, sure as shit. Two by two like Jesus himself."

At home Greta had managed to avoid Red. She'd been more perceptive than she knew. She looked out the window and tried not to listen.

"So I keep them two butts to this day. Like I say, if I was ever dying, you know, I'd just smoke 'em and die—me and them butts—and end up perfect!"

What the fuck does that even mean? Greta thought, outraged anew to be in the same vehicle as that stupid, fatuous buffoon! Red looked at her from the corner of a discharge-caked eye. Somewhere in his dull brain, it seemed, he expected her to compliment him for ending up perfect.

"Well, I hope you do," she said, with as much false enthusiasm as she could muster, her voice adopting the playful tone that was her prime defense in awkward situations.

Red gave her a lewd wink. She lowered her eyes but caught sight of his unfortunate belly that, exposed and obscene, had worked its way free of a t-shirt too short to contain the fish-white flesh. She gave a little cry, bit her tongue, and tried to put the image out of her mind. Then she felt his thick hand on her leg.

"There, there, girl," he said for some reason. She froze. He removed his hand instantly, but with a possessive air.

The spreading wasteland of what Greta understood to be Wyoming offered no distraction. She cranked her earpods until U2 rattled and banged in her head.

The van pounded onto a ribbed cow-track. As was typical, Red didn't bother to slow down. The sensitive equipment in the back of the van slammed against the sides and floor. Red ignored the racket. Greta did too. The pointlessness of the road trip had sapped her strength.

Vern Balstad was trolling survivalist websites for clues to where Doug Pepper might be, convinced that somehow those people were in league with Pepper and, therefore, knew his location. Greta could see Vern's point. Doug was from Northern Minnesota, after all, and for that reason alone could be classified most probably as a camouflage-wearing survivalist fanatic. But so far, the tips were sadly lacking in credibility and there was no way Pepper was anywhere near this godforsaken Wyoming desert.

The rutted cow track wound back and forth pointlessly for miles. Greta considered screaming for Red to stop the van. She would get out drop to her knees and retch into the dirt. It would be a relief to, in some manner, however obliquely, express her horror at her situation.

"That's it!" said Red.

Greta saw an utterly derelict shack. Red slowed to a stop. Dust flowed through the vents of the van and covered them in a brown, humid mist.

Greta coughed. "God damn it!"

"Nice talk!" Red stared at her unsympathetically. "What d'ya want to do now?"

The shack was no bigger than a tool shed. Greta prayed to God there was nobody in it. She stepped carefully onto the soft, powdery ground. The shack's cement-block foundation had crumbled, and the walls were rotted plywood. There was no porch, and the door consequently opened onto a three-foot drop to the surrounding dirt.

An inhuman scream shattered the stillness. Greta stopped and tried to calm herself.

"What the fuck?" said Red.

"Shut up!" Greta held up a hand for silence. A scuffling erupted behind the wall. Greta tried to look in a window, but it was too high for her.

"Hello?" she said, softly.

Red slammed the plywood siding with the flat of his hand. The windows rattled. "Howdy in there! I hear you in there!"

"Whoa, there girl! Whoa!"

"That's somebody inside," said Red. He slammed the wall again, then stood on an oilcan and cupped his hands against the pane to cut the glare. A gauze-like curtain blocked his view. "Shit!" he said. He hammered the shack with his two fists in a sudden fury producing a staccato booming that seemed to spur him on. "God damn!" he said at last, out of breath. An unknown substance began to rain down from the roof. The door flew open, banging the wall. It bounced back so hard it nearly closed again. Greta felt faint. In the doorway loomed a huge man in a wheelchair. He smiled at Greta, then at Red.

They stared.

The man was maybe fifty. He had curly hair and he wore a purple bathrobe. The robe was too small and it barely covered his shoulders and looked like a shawl except that it was tied at the middle and hid his private parts. The mottled red skin of the man's chest and stomach were exposed to the world. His eyes, behind thick wire-rim glasses, bulged like jellyfish.

"The TV people!" he roared. He leaned down and stretched out a fat paw for Greta to shake. His hand was cold and dripping with sweat. She jerked away, wiping her hand compulsively on her jeans until she forced herself to stop.

He grinned into the sun, and trumpeted the phrase, "The TV people!" over and over again.

"You're Mr. Ezra Justice?" said Greta doubtfully.

"Come in!" he said as he backed his chair into the shack.

Greta and Red set their equipment inside. Red scrambled through the doorway. Greta with evident strain lifted herself inside. Food and dirty paper plates covered every surface in the cramped room.

"Don't start hooting now, Henrietta," said Ezra, addressing what Greta now recognized as a large bird in a cage that hung from a floor stand by the wall. "We got company!"

Greta stared. The bird was, in fact, a chicken. The poor creature seemed oblivious to its confinement and to the visitors, too. Unconcerned, the chicken pecked at the floor of its cage.

Greta felt like she was sinking. She didn't trust herself to speak. She walked to the cage. Much of the wire was caked with something. She pretended to examine the chicken closely. The bottom of the cage was papered with film scripts filthy with chicken lime.

"Good girl!" said Ezra for no discernable reason. He smiled brightly when Greta turned around, but she couldn't reciprocate. She felt as if a smile would crack her face.

"Mr. Justice," she said, striving for a professionalism she didn't feel, "you say you have some information on the thief of WEE-TV's news-gathering equipment."

Ezra Justice pursed his lips. His fingers pounded nervously on the armrest of his chair. At length, he turned to Red Bertram, setting up his camera in the middle of the room, and said, "I'm a good shooter. Maybe one of the best. How'd you get bankrolled?" He laughed to no clear purpose, and Greta wondered if he might be insane. Could she report that?

Stacks of *Soldier of Fortune* magazine covered the floor, and strands of color sixteen-millimeter movie film draped like long ribbons over furniture. Some of the film was taped to lampshades, some dangled from walls. Several spools of film were draped over a hobbyhorse illuminated by a shaft of sunlight. The carved horse, painted brown and pink, boasted a gold bridle and flaring nostrils. Greta decided it was one of kind, maybe an antique. Bolted to the horse's feet were rockers treaded with sections of thick rubber from the gigantic tires of a heavy vehicle.

How could anybody confined to a wheelchair have any clue about Doug Pepper? thought Greta, horrified, especially Ezra Justice who couldn't have strayed from this pigpen for years!

He rolled across the room toward her, his wheelchair snagging and crushing snarls of movie film and paper plates.

"You know, times are tough," said Ezra. "Tough. Take me, for instance." He hunched deeper into his chair and glared from below bushy eyebrows. "Ever try doing a movie where you just can't remember the *denouement*? Well, it must be the depression. Hell, the whole economy's going through it!"

He lit a cigarette, a marijuana cigarette—Greta identified the smell. He took a long drag.

"Mr. Justice," Greta said impatiently, "this Pepper. When did you encounter the man?"

"Came by here Tuesday," Ezra Justice said promptly. "Came about four. Asked a lot of questions about photography. I'm knowed around here. I was on top. Before this." He slammed the armrests of his wheelchair with his fists, shaking the chair. "Before this!" he repeated savagely. Instantly, his face softened, and he said, "Knew who I was. Wanted me to go along. But I was too busy just then."

He looked Red Bertram in the face for a long, embarrassing moment. "You do porno?" Ezra Justice said. He turned to Greta and stared at her with the same fierceness. "Any of your stuff? No? Too bad. Need a star." Ezra scanned the room with mollusk eyes. "Not sure where all these pieces go. Toke?" He stuck his arm out from his chair, but then quickly brought the dwindling reefer back to his lips and took a long hit, holding it in his lungs for an eternity. Abruptly, he wheeled around and disappeared behind an Indian bedspread hanging from the ceiling. They heard him rummaging in what must have been the kitchen.

The hen pecked the floor of her cage.

"What'll it be?" Ezra called heartily. "Hamburger Juniors and champagne? Scrambled eggs and applesauce? Cabbage and ketchup?" Red smacked his lips, about to say something, when Ezra rolled back into the room. "I'm out of everything."

Greta thought it must be his abrupt shifts of mood that left her feeling so out of balance and uncertain. She could imagine what Vern Balstad would say if he thought she'd made a mistake with her coverage of this visit. It was quiet in the room, except for the pecking.

"If I could just think of the point," Ezra said suddenly, and then lapsed into silence. The room was almost dark. Only the chicken seemed unaffected by the mood.

"Well," Greta said, clearing her throat, "about Pepper. He contacted you?"

"He must have read about me. Could be in some magazine," Ezra said. "He wanted to make some money. He came in and fed Henrietta over there, and then he sat right here at the table and had dinner, and then he went to sleep on that couch." Ezra pointed to a broken-down sofa in the corner. It, like the table and floor, was buried in stacks of newspapers and filth. On top of the newspapers were several shoeboxes that had been reinforced with engineer's tape. The boxes were open and appeared to be filled with objects of uncertain purpose—rusted bolts and clamps, plastic buttons, wooden spools, and other, completely unidentifiable things. "You probably ought to get a shot of the couch," he said to Red.

With lightning speed, Ezra reached up and grabbed the video camera off the tripod.

"Hey!" Red screamed. But it was too late. Ezra clutched the expensive camera to his naked chest.

"It's like the baby Jesus!" he said in a hushed voice, rocking the camera back and forth. "A memory chip! No more mess!"

With a snarl, Red pried the camera from Ezra. Ezra didn't actually resist, but Red, flushed and sweating, had to break his grip one finger at a time.

Ezra's face glowed like someone witnessing an unutterably beautiful vision. "It's harmonics, yep, that's the trick—buzzing it up. And that's what I'm into here and now. And have been for many years. I don't bootle around. No, sir. I go on all fours. Yup. Always."

"Fucked-up fucker," Red muttered, as he wrenched the camera into position and secured it to the tripod. Ezra didn't seem to notice. He glanced sharply from Red to Greta and back again, as if he were just waking up.

"How much for that camera?" Ezra said.

"Hey, fuck you, bud," Red growled, breathing hard. He wiped the camera down with his shirttail. "The US Marines're 'bout to land on your fat butt!" Red aimed a finger at Ezra and stabbed the air. "You don't touch my camera, got that? I think you're some kind of fuck-up!"

"Red!" said Greta.

Red's eyes scrunched into narrow slits. "I don't care. He's a nut. Nobody touches my camera."

Ezra Justice shook his head and slumped further in his wheelchair. He tweezered the last of the joint. "You say you don't care but you've got hope hanging all over you like yesterday's dirt," he said. "I can see it. Yes I can." He raised his voice, talking faster. "These things guide them in the necessary conventions of living! The mothers, the *children*! How I love them!" He lit another joint with a simple flick and sucked it until thick smoke curled from his mouth as he spoke. "Thank God for television! And the commercials, too! And," his voice shook and he raised his arms, "is it any wonder I numb my consciousness under this pressure, like the legion minions that populate the bars of the New York night? No, I say! We are the signposts on the pathways of purchase, power, and prosperity! They're all the same thing!" He stopped and looked at Red and Greta. "Look," he said, "visit me soon. Anytime. Bring along your camera."

"Yes, Mr. Justice," said Greta, crisply, "if we might record a short interview about Doug Pepper?"

"How's that?" Ezra's eyes lit up. "Oh, between five-ten, six feet, say one-seventy, blond, you know, eyes, blue, like in the ad. Though it's hard to . . . but no matter! Ask away!"

"He's ready for the booby trap," Red muttered, but Ezra didn't seem to hear. Red giggled, then began to laugh in a giddy way, which nearly drew a sharp comment from Greta, but then he stopped suddenly.

"Just start shooting, Red," said Greta.

"Okay," he said, wiping tears from his eyes. "We could have you move that wheelchair up and down in front here, bud, like so." Red gestured back and forth to give Ezra the idea. Ezra wheeled obediently to the wall, then backed up his chair, turned around, and returned. He did the maneuver a couple of times as Red sat on a stack of newspapers and rolled the camera.

"Do it again," Red said encouragingly, as Ezra seemed to tire of going back and forth, and Red kept shooting. "Okay," Red said, standing up, "that ought to do it."

Greta smacked her lips in exasperation. "Red," she said, evenly, "Vern wants a little better story than the one on the car lot. Could we get a little variety, some interesting shots, maybe?"

Red breathed out slowly through his teeth. "Well, it's not working," he said, in a threatening voice. "There's not a goddamn thing to shoot. Why don't you have him do something, then, for a change? I'm not doing your job, too, sister! Not anymore!"

"*Red!*" said Greta, furious at this breach of professionalism. She snuck a look at Ezra. Ezra glanced away, then chuckled as though he'd heard a joke.

After a long silence, Ezra spoke up. "Well, there's my horse."

"A *horse?*"

"Well, not a *horse* horse. *Pinto* over there!"

She saw that he meant the rocking horse.

"Makes me dizzy," said Ezra, wheeling toward the wooden horse. "He's a good little pony. He's my *calico* pinto." It was a distinction without substance as far as Greta could see.

"Lovely," she said.

Red didn't move the camera. He left it on the tripod and zoomed in and out a few times while Ezra pulled himself up by the reins, muscled onto the back of the wooden horse, and rocked foolishly back and forth.

Greta felt very tired. There was something very much to the point she should ask Ezra. She couldn't think what the question might be.

"Whoa, Pinto!" Ezra said, and repeated it time and again. "Did you get that? Whoa Pinto!"

Chapter 20

Bob Tratcher was watching the story for a second time, this time in the presence of Vern Balstad. Bob had seen the piece earlier and he'd decided to run it. But now, here in Vern's office, the story seemed to have gotten worse. Bob couldn't see why he thought it broadcast-worthy it in the first place.

On the video, Greta's hair was wild. She had a dazed expression and an unhealthy gleam in her tired eyes. She started the story in front of Ezra Justice's shack with a short introduction.

Unfortunately, she used some biblical reference, which underscored an impression she wasn't so much reporter as religious nut.

"The Bible says that evil spirits are doomed to wander the waterless deserts," she said. "But, just a few short days ago, Doug Pepper sought his oasis from the storm here at the home of Mr. Ezra Justice of rural Solar, Wyoming, finding—only temporarily—a respite from the stormy seas of his chaotic life."

Bob did, it was true, admire her syntax. When she wrote sentences like that her subject seemed a lot more important. But in the very next scene she had a fat guy on a rocking hobbyhorse! *What the fuck*, Bob thought. Red Bertram shot a whole interview on the horse. The movement made him seasick.

"Mr. Justice is a creative genius who collected this valuable antique horse and often sits on it, as now, for ideas," said Greta. "It's ideas—ideas about television production skills, and other very important abilities—which Pepper sorely lacks. That is certainly what lured him to this humble abode in the great outdoors."

"Well, yes, Greta," said Ezra Justice, his face shifting left and right, and sometimes going out of frame when Red didn't move the camera fast enough, "what hits me, being a professional, though not working so much as I'd, maybe, like, just now, is the wonderful idea of television." Ezra looked down on Greta self-importantly from atop the huge toy, as if he were the great Smiley Burnette himself.

"Did you talk to this Pepper?" Greta said.

"Well, I didn't say anything to aid and abet 'im."

"No, but say what he said and you said."

"Okay. He agreed I've got plenty of good, solid experience, which ought to be in real demand. Say you want to think about corn flakes. You hire me—boom! I got you thinking about corn flakes. That's being a professional. But you gotta *know* though."

Greta showed a messy table and a couch stacked with junk. She seemed to believe the items proved Pepper had visited the shack. She walked to the table. "Mr. Justice was duped into feeding an apparent wayfaring stranger a delicious meal of sauerkraut and russet potatoes unknowing his true identity as a true-blue criminal."

"Greta said this wacko Ezra knew who Pepper was," said Balstad. "Then she turns right around and says he didn't know?"

"Well, she did and she didn't," Bob Tratcher said. Vern didn't follow up. He seemed fascinated by the close-ups of the caged chicken, which, regrettably, appeared on the screen for a lengthy period, though Greta never explained.

Somehow, Greta wrapped it up. But Bob wasn't watching. He stared at Vern, whose eyes were as dark and empty as caves. Bob thought he might be asleep, except for a thick index finger that tapped on the armrest of Vern's luxury chair as the TV screen went black.

The room was quiet except for a little sad-sounding street noise.

"What's this 'corn flakes' bullshit?" Vern said, in a low growl.

"She's crazy, Vernie!"

"Not her, you idiot, the fat fuck! On a goddamned hobbyhorse! People more or less saw this shit. Saw it right here on my channel—family heirloom, entrusted to me as a precious and priceless family heirloom as my daddy's dying wish. And what do you put on my TV? A goddamned idiot! Couple of 'em. Absurdities!"

A muscle in Vern's jaw twitched in a slow, rhythmic way.

"Well, sure—"

"That little bitch thinks she has me . . ." Vern leaned forward and glared at Bob. "Thinks I can't fire her ass, equal opportunity and shit. Thinks publicity'd kill us, scotch the Kleizer deal, too. Little bitch thinks I'm scared to stub my toe. Wait'll she finds out about Tanya Thorpe. That'll knock her on her butt."

Bob nodded hopefully. "That's good! Replace her and Red too. Like I said, that Tanya'll run rings around Greta B. Jones any day of the week. We'll see some real reporting out there now!"

"How would that be? I fired the bitch," said Vern. He punched a button on his telephone and lifted the receiver. He stared at the dial and then looked Tratcher in the eye. "*Handle it,*" Vern said, his voice a coarse whisper, his hand covering the mouthpiece. Then he waved Tratcher out of the office. Bob left fast.

* * * * *

TANYA THORPE EXAMINED herself in the mirror. She looked sad, she thought, sad enough to break down and weep. She didn't want to cry, though, not here in public, at any rate. And yet, James was staring at her hair so fixedly he seemed to have tuned-out everything except the task at hand.

"I know I've let it go," Tanya said. "I did have a coloring . . ."

"Hair care is a way of being good to you," James said.

He seemed to come to a decision. Suddenly his fingers began to fly confidently over her mousy blond hair. "It's about staying present, Tanya, remembering who you are."

"Okay," Tanya said, doubtfully. She didn't appreciate being lectured by a fucking hairstylist, even a pricy one.

"I did say I just got fired, right?" Tanya said. She watched James's face. His expression didn't change.

"Just breathe, Tanya," said James. "That's all. Breath is breath."

James's Hair Faire was a Nicollet Mall boutique across the street from the TV station. Most of the women at Channel Three were regulars here. Tanya Thorpe had avoided the place. The name sounded cheap, and silly. Worse, since Cat Barnum, and this James, were an item, the connection was an obvious breeding ground for gossip.

But now, Tanya thought, she could use a little gossip.

"I'm a big girl, James. I'm very competent."

"Who colored you?" James snipped off a short strand with his scissors and held it in front of Tanya's eyes. "See that?" he said. "Never do that!" He gave her an appraising glance in the mirror. "I think highlights!" he said.

"Well, no," Tanya said. "Not now, anyway. I think there may be cash flow issues in the foreseeable future. Not that it wouldn't be . . . but no."

James smiled for the first time and met her eyes. "Tanya, this is our no-charge introductory offer."

Tanya shook her head. "I can't . . ."

James moved behind the chair and covered her ears with his two hands. He held her in place as he lowered his chin to the top of her head and rested it there and met her eyes in the mirror. "Tanya," James said softly, "some women are inspirational. It isn't so every day. But I feel it, Tanya! Let's you and me see!"

Tanya laughed with a giddy pleasure. "You're crazy! But do your worst!"

James said something French and his fingers moved even faster. He teased her hair this way and that. She watched a transformation take place. He sprayed a fragrant mist on her hair, protecting her face with the flat of his hand. He massaged her scalp and she closed her eyes and let herself relax.

"You and Doug Pepper are a lot alike," James said.

"That's hilarious," Tanya murmured, half asleep.

"Intensity-wise. You get frustrated but don't run away."

"No."

"Instead, you give more energy. Too much."

"Oh?" she opened her eyes, and examined a fashion poster on a far wall. It was beautiful.

"I suppose, for both of you, it's the price of being real."

James handed her a mirror and turned the chair around so she could study what he had done. For as long as Tanya could remember, her hair had been a gaudy picture frame for her face. But James, with a strange kind of brave confidence had carefully and deliberately clipped and coaxed her hair onto new ground. She could see her hair had begun to delicately enhance her natural features in a completely fresh and unexpected way.

"James," she said, "this is beautiful!"

"A beer?" James pulled two bottles out of a tiny refrigerator on the counter. "I had a cancellation."

Tanya drank hers in silence. She gazed at her reflection, pleased beyond reason at the change in her appearance. She had shed her corporate self. She looked unexpectedly *feminine*. And yet she retained an aura of authority. The dignity of the pretty young woman in the mirror was intact, but she was a stranger.

James sat on the counter by the blow dryer. He put the bottle against his face to cool his cheek, took a drink, and listened to the sound system. "What's next for you?" he said.

"Oh?"

"I say, what's next for you?"

"Hmmm. I don't know. Maybe I go back to Connecticut and live in my mother's basement."

"Now, that would be tragic!"

"Reporter salaries are a myth, James. I never made much."

"I'd sue the station! They had no right to fire you!"

"Honestly James, I almost think I deserved what I got."

Tanya had finished her beer, and James gave her another one. "Jesus, Tanya. You were the corner stone of that place."

"Uh-huh. I watched that place disintegrate and never said a word. That's the kind of corner stone I am."

"Nobody could have saved it, Tanya. The place is a snake-pit."

"I'm ashamed to tell you the truth. I hung on to the last shred of glory until they spit me out."

"Wow! I see why you're a writer," James said, laughing. "That's pretty good!"

"I thought I was doing God's work, being a journalist, and all. But now I know I was just there for the prestige. My whole self-worth was in that place."

"Nooooo," said James. "I've got to disagree, honey." He turned to the mirror and looked at her reflection. "Look at that girl. I see a whole lot of self-confidence there. I see a blazing intellect, too. And I see willpower that can handle this and any other shit God throws at you." Tanya didn't answer. She stared at herself. "And, Tanya, I wonder if I can share some personal information."

"Okay," she said.

"Doug Pepper, and Cat, and I are working on a project. It's got a lot to do with what you just said. Maybe you'd be interested."

Tanya Thorpe didn't answer. She stared at herself. She turned her head. "It's a wonderful cut, James. But I wonder if we could take off another inch. And maybe go a little more red. This is a part of me I've never seen before."

* * * * *

BOB TRATCHER WAS NOT the news director he'd once been. But he was a survivor. In fact, there were still parts of the job—the honest, straightforward parts—that filled him with real pride at being in charge, making a big contribution to day-to-day news.

There was a tap at his office door. It was a tentative, mealy-mouthed sound. Bud Vanderpein had finally shown up.

"Get in here!"

The door opened and there was fat, dumb Bud. His freckles stood out on his pasty skin. His hair was redder than ever. He wore an ugly sports jacket. It was a weird red, green and white pattern, like a semaphore signaling that Bud had finally lost it big-time.

Bud reminded Bob of one of those inflatable plastic clowns with a weighted bottom. You punched it and punched it, and even when you did, it still swung right back up in time for another smack. Bud stood there chewing on his lower lip. He tightened his face into a grin or a grimace. Bob wasn't sure which.

"You have yourself a seat, there, son," said Bob, motioning to the chair. "Just sit down."

Bud sat down, and Bob studied him resentfully. On *My Cup Runneth Over*, Patrice had finally had enough of Dr. Johnson Smith's manipulative behavior and was running from the room in very dramatic fashion. But how could Bob watch now, what with Bud sitting there like a lump expecting him to talk?

"Bud," Bob said, "you're using too many goddamn words. Which I've tried to tell you before."

Bud's eyes were moist. His face underwent a sudden change. He blushed behind those freckles. He gave a hard, unhumorous laugh. "What? Is there, like, a shortage?"

"Cut the crap, goddamn it!" Bob said. "You know it isn't *numbers*. Cram as many words as you want into sixty seconds if the desk lets you have that long. I don't care. But you, do you hafta use words people hafta look up because who the hell knows what they mean? He grabbed some of Bud's scripts from his desk and shook them. "Who're you trying to snow?"

Bud Vanderpein turned redder and bit his lip again. He leaned forward and for a minute Bob thought the fat reporter might try to jump him. "Bob," Bud said, finally, "all I'm doing is trying to communicate."

That was funny. Bob laughed bitterly. "Yeah? Then how come you said this?" He picked up a script with a word circled in red. "'*Tryst*'! I still don't know what it means! Tryst. Nobody knows what the fuck it means! You and some word geek."

"If you want to paint the world, you've got to capture the hues."

"Ha! Quit being stupid! I'm telling you for the last time to stop showing off and just talk normal! 'Capture the . . .' My ass!"

"Why are there hundreds of thousands of words, for Chrissake? Because it's all in the *details*, all right? How else does somebody get his thoughts across?"

"Because there wasn't television!" Bob said. "There wasn't television! And if you want to work here I'm telling you to stop it!" He pointed a thick finger at Bud. "It's that or the great nowhere for you, bub. Count on it! You're about to be the next Tanya Thorpe!"

Bud Vanderpein's face was glowing now but he nodded.

"Fine," Bob said. "I'm going to be watching you. Now I'm done. Just get out of here."

Tratcher watched Bud Vanderpein leave his office. He knew that Bud, and not a few others, took him for a boob. They laughed behind his back. But they'd stop laughing soon. Bob had real suspicions about Bud. Stupid, and fat, and geeky and lousy at live-shots as he was, Bud Vanderpein had perpetrated a huge conspiracy in the newsroom. Bud was the Phantom Scripter!

Bob picked up the transcript of the Phantom's latest invasion of the newscast and read it to himself. "Experts say, a 'weight attractant' in the cement drew the victim to his death, which will last a long, long time." Ned Storm, the anchorman, had read that line without a glimmer of doubt on his face.

Bob had cracked the case when he read an article that said you could tell who wrote something by the words they used. Even Shakespeare, the article said, tipped his hand that way. Bob knew only one person who would say, "weight attractant" when he meant "gravity."

Bud Vanerpein would be going down.

Bob leaned back in his chair. He imagined the shock on Vern Balstad's face when he finally had the facts. Until then, Bob knew he had to play his cards close to his chest and keep his eyes open.

* * * * *

"—ONES, MR. BALSTAD?"

Vern jumped out of his skin at the sudden squawk. Flo's voice on the intercom was like fingernails on a chalkboard. Flo knew what she was doing, too. That cheap box was like a knife she wielded like a slasher, jabbing and jabbing at Vern. She clipped off half the information, and when Vern asked her to clarify—say, repeat, all seven digits of a phone number, she played dumb!

Vern was high-octane, he knew, like a racehorse, and these little annoyances had been building for a terribly long time.

Doctor De La Tremaine, the noted marriage doctor and mood therapist, cautioned that, when it came to women, Vern was often his own worst enemy. For example, as the doctor explained, Vern had failed miserably to pacify Bunny. As a result, she'd taken him to the cleaners. Lately, he'd been visiting the doctor for an occasional tune-up. Sometimes he came up with a decent ploy and Vern put it to use. To get control, for instance, Vern had been making an effort to believe the goddamned intercom really *did* short out more frequently than any sane person would credit, albeit only when Flo operated it. To believe that was to gain control, the therapist said.

Oh, but no, no, no, no. Flo was fucking with him. Vern was pretty much helpless, too, since Flo was protected by all sorts of Human Resources shit that Alva Avery nagged about for an unpleasant forty-five minutes.

Vern thought about Theresa, the receptionist, in the lobby. There was some chemistry there. Vern was certain Theresa felt it. She'd mentioned spirituality and sharing and putting trust in something bigger than the individual. Vern could read between the lines. He might have to look sorrowful, confess to some vulnerabilities, which he could think up later. He'd have her on all fours by the third dinner or he wasn't the man he thought he was.

Spiritual girls like that didn't fuck with you about intercoms. Their moral standards were higher than that.

". . ."

Vern rose from his chair, sped nimbly across the light-blue carpet, and flung open the door. In the force of the impact, the doorknob dented the expensive paneling in the reception area. Flo concentrated on her nails as though they were game stats.

Vern waited. Would she have him believe that his arrival had escaped her notice? She buffed the tip of her right index finger, repeating the motion again and again. She did not look up.

"Say!" Vern said.

Flo lifted her eyes with a studied bovine disinterest. Was she tired, or bored, or sick, or just stupid? No! It was the most grievous kind of disrespect!

"Get the hell in here!" Vern shouted.

Flo strolled into Vern's office, coolly indifferent. Vern sat in his big leather chair and watched his secretary. She had to be at least fifty. But she worked out or took injections. Her breasts were exceptionally firm, and he knew from experience that her body maintained a suppleness often lacking in far younger women. She dressed to draw the eye to her sexy figure and this was, of course, no accident. It was a ploy and a provocation.

But her days of parading her lazy ass around the office while her work piled up were ending.

She stood in front of his desk, her big brown eyes registering nothing. Vern watched her fold her slim white arms across her sizeable breasts and felt the familiar, unwelcome thrill as she squeezed her arms tighter and tighter squashing her tits. It brought to mind a kaleidoscopic montage of sexual images but he forced himself to focus.

"Well? What the hell is it?" he spat.

She stared at him a second longer than was tolerable. "Greta B. Jones is on the phone," she said, in a monotone. "You want to talk?"

"How long? How long would she have been on hold if I hadn't come and got you?" Vern jabbed at the phone. "Greta?"

Flo scratched herself, trying to eavesdrop. Her fingers moved up and down her butt. Her slatternly personal habits were disgusting and yet Vern never seemed to get enough. He gave her the eye until she flounced across the carpet and slammed the door so hard his liquor bottles rattled in the cabinet. He promised himself to proceed with her dismissal without delay, legalisms or not.

"Greta?" Vern shouted into the phone.

"Is that you, Mr. Balstad?"

"Me or the Count of Monte Cristo. What is it?"

Vern heard a gasp or a sob. "Mr. Balstad, what are we gaining from this? It's a good idea, but I just don't think we're going to find him. Every lead is a terrible dead end! One crackpot after another! Maybe they only want to be on TV! I don't know! That taxidermy surrealist we filmed? Beau Bardeaux? He said Doug Pepper is black! Believe it or not! *Black*! Bardeaux said he sold him 'Bear-Moose with Beavertail in Blue and Red.' He wouldn't hear of Pepper being white, even though I *knew*. And he said terrible things!"

Greta broke down and sobbed in earnest.

"You sending invitations to your pity party?"

"What?"

"You listen to me! I've about had it with all the 'Waaa waaaa waaaa, and poor me.' There's plenty of people who'd love your job, Greta, and'd kiss my ass to get it!"

Greta had been out on the road for better than a week. WEE-TV had simultaneously broadcast minute-long public service spots showing pictures of Doug Pepper and offering a reward for information leading to his capture. It was a good ploy—part of Vern's new plan to brand every aspect of Channel Three, even the search for that desperado. True, despite excellent tips from the Internet, none of Greta's stories had turned up anything. But Vern had bigger problems.

The network's top reality show *Snackers*, had tanked. It had been huge in the Twin Cities. In fact, station revenue estimates based on *Snackers* had convinced Foster Kleizer and Associates to buy WEE-TV. But, unexpectedly, the network had pulled the show, accusing the klutzy and comical entrepreneurs, of turning *Snackers* into an infomercial.

Take the Buccaneer Burger. They praised the taste and extolled the metallic wrapping that *changed color in the light* in smarmy, fake dialogue. Yes, the pandering was embarrassing, Vern thought, but pulling the show had destroyed his financial projections! Foster Kleizer and his henchmen were weaseling, too.

Vern smiled a bitter smile. Sure, he was under siege. But he would make progress anyway. The worm had a turn up its sleeve in the face of catastrophe.

Snackers's demise forced Vern, thinking outside the box, to see Doug Pepper, criminal low-life that he was, as a potential game changer.

Vern realized he could expand the search for Pepper, turn it into its own reality show! He'd slow the pace somewhat, play a little-cat-and-mouse, add some red herrings, flesh it out with some travelogue bits and maybe add prize giveaways!

And the Good Lord God had added His two cents as if confirm Vern's eureka moment by revealing a stool pigeon in Vern's own newsroom, a stoolie with real info about that bastard Pepper!

Oh, this person was playing hard to get, of course, insisting on communicating anonymously. But so be it. Vern could play that game, too, especially since the guy was naming names and confirming revelation after revelation and pointing out where the bodies were buried.

This source, whoever he was, confirmed that that Doug Pepper was the *Phantom Scripter*! That had been Vern's suspicion all along! The mysterious newsroom rat had gone even farther. He listed the IT flaws that had allowed Pepper to invade the station's Venus server and rewrite scripts anytime he wanted!

Naturally, the newsroom computer consultants about crapped when Vern explained point-by-point how the system let hackers in the backdoor!

For that reason alone Vern loved the mysterious informant, so far only a muffled voice on the phone.

Soon, if Vern's source kept his ear to the ground, there'd be hard data as to Doug Pepper's exact whereabouts! No more guessing, no more of Greta's confused attempts to sort out the true clues from the spurious. She'd be on Pepper's trail while it was hot!

"I'm going to tell you something, Greta!" Vern yelled into the phone, "This deal on the stuffed bunnies was garbage. Here's a guy who thinks he knows something about the whereabouts of that bastard, and you make him sound like a crackpot! That's no go, honey! I want some real reporting out of you. I'm paying good money to scare up tips for you! I got a two-column banner ad in *Soldier of Fortune* and a pop-up on the website, and those don't come cheap. You blow this and you're done!"

Chapter 21

Bud Vanderpein had butterflies. It was almost six. At about 6:01 he'd be live from Larchmont High with another great chance to fuck-up on air. As the seconds ticked away his terrorized brain pounded him with loser scenarios.

All afternoon, assorted neighborhood loudmouths, meeting in the gym, had shouted at each other. Larchmont had a gang problem, apparently. But the big issue, as far as Bud could see, was that everybody at the meeting hated everybody else at the meeting.

But, thank god, the tedious speechifying had ended. The bleachers had finally emptied. Only a few ragged teenagers remained. They were loading folding chairs on to carts.

On Bud's little television, a commercial aired. Master control chattered in Bud's earpiece.

Bud rehearsed his opening line.

"The citizens of Larchmont nearly came to blows this afternoon as they shared divergent views on key provisions of a new proposed curfew ordinance . . ."

The acoustics were terrible. Someone was dribbling a ball and it echoed through the old gym like a jackhammer. The kid under the basket had a king-size tattoo on his neck. He was a bruiser in a tank top.

"Hey!" Bud said, waving.

The assistant director said something in Bud's earpiece, but Bud couldn't make out the words. On Bud's screen the flaming three tumbled through space. The show was on the air. He'd be on camera in a minute.

"Hey, chief!" Bud raised his voice. "We're going live! Stow the ball a couple minutes, okay? Live mike!" Bud pointed at the microphone, smiling. The pounding didn't stop. "Did you hear me? Shut the hell up! I'm going live!"

That did the trick. The place quieted.

"Thirty seconds," said Bud's earpiece.

A basketball hit Bud in the head. "Whoa!" said the videographer, covering the lens to protect the camera. "Watch that!" Bud saw stars. He glanced over his shoulder and turned to the camera.

". . . Bud Vanderpein, in Larchmont."

Bud started his opening line. Something moved at the corner of his eye. He concentrated on his words and then he felt a wet, lingering touch on his left cheek. On the monitor he saw a finger at the end of a long arm extending to his face.

"Coochie coo!" a voice said. And then another basketball hit Bud in the head.

* * * * *

BOB TRATCHER WATCHED the monitor in disbelief.

Instead of giving a report, Bud was losing a wrestling match. Bud was down. A couple of bruisers slammed their fists into his soft gut. He understood how they felt. Bob shook his head. There was nothing he could do for the fat slob.

"Cut Bud!" Bob said into his headset.

Ned Storm, stammering and unnerved, skipped ahead to the next story.

"God," said Bob, slumping back. He punched "preview" on the monitor to watch the gym feed. Luckily Bud's photographer had the sense to keep shooting. Bob, in a sudden stroke of genius, ordered master control to record the violence. He'd deal with it later. He still had a show to get through.

Bob had had a couple monitors installed and controlled the show from his desk. Except for the Bud hiccup the show proceeded smoothly.

Ned Storm started talking about a gang that hacked computerized parking meters. The cyber-thieves enjoyed free parking using wireless devices that added hours to the meter with a single click. Minneapolis had lost thousands of dollars! Bob wondered how you got a clicker. Then, it dawned on him the meter hack piece was the show's last story. Bob looked at the clock. He'd lost two minutes by canceling the Larchmont story! In about thirty seconds the news would end. The station would sit on a station ID for a minute-and-a-half or more, dead in the water. Then Vern would call down and ask what-the-hell in his most abusive sarcastic tone. Bob had no choice. He shouted into his headset, "Switch to the live remote! Back to the gym!"

* * * * *

R. MATHEW DESMOND was a replacement at the assignment desk. His predecessor, Seth Peterson, had abruptly quit. That put Matt under a lot of pressure. Seth had been a guy loved by all in the newsroom. No matter what Matt did, he couldn't compete with that.

But with a WEE-TV reporter taking a beating on live TV, surely a major breach of journalistic ethics—at the very least, the police should have been called—Matt stuck his neck out. He ducked his head into Bob Tratcher's office to lodge a protest. The look on Mr. Tratcher's face made him turn around without a word and sit back down at his desk.

* * * * *

BUD WAS ON THE FLOOR. Ned Storm paused a moment, obviously at a loss for words, then, shakily, he began to ad lib some kind of an explanation based on what he thought he knew about the meeting in Larchmont. Bob Tratcher licked his lips. It was going to work.

One of the teenagers glanced at the camera and seemed to know he was on television. "Hey!" the kid shouted. His adolescent voice sounded hollow. Luckily the videographer panned with him as the kid moved. "Hey! We're on TV!"

Another young punk, apparently exhausted from pounding on Bud, joined his pal in front of the camera.

"Hey, you look like shit," the punk said to his pal.

They mumbled some things that Bob couldn't catch. One of them grabbed the microphone from the floor. He jabbed a knife at the lens. "Your man is all right!" he said. "But tomorrow is another day! If nobody listens to our demands, fat boy here gets it!"

Chapter 22

Tanya Thorpe sat in the Laramie airport feeling aggrieved. If "traveler's remorse" were a real thing, she had it. Taking off from Minneapolis only three hours ago she'd had a sense of purpose. The plan was for her to produce, and maybe even give some polish and coherence, to stories that Doug Pepper had, heretofore, failed to concoct and then structure adequately on his own. But fuck it. She was going home.

She chewed an unripe apple, an unappetizing Granny Smith, and watched her jean-clad neighbors in the airport lunchroom swallow sad and deflated burgers and chilled salads as they laughed and talked in picturesque Western lingo.

Tanya realized she'd been drifting since she got fired, becoming more and more unmoored, and grasping at anything that might offer meaning. So, she had signed on to Cat and James's feeble attack on commercialism and greed. Oh, but it was all nonsense.

Tanya tossed her apple in a garbage bin. She wasn't hungry anyway. Doug Pepper was supposed to meet her plane but, of course, he was nowhere around and she'd been left to tow her suitcase around the gift shop and wonder where the hell he'd got to. She'd hoped to spot him by keeping the airport's main entrance in view but now she had to pee. If she missed him, tough shit. Everybody on the concourse dressed the same. Surely they couldn't all be cowboys?

"Might I be of help, miss?"

"No, I . . ."

It was Doug Pepper. He was wearing mirrored shades and a beard and some stupid baseball cap that said "stunt double." He put his hand on the small of her back and guided her toward the revolving doors.

"You look like a gay hustler," she said.

He grinned so that his precious white teeth showed. "Anything to pay the bills." He left her side and sped toward the doors and disappeared among the cars outside. She watched in amazed silence. He was behaving with the same hubris and unembarrassed arrogance he'd showed at work. She dragged her suitcase onto the hot sidewalk narrowly missing an elderly couple, who seemed to take offense. Pepper was a hundred yards away at a large van.

She could turn around and take the next plane to Minneapolis. But the puffed-up bastard needed to know why she was leaving. She gritted her teeth and headed across the asphalt.

"How was your flight?" Doug Pepper said as she opened the passenger door to his shiny van with a huge dragon painted in dayglo colors on the side. She could smell his aftershave. His vanity included a yen for assorted toiletries. She'd forgotten that.

"Fine. I'm not staying. No! Get back in your van! I'm not staying!"

Doug zipped to her side. "Not staying? You flew out here to tell me your not coming?"

Doug looked good, Tanya thought. Sunnier, somehow, as though being on the run was a health regimen. "Thanks for being late. It gave me time to think," Tanya said.

"It takes awhile from Fort Collins or I'd have been here! What are you saying? You're mad?"

Tanya had never been out West before. There weren't any trees. There were rolling hills, brown hills. "I'm no loony-tune diva-type who's going to set off and go rampaging across the landscape for Internet morsels for YouTube!" she said.

"What?"

She felt hollow, homeless. She felt herself tear-up. She'd so lost it, hadn't she? In the newsroom, with the job to prop her up, Tanya had always acted like a queen, never a doubt in her level head. And yet everything had slipped through her fingers. She was reduced to standing in the middle of nowhere with this complete goon mooning over her, with no hope, no plan. She'd been that stupid.

Doug put a hand on her shoulder. Tanya saw tears flowing down his cheeks for unknown reasons. She pulled away from him and cleared her throat, then quickly opened the van's passenger door and inspected the interior. There were sleeping bags, and camping utensils. There was no tripod, no light kit. "Where's all the gear? I thought you stole a Roving Eye van."

"I torched it," Doug said. "In a manner of speaking."

"I'd better get going. I can book through Denver," she said.

"Yeah, okay," said Doug. But he blocked her movement, either intentionally or not, by holding his body against her.

"Look here," she said. He met her open mouth with a growling animal surge, and his smell and his tongue somehow triggered an unexpected reservoir of something in Tanya's fanatically trim, gym-honed body. It was a stupid thing to do, yes, but she'd wanted him before, and she wanted him now.

* * * * *

BONNIE LEE THAYER DROPPED her purse on her desk in the WEE-TV public relations department offices. She sat down with a thud.

She glanced at her ancient Snoopy telephone. The cute cartoon dog was a purposeful counterpoint to her framed Ansel Adamses and muted colors. Snoopy's brash red dog house and cheeky smile proved that work could be fun! She shoved him to the edge of the desk so she could spread her newspaper.

Anton Silph's column was long. The paper had squandered an incredible amount of space on that foolish man.

"OH, WOE IS ME! THE TROUBLES AT THREE!"

Bonnie Lee's small hands crinkled the entire arts section. The thin blue veins running to her frail little knuckles throbbed. "Shit a brick," she said. She dared not throw the newspaper away. It was her job to somehow fashion a coolheaded even-handed, and utterly convincing response. Somehow.

"TV News can't be anything more than a kind of table of contents for the events of the day," Silph lectured. "Unfortunately, TV news as it plays out in the Twin Cities, has the news content of a fortune cookie. WEE-TV is Exhibit A. In a ratings slump, struggling to improve the bottom line in hopes of selling itself to an investment firm, Channel Three has resorted to shameless self-referential hype."

How did Silph know about the sale?

"Veteran street reporter Bud Vanderpein, as almost everyone knows, is held hostage by attention-starved street toughs. WEE-TV panders to this sick community of misfits, turning over news time to the teenagers for their rants, night after night. This is a new and frightening demonstration of disdain for the public, and more to the point, greed. I wouldn't be surprised to see station manager Vern Balstad offer the creeps their own reality show. After all, they seem to be boosting Channel Three's ratings!"

Bonnie Lee Thayer lit a cigarette and held it between thin fingers. Her hand steadied. Channel Three was a battleship caught in the periscope of a submarine and the torpedoes had been launched. Her only defense was distraction: to stand on the deck, metaphorically speaking, waving her hands and babbling in loud tones in an attempt to avert the inevitable impact. Good luck with that.

But Bonnie Lee would not give up.

She lifted the receiver from Snoopy's paw and tapped Anton Silph's two-digit code.

"Hello?" Anton's throat was leather, cured by nitrates and tars and years of chronic drunkeness.

"Tony, honey," said Bonnie Lee, "how're you?"

"Bonnie," Tony rasped, in the voice of a dried-up frog. "How can I help?"

"Tony, what are we *doing* to each other? I tell you something, something *true*—and you go ahead and print *this*!"

Bonnie Lee had lived north of the Mason-Dixon Line for decades but a pinch of Atlanta spiced her patois when she thought it needful. "Could you just please, please tell me what I can do to make you understand that WEE-TV *always* broadcasts in the public interest, before your column just *ruins* us?"

"The facts are the facts, kid. You know better than to take it personally. Come on. Lighten up. You'll live longer."

The level of condescension in that man was absolutely staggering. Bonnie Lee hated Anton Silph, and more now than ever.

"Tony, please listen! Am I just being *foolish* talking to you? Tony?"

"Bonnie?"

She gritted her teeth. "Tony, Bud could be murdered at any moment. What would you have us do? We're walking on *eggshells* to save that young man! And you call it a cynical ploy. Please don't distort the record like this!"

"Let me call your attention to the ad adjacent to my column, today. I don't know who on your staff wrote it. But if it's not the very last word in cynicism, I'll eat today's final edition!"

Bonnie Lee said, "Fuck it," under her breath, and hung up the phone. The Silph column was a mockery. She herself had written the ad, of course. It had run several times in various forms over past weeks and she was proud of it.

"IF YOU THINK THE NEWS IS JUST HEADLINES," the copy read, "ASK BUD. Ask Bud how it feels to live at the point of a gun. Ask Bud how it feels to live on dry crusts of bread like the hostages in the Middle East. Ask Bud what it means to long for freedom. Ask Bud about the tragic plight of American minorities and their desperate struggle to survive."

Bonnie Lee's copy ended with a pithy paragraph. "We just hope and pray that someday soon we get the chance to ask Bud these questions. And one thing is sure. Bud's a great reporter. He'll have the answers!"

There was some beautiful language there. And the audience was obviously with her, Bonnie Lee thought. The news had enjoyed a substantial ratings bump lately.

And yet, within the tight community of wordsmiths in Minneapolis-St. Paul, no, the ad wasn't appreciated. In fact, some naysayers, like Mr. Anton Silph, maligned her for it. "Fuck a duck," Bonnie said. She pulled Snoopy close and stubbed out her smoke on his little paw.

Chapter 23

The Minnesota Prairie, dreary as it might seem to those who didn't comprehend the beauty of cattail and willow, and the gleam of marsh and creek, was, Tanya knew, a heavenly wilderness.

Wyoming, by contrast, had no such loveliness—subtle or otherwise. It was dry, endlessly flat, and downright ugly.

Oh, yes, at times there was a nearly imperceptible rise in elevation as the land rose and dipped like an interminable wave. Sometimes Tanya thought she glimpsed silvery mountains in the far distance. Jagged, glowing with light, they seemed to promise a serenity she didn't feel, but they were always gone in an instant. If she and Doug ever reached those mountains, Tanya thought, maybe the two of them would be transformed.

Yet Doug's van had a great sound system. The leather seats were heated and as luxurious as the fanciest office chairs. And Doug's hypermasculinity seemed to work to Tanya's advantage. He wouldn't let her drive or even cook beans on his ridiculously complicated portable stove.

She was feeling quite pampered, in a provisional way, as though she were on a luxury vacation to a third-rate destination as the withered wasteland moved outside her passenger window. Sometimes Tanya dozed, isolated within herself, eyes closed, mind drifting. Those dreamy states were a bulwark against the uncertainty that sometimes rose in her like an ocean.

"How are your ankles?" Tanya said.

"My *ankles?*" Doug said.

"Your terrible shin splints. It's all you used to talk about. At the station?"

"Hmmmm, no. Anyway, I don't jog now."

The sun had turned Doug Pepper golden and brown. He was practical and energetic. But in an odd way he seemed less a person than a set of circumstances. He was a closed book, a self-involved loner without a speck of spontaneity. She'd forgotten how boring and predictable he was. She'd misjudged what an effort it would be to work with him, blinded as she was by James, and by Cat Barnum's vision of excitement and groundbreaking stories chronicling the lives of real people as played out on the back roads of America.

Tanya just didn't feel up for kissing Doug Pepper's ass, and propping up his fragile ego every ten minutes. The whole enterprise, in her estimation, was really, really shaky. Even Cat Barnum, the impregnable bastion of calm and cool ideas was edging closer and closer to the brink of desperation. Cat'd pulled his latest story idea from the "schedule of events" section of the Triple-A travel magazine!

Tanya dozed. The van crunched over gravel and stopped. They were at an old-time grocery store. Good. She was thirsty and had lately developed a taste for beef jerky. She opened the passenger door and got out.

The gas pumps were antiques. They looked like skinny red lamps. On top of each there was a glass bulb decorated with a flying horse. "Mike!" said Doug, to a guy in a blue denim jumpsuit with a nametag. "We're here for the Tree-lunking Festival!"

The store itself had a porch and flowers boxes under the windows. The place had fresh paint and a cheery feel, though Tanya was glum.

"Tourists, huh?"

"Yessir," Doug said. "I guess that's right."

Doug wore his cheerful boyishness like an old t-shirt. It was serviceable, but a little ragged, since he wasn't a kid anymore and often came across as needy, Tanya thought. Still, she preferred his affable glad-handing to the courtly, flirtatious treatment she got when Doug was feeling talkative.

"Why'n'cha talk to the mayor?" said Mike. "He's my brother. Hey, Eddie!"

Eddie was inside the store. He came out with a toothpick in his mouth. "What's up?"

"These here are tourists," said Mike, unexpectedly putting an arm around Tanya. "For the Tree lunking!"

"Ah, so," said Eddie. "Too bad."

"Yeah," said Mike.

"Late by a week. To the day," said Eddie.

"Sorry," said Mike.

Cat had texted Doug a paragraph about the event. "Triple-A says it's now." Doug showed Eddie the screen. Eddie shook his head.

"That's just wrong," he said. "It's all over."

"Too bad," Doug said. "We're with a TV station in Minneapolis, see. This kind of festival really grabs the national spotlight these days. You handle it right and people eat it up. How's it work? You run around in the trees?"

"Well, there more to it," said Eddie, "but, yeah, in a manner of speaking."

"Perfect. I would of climbed up there with you, and caught the vibe, if you will. Before you know it there'd of been calls from *The New York Times*. I'm serious."

"No kidding. I wondered how . . ."

"That just happened with our 'Hydraulic Wars' story," Doug said.

"No kidding," said Eddie.

"We wrote to 'Is that Weird or What?'" said Mike. "They didn't answer back."

"Did we do that?" said Eddie.

"Yep. And I told you at the time. Registered mail, too. But nothing."

"Damn. Strike two," said Doug.

Mike and Eddie nodded.

"I often wished we'd of waited," said Eddie. "We could have fostered a delay." He held his toothpick up to the light, examining it.

"You didn't know," said Doug.

"It's only mostly locals anyway," said Eddie. "This year, nary an uptick at the store. They spend what they gonna spend." He shrugged. "It isn't brain science."

"But a whole world waiting out there," said Doug. "An unknown world."

Eddie tossed his toothpick and they stared at it lying in the gravel.

"Tree lunking's quite a little show," said Mike.

"Yes. Yes it is." Eddie put his hands in his pockets. "On the other hand, the season's way too short."

"It's two days," said Mike. "The weekend."

"I know that," said Eddie.

"People have work. Younger ones have track. We were almost champions," Mike told Doug.

"But it could be longer."

"Okay," said Mike.

"I'm gonna see about something," said Eddie.

"How so?"

Eddie landed a playful but audible punch on his brother's bicep. Mike rubbed his arm. "Some more festival!" Eddie said.

Mike nodded. "Yeah. It's already done."

"I know that, but as mayor, my thinking is there's possibility. Options. It's not that hard to figure out. Call District One. Talk to the chief. Tell him I said so."

Tanya and Doug followed Eddie along Main Street. "Mike'll talk to the volunteer firefighters. They're a good bunch of boys. We'll get something going for sure. No problemo. All of our top Tree Lunkers live right here. Despite efforts. At the firehouse you'll see quite a few. You just won't believe what they can do."

The prairie stretched past the edge of the town's last unexpectedly green lawn and on and on to the horizon, broken only by a grove of trees at the top of a distant rise. The three got closer to the trees and the wind picked up and Tanya saw the trees transform themselves into a shape-shifting, sparkling light show. They bent and danced and the wind made the whole grove moan.

"Those are *some* trees," said Eddie.

The trees were a lot farther away than they looked, and Tanya and her companions marched on. She wondered how the giant oaks got there in the first place. Nothing but grass grew for miles in any direction.

From Tanya's viewpoint the trees were beautifully silhouetted against the sky and prairie. At last she and the others stood in the shade of the giants. The wind died and then picked up. The creaking, rustling branches made Tanya want to lie down in the dry grass and take a long nap.

"The trick's to get up highest or farthest out on a limb," said Eddie. "Or, anyways, use up the most rope. A Tree Lunker has a rope around his middle. He's gonna get points for each three feet of rope he pulls past the baseline painted there on the tree. Gotta be one of the eligible trees, see, the tallest and strongest. You can really travel up in them. You always gotta do another three feet, remember, or forget it. No Points. It's what keeps it interesting!"

"Wow. Okay."

"Now and then we lose somebody up there. Because it's dangerous, is why. You try a route, you don't know if it'll hold you or not."

"No. I see that," said Doug. "Going out on a limb, so to speak."

"Young kids do best. Cause they're lighter."

"You let kids do that?" Tanya said.

"Well, eighteen and over. Or a note of permission. 'Cause of the Pelaski rule."

"'Pelaski'?" said Doug.

"Can't talk about it. Cousin of mine. Just can't talk about it."

"Oh," said Doug. Birds twittered in one of the trees. "Sorry."

"That's Tree Lunking, though." Eddie shook his head. "That's how it's played."

"People actually die?" said Tanya, shielding her eyes against the glare as she examined the upper branches.

Eddie gave her a serious look. "Foscel has known some tragic times on account of this sport," he said. "Over the years. Yep. You gotta be smarter than the tree, or heaven help you."

"It's a challenge, that's for sure," Doug said, staring at the branches. "But so's baseball. Ever think of another sport?"

Eddie shook his head. "No. Look around at all the flat. When you live with all this flat out here, you kind of want some up-and-down. A little vertical. The trees here give us that. It's a blessing."

"Yeah, but tennis? Soccer? They're safe."

Eddie looked out across the prairie. "Sure. But I don't know. Prairie's like a hole you can't climb out of. A man needs something *upwards*, see, in lieu of horizontal. It's just a matter of desire, you could say." He swooped his arms out at the view. "A man needs more than flat."

Doug didn't answer. Tanya couldn't wait to get Eddie on video. He was a hick-town philosopher and that would definitely play well, she thought.

"You want some *here* instead of always just *there*," Doug said.

"That's right," said Eddie. "That's right, Doug."

Doug jumped at a branch and did pull-ups. Tanya watched. The hot wind began blowing from across the prairie.

* * * * *

THE VAN'S BACK SEAT made a nice couch so Doug unbolted it and put it in the grass. Doug and Tanya sat under the open sky and watched a kettle of food cook on the kerosene flame.

"This'll be kind of a sociological report," Doug said. Tanya kept quiet. He grabbed his notebook. "Yeah," he said. "Plenty of possibilities. Right? Right, there? Hey?"

Tanya's eyes were open. She wasn't deaf.

Doug decided to let her be.

"We're going to need you up in a tree, Doug," Tanya said, finally.

"Okay. Trees aren't my thing, actually. Heights neither."

"Who's the producer here, Doug?"

"No! Sure! Of course! But not too high, though."

"And why aren't there any women, I want to know."

"There could be. You don't know. You could go up."

"I'm the producer!"

"Well, truthfully, we're more a partnership, right? But yeah! I'm game. You want me up there, I'm right up."

"I'd like you to use the big camera. The zoom lens'll give us flexibility so it's worth it."

"I'll have to stop you right there, Tanya. I just have my iPhone. I shipped Cat the Sony. Servo's out. Nothing but error messages."

"'Servo'? It's solid state!"

Cat shrugged. "True. If it were the servo I could've fixed it with a screwdriver. As it is, it's probably the motherboard. It's toast."

"Jesus H. Christ!"

"Blasphemer!"

"How long have we been stuck with your fucking iPhone?"

Doug unzipped his hip pouch and put phone and accessories in his lap. "There's even a little telephoto, Tanya. We're fine. Believe me! Here's a wireless clip-on mic! We'll get sound up there."

Luckily, Tanya took it in stride. Doug relaxed. Chances were, she'd matured since her days as a star reporter when she was impossible to please, no matter how you tried. Even when they were lovers, she'd said hurtful things. She was still Little Miss Professional no doubt, Doug thought, but maybe softer. She didn't need to know that the big camera was in a blue bag at the back of the van.

"I've got a story idea, Tanya," Doug said. "Kind of funny, I got it in the bathroom at the Foscel Grocery."

"I can't imagine!"

"Well, listen! Mostly, it's for guys. Picture this: You're sitting on the stool in some foreign stall. Filthy, see. All stained and shit. Like, in bars."

"I'll take your word for it."

"Like I said, for guys. A pen's falling out of your pocket with your pants bunched up, and you get inspired and write something."

"You do that?"

"No. But people. In general."

"Graffiti? Bad, bad idea."

"Not graffiti. More poetry. Listen to me! This guy sits there inspired and so he writes lines above the toilet paper dispenser."

"Women don't have the time. There's someone waiting. Inevitable."

"Tragic." Doug opened his notebook. "'Beware of people who dress the same unless they're identical twins. For it's too easy for men in a crowd to pardon their mutual sins.'"

"What's that? No, forget it."

"Huh? You should like this stuff. You're the writer!"

"Too wordy. This is TV, Doug."

"Okay. 'Did Viagra kill the dildo?' That's pretty good. Short."

"Poetry you say?" said Tanya in a sarcastic tone.

"'Fish gotta swim, birds gotta fly, man's got to ask himself, why, why, why.'"

"Well, it rhymes."

"This stuff is everywhere," said Doug. "Since I've been on the road? What if there's some rootless hobo poet, like Jack Kerouac, who stops up in Steamboat Springs, and then heads to Gunnison and Moab or Price and leaves his stuff in stalls for, like, the very select audience who'll be looking. Wouldn't it be a great interview?"

"And this guy, he's real?" said Tanya.

"Sure. Maybe. 'The mind and body are not tangential entities. I must pay them both heed in order to succeed.' He's like a traveling preacher. Everybody's got to take a shit. He's got a captive audience, so to say."

"I imagine. Why don't we get Tree Lunking done and look into it then, okay?"

"'When solutions are blocked behind doors that are locked and the future is barren and broken, then faithfully ignore reality and you will see other doors open.' Yeah. Like a preacher. A prophet in the wilderness. Except his reward's in heaven, since how's he going to meet his fans? Unless he hangs around johns, which I hope he doesn't. But what if we find the guy and have a reunion and people say how much he meant to them at a low point. And he's old and all but his face just glows with gratitude since he knows he's helped so many not expecting any thanks."

"Pretty touching. But I'm going to sleep now. Big day tomorrow."

"Okay. You're going to sleep on this side, finally?"

"No."

The fire seemed intimidated by the darkness. Doug watched it quiver and shrink. He heard Tanya stumbling around, and then made out her shadow taking her sleeping bag out of the van. He felt good. She'd hurt him in the past, but the past was past. They were alike, both trying to make it in the face of frustrations and unimaginable hurdles. He would have to be more protective of her in the future.

"Doug?" said Tanya from the other side of the van, "Is the handwriting the same everywhere?"

"I don't know. Probably. It's too small to say."

* * * * *

GRETA B. JONES WAS on the cell again from somewhere out west.

Vern Balstad put her on speakerphone and swiveled to the window. He didn't care if she heard him or not. He was sick of her intolerable, shrill, harping. Oh, Greta was a champion whiner. Vern's blood pressure boiled over whenever she was on the line bitching about what was wrong instead of what was going right out there.

Today as he counted pigeons on Lowenstein's window across the street, Vern felt a pleasant lethargy even that waste of a paycheck couldn't disrupt.

Vern had Doug Pepper by the balls.

"Foscel, Wyoming, that's right, sister!" Vern yelled.

"Where?" said Greta, in a tone of regret.

Vern turned his chair around and leaned into the phone and shouted at the blinking LED. "And don't ask me what about my sources because it's need-to-know, missy! You think you're the only one has sources. No, sir. Not this time!"

There was a stifled sigh on the other end of the line. *You'd think she was the one that lost thousands of dollars worth of expensive TV gizmos at the hands of Pepper*, Vern thought.

"But Vern, we were just *in* Wyoming," Greta said.

"Well, great, goddamn it! Now you're going *back*!"

Greta didn't answer right away and Vern knew she was whining silently, which was another one of her tricks. Well, she could pregnant-pause all she wanted for the good it would do her.

"Vern, you said he was in Kansas," said Greta.

"That was a lead!" Vern shouted. "We had a lead who said Kansas, okay? What do you think I am, a GPS? I get the leads, sister. *You* check 'em out!"

Foscel, Wyoming, wasn't just picked out of a hat by some doped-up crank reading *Soldier of Fortune* on the crapper. Vern's source in the newsroom had come through big time. This was *spy-quality info* divulged by a newsroom stoolie ratting-out actual friends for the higher good, namely nailing Pepper. Vern had had his doubts, of course. But the anonymous voice on the phone proved he had the goods. For instance, fingering Doug Pepper as the Phantom Scripter. Sure enough, no more Scripter scripts after Pepper got canned!

"You tell Red Bertram to hot-foot it to Foscel, sister. I don't want you phoning me with a sob story. You hear me? Drive all night, 'cause you're on the clock, now, missy. Just nail Pepper and everybody's happy. Understand?"

Vern slammed down the receiver. He stood up and stretched. He felt invigorated in a small way. Could be he would have been a great newsman himself, if he'd had the breaks, telling people what to do, getting the headlines here and there. He'd recently taped a jumbo US map to his wall and he stared at it now. There was Wyoming. What if that Pepper stared straight up in the sky right now and saw Vern looking down at him in that god-forsaken state? Vern had to laugh. It would scare shit out of the dumb fucker. Probably, Pepper would turn into a quivering mass of jelly, realizing Vern could rain down vengeance from above. Vern stuck a pin into Foscel's little black dot, and let loose some little mouse-like yelps as if it was the death-shrieks of Doug Pepper miles below.

"That bastard ruined my life," Vern said to himself. But his voice had a new, philosophical tone. He heart was curiously buoyant. "But if you let that kind of thing get you down, pretty soon they've got you."

* * * * *

THERE WAS A THUNDERSTORM. Nobody could go up in the trees. No rain fell, but the sky was a churning black mass. There was lightning.

"The wet don't last long around here," Eddie said. "Though we could use a good lot of it."

"I don't think we'll get it," said his brother Mike.

"Who asked you?" Eddie said.

"On account of rain lacks a force of will," said Mike. "It's more like you gotta be optimistic and pray."

"Mother Nature's her own boss."

"Nope. It's apples to oranges. It's prayer missing, anymore."

"Uh-huh," said Eddie. He lit a cigarette.

There was more thunder off to the south. The sun shown briefly through the clouds but the sky darkened again. Eddie took a call and nodded and thanked somebody. "Well, it's too bad. We've got the volunteers but it looks like today just isn't going to happen. Sorry."

"But tomorrow is another day," said Mike, standing up with a grunt. "I got to get back. The new help is no help."

"It's hard to find good people," Eddie said.

"Think we'll get up tomorrow?" said Doug.

"Oh, sure," said Eddie. "The trees'll still be here."

The night came early but it didn't cool down much. Eddie had brought some sandwiches from the store. They were still good. Eddie and Tanya and Doug emptied the cooler and ate.

"You and your brother have a good time," Doug said.

"We're all we got," said Eddie. "The folks passed on."

"They left you the store?"

"No, that was more desperation. Mike doesn't like this, but daddy went a little nuts way back when. Pitiful thing, too. You've heard of a 'plague of locusts'?"

Doug and Tanya nodded, chewing.

"Well, we had sheep and grain. Dad did okay. Some years were better, never too bad. Then daddy worried about a coming plague."

"Oh! Like the bible."

"Moths," said Eddie, nodding.

"I never heard of that. Did you?"

Tanya shook her head.

"No, that's right," said Eddie. "Dad never worried about grain, like the Mormons and their seagulls and all. His idea was moths and sheep. Moths leaving the ewes and their lambs to freeze to death overnight, their little pink bodies sprinkled all over the slopes. We warned him, too, there wasn't any such thing, but to no avail. Plague moths, plague moths. It's what he had on his mind. And then he sprayed bug spray on 'em and killed the flock. All three hundred head on the hillside, wool still on, but dead."

"Oh," said Doug. He glanced at Tanya but it was dark, He couldn't tell what she was thinking.

"That was hard," Eddie said. "Me just a kid. Mike, too, 'course."

Eddie got up slowly and refused the offer of a ride, heading back to town across the prairie on foot. Tanya and Doug walked to the van. "Was he bullshitting us?" Doug said.

Tanya sounded as though she'd been crying. "I'd rip his guts out," she said, "if he was."

Chapter 24

THE GROVE WAS A BEEHIVE. There were climbers in the trees. You could see their shirts sometimes—flashing reds, and yellows, and blues—through the leaves of the giant oaks. A coil of rope sat at the trunk of each tree and each rope inched upward as the competitors chose routes.

"It's a perilous journey sometimes," Eddie said, "going up there. You just don't know if the branch'll hold you or not. And sometimes . . . well, but that's the fun of it, too."

"'Tree Lunking,'" Tanya said, "that's a play on 'spelunking,' the word for exploring caves?"

"Hmmm, you just might have a point there, Tanya," said Eddie.

"So give me this guy's name again?" Doug pointed to the rope, moving up the nearest trunk like a lazy snake.

"This is Kory Jordan Chase, one of our best. You might have a little trouble keeping up with that boy, especially with his head start, but I had a talk with him and he knows you'll be up. Fireman. One of our best."

"Great! Fine."

"Really ought to have a harness," Eddie said.

"No."

"And a decent camera," said Tanya.

Doug pulled out his iPhone. "This is all I need."

"That's just remarkable," said Eddie, looking at the phone. "And so small!"

"Remarkable until he needs to go tight on somebody in another tree," said Tanya.

"Which is exactly why I got this," said Doug, pulling the tiny telephoto from his pocket. "It'll pull in a bird's eye at a hundred yards."

"If that don't beat all," said Eddie.

"It's sure better than hauling up twenty-four pounds of camera plus batteries," Doug said. Doug climbed to a low branch and sat there.

"Now, you take it easy up there," said Eddie. "A tree can fool you. Looks green up there. But there's a lot of it dead, too. Work from fork to fork where the branch is strong. But don't get too comfortable either. A tree's restful. But the trick is to stay alert. Before you know it you're careless and it's a long way down. Just be smarter than the tree. You'll be okay."

"Got it," said Doug.

Tanya and Eddie watched Doug work his way up. Pretty soon he was hard for Tanya to see without hurting her neck. "How do you know who wins?" said Tanya.

Eddie smiled. "I'm the judge, Tanya. I referee disagreements. You gotta pull the rope past that red line on the trunk. But we round it off, so you need a full three feet for a point. Then it's a question of counting up each three-foot section of rope and you got your winner."

"Right. Some people take chances, I imagine, going for that last three feet?"

Eddie shrugged. "Well, you gotta use up your rope. It's how you keep score."

Tanya nodded.

"No guts, no glory. Sometimes you gotta go out on a limb," Eddie said, laughing, "so to say!"

* * * * *

GRETA B. JONES'S BONES cried out for a shower—a shower with a massage head and great water pressure and reliable heat so it didn't turn into an icy blast in two minutes and give you a heart attack. Yes, and Greta wanted a Jacuzzi, too. She imagined the hot jets soothing her aching muscles, tense from hours in this fucking van with Red Bertram.

Just now, he seemed to be dozing, weaving all over the road. But she could already see the town. The buildings needed paint. A vacant lot surrounded by a rusted Cyclone fence stretched an entire block. The ruins of something were piled in the weeds. The town had the charm of a mildewed mattress.

Red slowed with a jerky pumping of the brake pedal. The street widened. A banner stretched across it. "Tree Lunking," it said. But the date was last week.

"We're too late, it's over," said Greta. "Let's go back to the highway."

"I need ciggies."

Without warning, Red breaked to a screeching stop in the middle of the street. "What the fuck?" Greta said. "*What the hell are you doing?*"

Red stared calmly through the windshield. "That sign up there'll catch my CB!"

"What?"

The van was almost directly under the cracked canvas sign. "You heard me."

Greta had thought of sabotaging the CB radio by bending its huge whip antenna into a hanger. Red held endless gabfests with idiots as far away as Arizona calling himself, "Bullpucky." "Well get out and look!" she said.

"I'm driving," Red said.

"Not now. You're stopped! Without my seatbelt I'd have gone through the windshield."

Red laughed. "Squash your boobs."

An oath strangled in Greta's throat. "You drive to the curb this instant."

"Nope. Not with that attitude."

Greta stifled a shriek. Three smiling men walked toward the van. They were certainly Chamber of Commerce types, Greta surmised, with red faces and each with a defect in teeth or hair in need of cosmetic attention. This, then, was the Foscel, Wyoming, ruling elite. Greta shaped her mouth into a grin and hopped out.

"Quite a rig you got," said one of the men.

"I'm Eddie, who you talked to. You're real welcome! Miss Greta?"

Greta lowered her eyes, but her flirtatious giggle registered to her ear as a yelp. She was off her game, and Red Bertram was clearly responsible. "Thanks so much," she said. "We're about to park. My photographer was just a little fearful of snagging your sign. Awfully sorry."

"There's no need. We'll be taking it down anyways," said Eddie.

"Yes! Unfortunately, Mr. Mayor, we were contemplating the sad news that we missed your event."

"No, didn't your friends tell you? We're having more Tree Lunking for the cameras."

"There's a crew here?" Greta said, her heart beginning to race.

"That's right! They didn't say anything?"

"Well," Greta hesitated, "we weren't sure if the reports . . ."

Red finally maneuvered his bulk out of the driver's seat and waddled over.

"They're here," said Greta.

"Well, if that ain't the ding-dangdest thing," Red said.

* * * * *

DOUG DOZED ON A BRANCH. His Tree Lunker, now at a high point in the tree a few feet above, had stopped moving. Doug hoped the guy was scared, or too wise, to move any further along the increasingly skimpy outer branches of the tree. The limbs were shakier than Doug had imagined they'd be. He hadn't banked on this unwelcoming set of leaves and branches or his fear of heights.

The branch swayed with every little gust. Down below Tanya was shooting coverage with her iPhone. She wasn't sympathetic. She offered to take over if he couldn't handle the tree.

Every handhold was a threat. Doug couldn't tell what was brittle, or rotten. It'd be easy to lose your balance, he thought. One bad guess and your handhold could snap and you'd go bouncing down through the branches until you hit the ground.

Doug could see a climber's rope in a neighboring tree moving up the trunk at a respectable pace. That guy was sure to be the winner. Doug knew he should get over there now and follow that Tree Lunker step by death-defying step. If the guy hit a rotten patch so much the better! *If it bleeds, it leads.*

On the other hand, Doug thought, Tree Lunkers at least had a rope tied around them that they pulled up as they climbed. It wasn't for safety of course but it might stop a fall.

The rustle of the leaves became hypnotic. Doug managed to wedge himself securely into the fork. The light breeze rocked him back and forth in the pleasant and comforting heat. Doug imagined he was riding a long, skinny elephant.

His iPhone began to buzz. It was Tanya.

"Hey!" Doug said.

"Doug! Doug! They're down here!!!"

"Huh?"

"Greta! Red! They're here!"

* * * * *

EDDIE TOLD GRETA he had obligations. Mike guided them over the rough ground leading up to the oak grove.

Mike was a tall and pasty man with hands in his pockets. He had no hair to speak of. He yapped, and yapped about who-knew-what. Greta was exhausted but she kept smiling and tried to avoid the rocks.

"Father Mack could have done anything with that well," Mike said. "But, instead, he donated it to watering these many trees and all the houses in town! Well, it was such a blessing, as you can see! And it still is to this day! He was a very insightful man, Father Mack. That grove looks like—and most certainly *is*—a temple of the Lord Jesus Christ!"

Greta nodded, though she couldn't have a repeated a word he said.

At last, they stood in the shade of one of the huge trees. For a blessed moment Greta had forgotten Red. The prairie and town looked lovely from the low rise. Red tapped her on the shoulder. Greta startled at the unexpected touch. She tensed and closed her eyes but gave no sign that she noticed Red. She felt the tapping again. It was like a lewd caress. Mike turned toward a particularly lovely and massive tree in the distance, saying something. Greta aimed a quick, blind disciplinary swat at Red. The blow connected with his face in an unexpectedly loud slap. Red cried out in pain and with no warning grabbed Greta's shoulder and squeezed hard. Greta whirled and hissed in his face. "*What the hell do you want?*"

Mike and his friends stepped back discreetly. Red spoke respectfully. "I just want you to listen," he said. "I want to explain something. Mr. Balstad doesn't want to catch Pepper. No way. He wants to play cops and robbers."

Greta could feel the weeks of revulsion for Red rising in her veins as if there was a boiler somewhere inside her body that was about to blow. "*What are you talking about? Of course he wants to catch Pepper!*"

Red shook his head. "No way, no way. Look, we've got to chase Pepper. Sure, corner him a couple times, maybe. Like it looks like maybe now. Only the last thing Balstad wants is we collar him for good, see, 'cause the party's over then, see? What's he supposed to do then? No, it's gotta be cat-and-mouse, us and Pepper, and a shitload more crappola stories. That dumb fuck running like hell in every one of 'em."

"*What the hell are you saying! Are you insane?*" said Greta.

Greta felt hot and her vision was blurry. She could barely think. And yet, in a strange way, she saw with crystal clarity what Red Bertram was trying to pull. His plan was to stay on the road forever, living on per diem, not showering, building on the immense trash heap that had turned the van into a sty. In an instant she calculated the consequences of riding back and forth across the country forever, stuck in the reeking van with Red. She would not be able to help herself. She would kill him and do it with a smile.

"Listen, you dumb broad," Red said, in a whisper, his face red, his voice rising in pitch, "You have the cops grab that dufus and the whole fucking deal's over! That dumb prick sent us out here to do stories!"

"*You just shut up and shoot, goddamn it.*" A spray of Greta's saliva landed on Red's chin. She couldn't help herself. "*You never talk to me again. Do you understand? You're shit-canned the minute we get to Omaha!*"

Red grabbed her shoulder again. "You fucking prick-tease!"

Greta didn't think. She felt cold, clean joy and with a loud cry, she kicked Red in the nuts. Hard.

She stepped back to be out of the way when he collapsed. He tottered and looked to the sky. As he reeled he reached out with his thick arms and grabbed Greta by the neck. He had surprising strength. She was in it now, fighting for her life. Jungle rules applied. Greta kneed Red in the crotch a second time as he pulled her down. She went for his eyes as she heard her blouse tear.

Greta gave as good as she got. Red suffered the worst of it, and that gave her a sense of pride. Mike, and the other dumbos from Foscel watched for five minutes before they made a move to rescue the fat slob.

* * * * *

"It's like the wrestling championships, ladies and gentlemen, between the beauty and the beast. Only maybe more like this tiny gal fighting a balloon. It's looking like not a fair fight, exactly, with a surprising lack of skill from our jumbo contestant Mr. Red Bertram, who should be dominating his weight class here today."

Doug Pepper had remained on a low branch of his tree where the perspective on the action was good. Tanya Thorpe was using her iPhone too and so their coverage of the fight was superb. Doug felt he had discovered a hitherto unknown skill at play-by-play announcing and so he laid it on thick.

"Cheating! Cheating! You're not supposed to bite!" Doug said, in his sports announcer's voice.

But then the fight was over. Eddie, Mike, and their friends held Red and Greta by the arms as they both struggled to land another blow.

"You fucking bastard! I'll cut your sack off!" Greta said.

Red spat at Greta but he missed.

There was no post-game interview, except with Mike, who said he better not say anything. But Doug was satisfied. And, at any rate, the police arrived soon after and the combatants were ushered into a squad car.

"Let's skedaddle," Doug said.

"They'll rat us out in no time," said Tanya. Doug swung around and looked her in the face.

"What did you just say?"

"Who cares? Move!"

Doug and Tanya loaded the van and headed out of town at top speed. "Probably, 'ratting us out,' even now." Doug said

Chapter 25

Bob Tratcher, news director, swallowed a pill from a little packet in his drawer. Right away, the bad feelings melted away into a pool of drowsiness and ease. He hadn't gone home, and was still sitting at his desk, though it was past midnight. Outside his door, the early morning news team was squabbling, sounding like turkeys at a trough. He'd planned on learning the mood among the troops with a little strategic-listening, but no. It was all smarty-pants sarcasm and "how long for sports and weather" out there.

Oh, Bob had just about had it with this operation.

Maybe the Wisconsin National Guard would take him back. He had friends, after all. Except there'd surely be a reduction in rank given the questions about certain recruiting practices that had come home to roost, and the pay was certainly shit.

But the pill was doing okay. Bob's brain became a little bird flying above the current unhappiness, which somehow became blurry and pinkish and okay. Everything was going good. He still had his job, and if Vern Balstad was ignoring him now, and left him on his own, maybe, to hang himself accidentally and twist in the wind forever, well, nobody, including Vern, knew him very well, and what he was capable of.

Bob was stronger than those kids out in the newsroom.

Seven, Bob's wristwatch said. Some of the day crew arrived, laughing and gassing without a worry in the world. Grab-assing, smarting-off. Yabbidy, yabbidy, yabbidy. Acting pure grade school while on the clock.

The old Bob would have gone out and stepped in it. He turned up the sound on his new TV instead. The engineers had had to hang this one on the wall it was so big. The morning news would soon be on, and that was good. Red Bertram and Greta B. Jones had sent a dispatch overnight and it would air all day. Vern Balstad had decreed they get high priority.

That was fine with Bob. Greta was a looker.

The golden "3" caught fire and flew away and then that adolescent-looking Wesley Bean said his hellos. Then the screen showed a street, lined by a few buildings.

"Foscel is this little town's name," Greta said. "It's sort of a fossil, though spelled different. What kind of people live here? We weren't too suspicious. What made us suspicious was Doug Pepper.

"Doug Pepper was here. Who's fault is that? We don't know yet. But if the town of Foscel is in on something with Pepper then "beware town," on account of they'll be brought to justice!

"But the weight of the evidence is not fully garnered by the authorities, and the wheels of justice have yet to suffer the full extent of the law."

Bob Tratcher drummed his fingers. He hadn't caught what Greta was getting at, though it was obviously critically important. His mind had perhaps wandered at a crucial point. He would have every chance to watch the report again and again throughout the day, however, as promised in the promos.

Red Bertram's poor video was even worse than usual on this report, consisting of shaky town scenes of interminable length. Bob sat up and tried to focus.

"Indeed," said Greta, "Doug Pepper would be in custody right now except for the efforts of certain people here."

"We didn't know for sure," said an elderly man, squinting in glaring sunlight. "Hell, we didn't know anything at all."

"Oh, no?" said Greta B. Jones.

"No," said the man.

The next picture was a close-up of a flat tire. "Since the beginning of this search," said Greta, "Doug Pepper has avoided capture because he is a devious sneak. Here is the proof. This flat tire on our van is just what he needed to escape town unpursued."

Surprisingly, since he was the cameraman, Red Bertram then appeared on screen. He looked much worse than Bob remembered. Red had a bad eye, and a cut on his face that probably should be looked at. "Yeah, yeah," Red said. "Somebody cut 'em. Used something sharp on 'em, see?"

The camera showed a wide shot of the van. All the tires were flat. "Yessir, whoever did it was unbeknownst to us, except it was Pepper," Red said, and wiped his nose. His nose too, seemed peculiarly swollen and lumpy. "Say what you will," Red said. "He's gone now. And we got flats."

Greta, face in shadow, stared from the screen. Her eyeballs were little dots of light. Her pudgy face looked somewhat bruised and beat to hell. "Certainly," she said, "this small spot on the map in the middle of nowhere isn't important. But because of what happened here today, it is important. That's because Pepper escaped for no good reason. The question is how.

"If this town can live it down, nobody knows, since they let a desperado loose. Only time will tell. This is Greta B. Jones for WEE-Three News, on assignment in Foscel, Wyoming."

Bob drummed his fingers and thought. The network whiz kid, Harrelson Fogarty, had done a story about Doug Pepper, a couple days earlier. Bob remembered it pretty well.

Vern Balstad had been interviewed and, like Greta, he looked like nine miles of bad road. He had circles under his eyes and was more pasty than usual.

"Well, Mr. Fogarty," Vern said, "there's every indication we've got him right where we want him. There's just the final necessities of taking him into custody."

"Just where is Pepper now, Mr. Balstad?"

That seemed to be a question Vern hadn't expected. He looked puzzled. Luckily, he took some time to think. He rubbed his chin and then made a sound, maybe a kind of laugh. "Well, Mr. Fogarty, I'm not at liberty to divulge those clues. Suffice it to say there's some fine criminal minds working on it."

Quite possibly there would be another bump in the ratings when the ratings came out. Bob hadn't ever thought much about ratings, but now he understood that they had to keep going up or he'd be out on his butt the minute Vern Balstad completed the sale of the station to the new people.

So stories about Doug Pepper were a good thing as long as there was a buzz.

Bob's door was a little open, and he was thinking about getting up and shutting it since he was planning for a nap. Surprisingly, though, somebody was standing there. Little Tammy Bailey. Bob put on his smile.

"Hello!"

"Mr. Tratcher, can I talk to you?"

"You just did!"

"What? Oh." She crossed her arms. "This is serious, Bob."

Tammy didn't usually require thinking about. She was pretty and bustled around. But unexpectedly, Bob thought he detected an unmistakably Vern Balstad-like disrespect he'd never sensed in her before. "Well, now, Tam Tam . . ."

"First off, nobody likes those creepy newspaper ads about Bud Vanderpein because they're playing into the hostage-takers plans and make us look like mercenaries."

"Now, you . . ."

"And these self-promoting stories Greta's doing have got to stop!"

Bob felt his blood pressure going up and his face was hot. He'd been warned about this. But prior to this moment he'd never before been yelled at by a young person especially a pretty one. Bob stood up, though if his size was normally intimidating, Tammy didn't seem to notice.

"You've embarrassed every single employee in this newsroom, Bob," she said. "You've cheapened us with pompous, banal rhetoric so transparently cheesy that, really Bob, it's hard to believe even you and Vern Balstad would stoop so low."

Bob heard her words through a haze of disbelief. He felt a pounding in his head. He opened his mouth to talk. No words came to mind.

"You're going to apologize, Bob! You and Vern both! And I mean on air and in print! Both!"

This tiny person had a beet-red face. She was actually yelling, walking back and forth in his office like she owned the place. Gesturing. It was a blatant display of naked hostility. It should have been impossible, but . . . there it was! With effort, Bob opened his mouth again. He made sounds but they had no meaning. Perhaps he would have become calm and lucid had Tammy given him a moment but her avalanche of rhetoric didn't stop.

Bob stumbled in an attempt to move around the desk. In a moment of insight Bob understood there was only one way to quiet this little woman. He didn't choose his actions, but in the confusion of the moment, Bob found himself suddenly on the floor. He grabbed at his throat as though he were choking. He was on automatic pilot knowing, yet not knowing, what he was doing. He moaned and clawed his chest and rolled back and forth. Through half-closed eyes he noted with satisfaction the look of horror on little Tammy Bailey's face.

"My God!" she shouted, "Don't die! Please don't die!"

Bob wished he could, just to pay her back. He held his breath until he saw stars and began to blackout. That was good. Now he really was gasping for breath. The paramedics would arrive, and he was more than ready for them.

Chapter 26

THAT THEIR BODIES were constantly in close proximity every single day hadn't been an issue for Tanya. Doug was there. That was that. But then Greta B. Jones and Red Bertram fell to scratching and spitting and rolling in the dirt. That, somehow, had changed the equation. It was such an unexpected coup! Tanya and Doug caught it all on video! Tanya felt an unmistakable bond with Doug Pepper now. They'd vanquished their oppressors completely and utterly, condemning Greta and Red to the public shaming they deserved. Unfortunately, though, Tanya's relation to Doug seemed to have gone beyond mere satisfaction at their shared victory.

She'd begun to notice the way his lips exposed his teeth when he smiled. She'd begun to let herself study the little moves Doug's body made, the way his tight t-shirt stretched with the play of muscles along his back. She knew she was letting herself go. She would have liked to stop.

"I'm giddy," Tanya said.

"Huh?" Doug said.

"Forget it. Nothing. It's just these last few days. Victorious! Us! Hooray! I just must have suppressed all my feelings. Then presto! I'm letting my passions run wild, I guess! About Red and Greta and Vern Balstad and Channel Three. Ha, ha. Silly. Forget it. It's . . . overwhelming."

"Wow!" Doug said. He watched the road. Tanya couldn't read him.

"Don't go thinking it's anything more than that," she said.

He looked at her. "What?"

"I know you, buddy. You're the one likes to be in control."

"Okay, now you've completely lost me."

"I mean, dominate. Well, this is a fifty-fifty deal." She looked out the window. "You do, you know."

"It better be fifty-fifty. Maybe sixty-forty. I can't write these stories," Doug said. " I'm not going to even try! You just better carry your weight, Miss Tanya."

He was smiling. She realized she was too. "Okay," she said. "Just so you know."

It was the shortest non-argument Tanya had ever had.

"Let's drive into the badlands," Doug said. "We'll kick back awhile. Lay low. Celebrate."

"Sure," said Tanya. Reality was bound to hit soon enough, she thought. Surely it wouldn't be the rosy scenario that seemed to be presenting itself.

The light had dropped out of the sky. Tanya dozed and imagined herself as master of her fate. She could make Doug Pepper her lover, or not. All she needed was an exit strategy.

At last, with clouds hiding the stars, it was too dark to see anything but pale asphalt in the headlights. Tanya tuned across the radio. There were no stations. She leaned back in her seat. In these close quarters, with nothing to distract her, Doug's presence was bothersome. He was too big, too quiet. His skin reflected the glow of the red dashboard lights.

They reached Paisley, bought some ale and beer and chips, and headed into the badlands on a bumpy dirt road.

They were on an endless conveyor belt to nowhere. She found an AM radio station, at last, but no music. The show was, *Mystery Theater*, and it was like listening to *Paranormal*. A werewolf was loose in a little town.

"*Is that the body?*"

"*Yeah, that's it.*"

"*What do you think, Officer Malone?*"

"*Wasn't any animal I ever seen done that!*"

Tanya allowed herself a smile. This would have scared her to death as a little girl. Even now, without Doug Pepper here, she'd have been terrified, listening to this foolishness on this lonely, dusty road.

"*That was Granny Spoon!*" cried Officer Malone. "*That's all that's left of Granny Spoon!*"

"*It's hard to tell!*" said Deputy Bibb, sobbing his heart out.

The van bobbed along with the road shining white in the headlights. They dove down a ravine and rose up the other side. Doug veered into what seemed to be a box canyon and stopped. He and Tanya laid out their sleeping bags, one on either side of the van. Tanya heard Doug firing up the stove.

"Hey over there!" Doug called, "I'm feeling sociable! Join me, for Christ's sake!"

There was a trace of moonlight, but it was too cloudy to stay and the boulders came in and out of shadow and sometimes seemed to be moving. Tanya could hear the hissing of the cook stove and see the flickering of the lantern, which silhouetted the entire van. She sighed and picked up her unrolled sleeping bag, and dragged it across the dusty ground. "I've decided to do a little experiment," she said, as Doug squatted over the stove. "But it's going to require that you behave like a gentleman. Do you think you can do that?"

"Why, yes, miss. Soup'll be ready in five minutes. Did you buy any wine in Paisley?"

"I'm serious!"

"Okay."

"We are colleagues," Tanya said. "There's no reason for either of us to be suspicious of the other. Our intentions are both good. We just have to be open and above board."

"Yes, I think so. And there's the stove and the lantern. It's just more comfortable over here. Plus, better protection from wolves with two of us."

"Well, if there were wolves," said Tanya.

"Could be werewolves. That was scary shit."

Okay. He was making fun of her. But she laughed. She spread her sleeping bag next to his, and they had their soup.

"Do you even know where we are?" said Tanya.

"Google maps is a little vague out here. There's mention of a stock tank *that* way, I think."

"Good to know if we befriend a cow."

"Better to be off the grid for a bit, I think," Doug said.

"What was that!"

"Huh? What was what?"

"There's little things moving around! See that? It's still there, in the shadows!"

"Oh! Rats? Maybe picas? See that? There's a hell of a lot of them."

"*Rats!*"

"Obviously nocturnal. Safer from predators," Doug said. He poured himself some tea. "Probably don't even like moonlight 'cause of owls."

"If those are rats, I'm not staying here."

"Oh, come on, Tanya. They keep the snakes down!"

"That's mongoose! Rats don't eat snakes, snakes eat rats!"

"Well, see? There's no snakes around here at least."

"This no laughing matter, Doug. Have you ever heard of the Hanta virus? It's the black plague! There's rat droppings all around us! Look at that! I'm not sleeping on this ground! You breathe even a speck and you're done!"

"Oh, for Christ's sake!"

"Yeah, for Christ's sake! Get a move on."

"They're probably picas," Doug said.

"For all you know picas are worse."

"Well, they're cuter."

Tanya put her stuff in the van and Doug had no choice but to follow. It was 10:00 p.m. They were back on the road. Somehow the badlands had grown a far more complicated network of roads in the last few hours. It was a labyrinth with the main road missing. They jolted over deep ruts. Doug braked at sudden jackknife turns from nowhere.

"Jesus Christ! This is a lot of work," Doug said. "And there're probably picas all over everywhere."

"Rats."

"What if we pull over and sleep in here?"

"There's no room," Tanya said.

"Yeah there is. We put stuff on the roof. I put my arms around you and we go to bed. I know you're attracted to me."

"Yeah? Fuck you! I'll drive if it's too much for you."

Tanya looked out the window. There was nothing to see but white shapes, which were boulders and eroded hills. The quiet of the last few minutes, growing longer and longer, was somehow embarrassing. She wished Doug would say something.

The point, Tanya thought, was that she didn't really know him. Surely they must have talked in the bad old days when they were getting it on regularly. What they'd said or hadn't said didn't seem to have stuck. In a nutshell, she knew zero about Doug Pepper.

On the other hand, that tanned body seemed to Tanya to be radiating heat like a sun-baked road.

"You ever get back to Bemidji?" she said.

"No."

"LOOK OUT!"

"WHAT!!!"

Doug swerved and threw Tanya hard against the door as the van came to an abrupt stop, leaving them in a roiling cloud of dust. They were off the road, tilted at an angle. The engine died. Tanya rolled up the window but it was too late. Powdery dust covered everything.

"You hit something!" Tanya said.

"No!" shouted Doug. "Thanks to your hysterics, we're in the ditch!"

"Back up! We've got to see what you hit!"

"Easier said than done." Doug turned the key. The engine started immediately. "Probably stuck," he said.

He backed up on the road. "Well, that's a blessing," Doug said. He put the van in gear.

"Wait!"

"Nothing, Tanya! Not nothing did we hit back there! Nada!"

"Well, you swerved. You must have seen it."

There was a loud crash in the back of the van. "Jesus Christ, what could that be?" said Doug.

"Not your iPhone."

"No. The cooler. Or the stove."

"You're not going to check?" said Tanya. "Stop. I'm choking on this crap anyway."

"You know, we'd be asleep right now except for your paranoia."

"Park. Right now. Park!"

"Very fine." Doug stopped the van and set the emergency brake.

"Great." Tanya got out of the van and brushed herself off. She started walking back down the road.

"I thought you were going to . . . Christ. First the rats. Now . . . *your apparition*." He slammed the door and joined her on the road. "Twenty bucks says there's nothing but a hoodoo back there." He extended his hand. "And from now on we zip our bags together. Deal?"

Tanya and Doug shook. "Okay. And when I prove there's something back down this road, you start acting like a gentleman. Finally."

The air was chilly. The chalk hills glowed. Their feet crunched on the rutted track.

They walked slowly choosing their footsteps carefully.

"This is much safer than being alone in that van with you," Tanya said.

"Really? Why don't you go back and see what fell in the van. I'll call you if I need you."

"You go."

"Seriously. You won't be any help out here. Go on! Get!"

"The equipment is your responsibility. This is mine," Tanya said.

"Halt! There *is* something." Doug lit his phone flashlight. "Hey! You!"

Tanya barely breathed. Doug lowered his voice to a whisper. "Tanya. Look there."

"You definitely needed back-up," she said, quietly.

"Hey there, sir!" Doug grabbed Tanya's elbow. "*Stay back*."

"Shut the fuck up," she said.

Doug laughed. "Don't stay back," he said.

Two eyes gleamed in the light of the phone. Then an arm came up. The eyes disappeared.

"Good Christ!"

"It's somebody in a rocking chair!"

"Wheelchair!"

"Rocking chair!"

"Easy enough to figure that out," said a voice, "if you stop standing there like a coupla school girls!"

"He talks!"

"It's a woman, Doug. Get some video!"

"Coupla gawkers! Turn off that goddamned light!"

"I can't, ma'am. I'm a professional."

"Excuse me, miss," said Tanya. "You're out here in a rocking chair."

"Good," said Doug. "Start obvious."

"I'll ask the questions," said Tanya.

"Okay."

"Nobody says I'll answer," said the woman.

"But what are you doing out here?" said Tanya.

"Rocking. My mama used to, now I do, because there's nobody else. Isn't a bad thing. Best not to trust people too much."

Tanya studied the pale, hunched figure in front of her. Doug moved for another shot. The ground was perfectly flat. The wooden rockers grated as they moved.

"You know, that sounds kind of Zen what she said," Doug said.

"Talk about me when I'm gone," the old woman said. "Otherwise, you can go direct."

"See?"

"No, I don't, Doug. She's *here*. We apologize miss, for being rude. You did give us quite a scare."

"Well, you had your brights on, and I thought I was no more than a bug on your grill. I hope you brought soap. We're real low."

"Milly! Milly!"

A man with wide, stooped shoulders and a shaved head picked his way along a path out of the dark, and then stepped onto the roadway glaring at Doug and Tanya. "Who're you? Milly, honey, now look what you've done!"

"How do I know what I've done, Doctor John? I don't know these people, any more'n you do. I guess they're from Nelson Brothers."

"No deliveries today, Milly. Damn. Where's you wheelchair, honey?"

"Rolled somewhere, John."

"Damn," the man said again, moving beyond the road and disappearing in the dark. "Honey?" he called from somewhere, "did you happen to notice which way it went?"

Chapter 27

Doug was still buried in sheets and shams and comforters. It was a volcano of bedclothes. Tanya couldn't see a single patch of his tanned skin. She'd been robbed during the night of her share of blanket and sheets. But it was a warm night. And Doug, she'd been pleased to note, had left her her pillow.

Now, She was dressed. She'd been up at least an hour. She leaned on the windowsill. The white cliffs surrounding the big house were ash from a volcanic eruption, Doctor John had said, though exactly when that momentous event may have taken place, he didn't seem to know. Tanya herself was convinced the deposits were limestone possibly left behind by some long-ago inland sea. None of this helped her get a handle on exactly where they were. Her phone's GPS app put them in the middle of a vast blank.

"Hey! Breakfast!" said a voice from the hall.

Doug stirred at the knock on the door. "Great Doc! Bring it in!" His voice was muffled by the pile of bedding.

Doctor John opened the door. "Food's in the kitchen, mister. Another ten minutes give or take. Then it's cleanup and everything goes into compost. So you're racing the clock, son. If you want to eat."

"Oh, that's not good." Doug's head revealed like a diver surfacing.

Doctor John wore a frilly apron, which clashed with his plaid shirt and jeans and work boots.

"Brings out your eyes," Tanya said to John. "Especially those little ducks."

Doctor John had great teeth, and he smiled. "How's the bed, there, Mr. Pepper?"

"I'll let you know," said Doug. "I need more time to be sure."

"Hah!"

"He's going to be sorry when he learns about the waffles," Tanya said.

"Oh, we'll save a plate. He looked like he was rode hard and put away wet when you guys turned in last night."

Doctor John's face was broad and red in the morning light, and he moved gracefully, Tanya thought, like Gary Cooper in that movie where he was supposed to be scared but acted grand and larger-than-life anyway.

"Don't make excuses for him," Tanya said. "He's always like this."

Doctor John laughed again, his voice filling the room. "Oh, it wasn't a best effort, I'm sorry to say. The batter's bad, account of I forgot soda. It's a sorry mess. So I made up for it with gravy and butter, which was their ultimate downfall, because of too much flour. Anyway, the gravy's glue, and there's nothing to be done. I pity your jaw, Mr. Pepper."

Doug had burrowed back under the bedclothes. Doctor John shook his head in a friendly way and closed the door behind him.

"He's just being modest, Doug," Tanya said. "Dip everything in coffee and it's pretty good."

Doug came up for air rubbing his scalp. "Everybody's entirely too cheerful," he said.

The kitchen was in the back of the house. The air was cool. A breeze tossed the curtains. Through the window, Tanya saw rocks as big as boxcars. Somehow, they must have gotten there on their own, she thought.

The doctor swooped pancakes over Doug's shoulder and onto the table. The old man was too kind-hearted, Tanya thought.

"You just eat up now!" John said.

He slammed down some syrup, too. Doug flinched and Tanya nearly splattered a mouthful of coffee on the tablecloth at the startled look on his face.

"Karma!" she said. "Karma pure and simple!"

"Sit down, Doctor!" An old lady, name of Amanda, walked into the kitchen. She was not the friendly sort, Tanya thought, having officiously assigned Doug and Tanya the same room last night, without regard to privacy, having apparently assumed they were lovers, on no evidence whatever. "Those two'll think you're the headwaiter."

Amanda set about scrambling eggs at the iron stove. Making food must be an obsession around here, Tanya thought. She'd peeked in the refrigerator. It was so packed it needed a filing system to identify what all those containers had in them.

"Plenty of batter left," Doctor John said. He poured some into a skillet and wiped his hands on his jeans with loud, satisfied slaps.

"Jesus!" said Amanda, though Tanya couldn't tell what provoked the exclamation. "Quit crowding me, you old goof!"

"You cook for everybody here?" said Doug through a mouthful of food.

"No sir," said the doctor. "It's self-help and help-your-self. There's plenty of Good Samaritans when a need arises. As sometimes it does. Otherwise, there's always leftovers, at least."

"Well," said Amanda, "Good Samaritans are fine, Doctor John. But I draw the line at martyrdom, which is where you been leanin' more and more these days."

"Shut up, Amanda."

"He's good-hearted," Amanda said, as she piled scrambled eggs on a plate. "And that's a blessing. But it makes him soft. No good—in this world. It's real lucky he has me to lean on. I'm not so nicey-nice. Eggs?"

Doug said, "Yes, ma'am. That looks good." Amanda carried the eggs to the table and served Doug, and then placed a full plate before Tanya who for some reason felt compelled to eat what the old lady served her. Amanda took a helping, sat down, grabbed a piece of cold pancake from a plate, rolled it up and gave her coffee a few stirs before she put the sodden fragment in her mouth.

She put a gnarled hand on Doug's arm. "Doctor John says y'all are a couple of fugitives." She looked him in the eye searchingly. "What does that mean? You look to me like someone Wyoming Human Resources might send to report on this place. Heaven help us if you are."

"Unless I miss my guess," said the doctor, shoveling pancake after pancake on a plate, "you're dishing yourself some crow, Amanda. They're in some kind of trouble back in Minneapolis, Minnesota."

"So *that's* what you two were jabbering about 'til all hours!"

"We're not criminals. I never said criminals," Doug said. "This is a carefully considered counter-cultural pursuit we're in."

Tanya smiled at Doug's choice of words. He sounded like a *sociologist*. The old man winked at her and stuffed most of a buttered pancake in his mouth. He had the jaw muscles to handle it. "Sounds like you bared your soul, last night, Pepper," Tanya said.

"Doctor John isn't the FBI, Tanya," Doug said, easily. "I know that."

Tanya prided herself as a judge of character. It'd been a cornerstone of her success as a reporter. Take Doctor John. She could see why Doug trusted him. He seemed holy, without being religious. He had gravity.

"When you're done," Doctor John said, "I'm going to repay this good man's forthright honesty with a little tour."

Minutes later the group walked out of the kitchen. Structural beams comprised of enormous split logs gave the hallway the feel of a mountain lodge. Floor tiles were the color of red clay. The place had a whimsical, but messy, feel. Nobody here seemed to worry too much about dirt, Tanya thought. Yet somehow the place was comfortable and inviting. You could walk around in white socks, Tanya guessed, and they'd stay white. The gloom of the long corridor was broken intermittently by light from arched cut-glass windows near the ceiling, that lent a cheery rainbow effect to the ancient, wallpapered walls.

Doctor John showed them the sitting room where elderly guests, men and women, busied themselves reading and knitting.

"Nice," said Doug. "Very nice."

An overhead projector flashed pictures on a wall. Almost nobody was looking at the images. Snapshots came in quick succession. A woman, maybe eighty, talked about the pictures. She seemed to remember the people in them. Here was Theo, fishing. There was Maud and Molly-somebody in an open air auto from the forties. Everybody in the pictures was young. Only a few of the shots were in color.

"This is Tony and the dog in the front seat," the lady said. She placed another photo on the projector's flat surface. "We were going to the beach. Tony loved to swim. Roscoe did too. My they had fun. There never was such a dog. Somewhere here we have him swimming, I think. I can't remember the year."

Doctor John steered Doug and Tanya back into the hall. "This is all part," Doctor John said in a low voice, "of what we think of as our 'living reflection library.' Our people love to remember. Reclaiming their private past helps that. We give them all the help we can. Old yearbooks. Photographs—stretching back to the Pre-Cambrian Epoch. People need this. Also they need to be listened to, appreciated and respected."

Tanya nodded.

"'Give everybody their due,' I say. We're all family here. It's the way it works."

"This is part of a church, or what?" Doug said.

"What? No, Doug! Oh, no. God's a given, here, of course. That He loves his people, that's a given, too. Sure. We all agree there, don't we?"

Doug nodded automatically.

"Sure! God does what He does, right? But don't forget the people, is all I'm saying. We more or less stick with the more secular symbols of sadness and joy," Doctor John said. "Personal expression is the thing. The theological we leave alone, pretty much."

"Like a church with no dogma, then?" said Tanya.

"Maybe so," said Doctor John, gesturing for them to follow him down the hallway, "haven't thought so much about it."

"Tanya!" Doug whispered.

"What?"

"You're the reporter."

"Yes?"

"Just that you gotta keep your eyes on this old guy," Doug whispered. "He could be up to something, here. Keep a suspicious mind."

Tanya smiled and might have said something but they were gaining on Doctor John so she just shrugged.

"What do you call this place, Doc?" Doug said. "There's no kind of sign by the road is there? Right?"

"No identification whatsoever. Just a family home is what we have here," said the doctor, putting an arm around Doug as they reached a stairway.

"That kind of surprises me, Doc," Doug said. "Seems a name like, 'Shady Rest,' or 'Sunset Acres,' maybe. Being as, you know, everybody's old, and all."

"Goodness gracious!" said the old man. "Lord love you, boy, you're talking sanitarium! Forget that! You want a label? Maybe 'club,' or 'clubhouse.' Yeah. Doug, you need to understand that the like-minded live here—each individual unique in his or her contribution to the whole. I'd offer clubhouse!"

Doctor John looked at Tanya and then nodded, as if she'd just confirmed the concept.

"Okay," said Doug. "That's a little strange."

"How so?"

"Well, in that you don't know who you are. I mean you're a group of some kind, yet there's no organizational creed, so to speak."

"True," said Doctor John, thoughtfully. "That we are. The house is in trust, owned in the main by, 'The Wyoming League for Home and Freedom.' But that's just for tax purposes. We don't call ourselves that, or anything."

""The Wyoming League for Home and Freedom'?"

"Yessir. If it makes a difference, you could call us that."

"So, somehow you're a group that works for home and freedom?"

"As the name implies, yes. That we do. In our little way."

"So people that live here, they're not inmates, or patients, or clients, then? They're just sort of members of the group?"

"League. Yeah. Exactly right, Doug. You nailed it."

* * * * *

DOUG TOLD HIMSELF that something was slipping by him. He walked beside the doctor as the old man recounted the history of the place. It had apparently been an orphanage and then a Catholic retreat. The

Catholics gave it up, and Doctor John bought in. Tanya should have been taking notes, Doug thought. As it was, she was looking around, and might, or might not, have been paying attention. Doug pulled out his phone and took some shots, and Doctor John didn't seem to care.

Still, the set up didn't smell right. What had happened to friends and family? They had a long drive to visit granny. How about getting sick? What happened then? Doctor John walked ahead talking to Tanya in his expansive way like a larger-than-life Santa Claus.

"This is the laundry," Doctor John said, happily, as they stepped down into a cellar carved out of rock. Tanya admired the appliances. Doug retraced his steps and then passed the main floor racing two steps at a time past the landing to the second floor. He entered a gloomy, carpeted hallway. He could see rows of doors on either side of the stairwell. The first door was locked. "Ouch!" Sudden pain froze Doug in place. The pressure on his deltoid was Doctor John's powerful grip. "Shit, Doc!"

"Sorry, son!" the old man said. "Up here is residential. Private, see. Bedrooms." Doctor John leaned against the wall, breathing hard.

"Jesus, Doc," said Doug, rubbing his shoulder. "You okay? Here. Sit on the stairs." He helped the big man sit down. Sweat rolled from his wrinkled forehead.

"People need privacy, Doug," John said. "Downstairs, you've got your run of the place. Up here, let's keep it private. Let me show you the backyard. Gimmee a second."

Doug sat down by Doctor John. "Jesus, Doc. Admit it. There's more to this place than meets the eye. Okay? You gotta fill in the blanks."

"I'm not reading you, Doug," said the old man.

"We don't need to see any backyard, or even bedrooms either. But I'd sure like to see the books. Bet they're interesting! Right, Doc?"

"How do you mean that, Doug?"

"Well, for starters, how much money is there, and where's it come from? Strikes me, out here in the middle of nowhere, you don't get a lot of visitors. All right? Some people'd pay a lot, I bet, to have bothersome relatives out of the way. 'People's Peace and Freedom Foundation?' More like a holding pen for folks that need to be kept out of the way. That about it?"

"Wyoming League for Home and Freedom, Doug. Man, you make the place sound like something from a tabloid headline."

"How's 'Elderly Fleeced by Sharpies' for a headline? May need refinement."

"The minute I opened my big mouth last night, Amanda said I stepped in cow poo. Looking like she about called it."

"Excuse me, doc. Tanya! I've got to get my reporter up here. Tanya!'"

Tanya was there in a heartbeat, looking up at Doug from the landing. He was pleased to note she'd been eavesdropping like a good reporter.

"You're such an idiot, Doug," she said. "We've been on the road quite a long time, Doctor John. Doug a lot longer than me. So don't judge him. He has PTSD or something."

"What!" said Doug.

"No offense taken," said Doctor John, nodding.

Doctor John put a hand on Doug's shoulder. "What the hell, Doug," he said, in extremely condescending tones, "I know you care. Ours is a complicated operation and you're new to it. You just can't know what you don't know."

Doctor John walked them through the rest of the building but Doug was in a daze. He was mortified. Outside, on a patio, they had tea and sandwiches Amanda made. Boulders towered over them.

"We had to clear quite a space out here," said Doctor John, with a smile that seemed genial or smug. "There's a lot going on. You're not aware, of course."

"I thought such talk was off limits," said Amanda.

"Well, but we might have come to an understanding," said Doctor John.

They followed Doctor John back to the front of the house and he worked the room like a politician—slapping backs, laughing like a maniac, joking around. There was a big story here, Doug could see.

"Well," said old Amanda, easing up to Doug, "well, well!" The big old gal put a heavy arm around him and dragged him so close he caught a whiff of face powder. "I don't care what you and Tanya did," she said, in a confidential tone. "I don't care who wants you. You're real safe here. Okay? If you're intendin' to stay, Doug, Doctor John and I could use a hand with some of the chores . . ."

"Amanda, *shut up!*" cried Doctor John, from across the room.

"One of us is confused, here, John," Amanda shot back. "Most likely you. We got us a pair of healthy young people here. If we're going to trust 'em, than I say trust 'em, and be done with it."

"Trust them, sure! But I see recruiting going on over there! Turning on that sly charm of yours when you know we don't work that way."

"How do I know how we work, John, we've been playing it by ear since day one," Amanda said, "All I do know I gotta conserve you, honey! You've got thirty-five people on your hands! Plus there's two or three on the way, don't forget!"

"And they're welcome," said John. "We've got plenty of room."

"Room? Yessir! Room is what we have! But there's only one *you!*"

Nobody seemed to think the flare-up was serious. People were smiling as if Amanda and John were a sitcom couple. "You give out on us, John, and we've got real trouble! You won't care, your earthly race forever complete, and, good for you, but there's these others. So if these two young people . . ."

"Tanya, Doug, good people, my apologies for our outburst! It's my fault," said Doctor John. "I've failed to convince Amanda of my invincibility! Furthermore, were anything to happen to me, she can hire help. We've got money, for God's sake. And this place is endowed in perpetuity. But she worries. And I'm afraid I can't fix that. I got a late start! I just don't want the rest of you to worry!"

Amanda ignored him. "He's a silly, silly old man," she said to Tanya with a smile. "He invented a switch, if you can believe that. A *switch!*"

"It was a breakthrough in nanotechnology, though," said Doctor John, having joined them, "at a quantum level."

"He made a pile of money, and frankly, he's had a swelled head since that day. He's just unmanageable." Amanda shook her head. "A *switch!*"

"You ever heard of photon absorption?" said Doctor John.

"No," said Tanya.

"Well, before me, there was no reliable—"

"Some of these folks related?" said Doug.

"Related? No, sir," said John.

The old man could be intimidating, Doug could see. He moved in, towered over you, cheerfully violating your space. Doug knew it was a power thing. "Nobody here's related," said Doctor John. "Oh, fourth cousins, maybe. See, Doug, when our people come here, they've pretty much run out of family. A bitter thing. But true."

In the corner of the room, the overhead projector was running, as it had been that morning. This time, an elderly gent was showing snapshots. They looked familiar. They were exactly the pictures shown that morning!

"Hold on here, hold on!" Doug said, his voice shaking. "They're not family, so how come he's showing 'Tony,' and 'Roscoe the dog'?"

"Doug, that's Ernest's boy, James. The cocker spaniel's old Narcissus. James loved that dog. This particular day is Fourth of July, lake Miniwashta, some year. Right Frank?"

"Fifty-two, Doctor," said Frank.

"I've got eyes!" Doug said. "How're you pulling this off? Same photos, different names and times? No way! This is a scam, Doc! A clear cut scam!"

"Keep it down in here, would you?" Doctor John said, taking Doug by the arm. He pulled Doug into a hallway. The way the light hit, Doug could see Doctor John was actually pretty old. "We share," he said.

"*Share*? You can't share that! It's pictures!"

Doctor John nodded. "Think of Carl Jung! Remember, he says symbols are everything! These photos? They trigger memories! I've seen it! But old black and whites and color snapshots are scarce! Photo albums get tossed, hard drives crash. It turned out most of these people came here with nothing! We use our only stack over and over. Could be play-acting of some sort, but memories come flowing out of nowhere even if, as you say, they can't be true. No, they're not *real* memories, I guess. Not, at least, if you mean that's Frank's dog Narcissus, there! No! But I've seen miracles in this room! A person just doesn't talk and then—boom!—out come the pictures and there's a fountain of recall that had to be just waiting inside! It's a real blessing when you see that happen!"

Doctor John had his arm around Doug's shoulder again. It seemed to be his favorite way of talking to people.

"Well, that's the goddamnedest thing," Doug said.

"You use what you've got, Doug. I learned that a long time ago. Sometimes it's best not to ask why something *is*. If it works, you just go with it. You nudge 'em here and there, and pretty soon, they're filling in the blanks. Frankly? I bet the memories they make in this room are a damn site better than the lives they lived. That's a sad thing. But a true one."

Tanya was across the room whispering with Amanda. Doug wished to God she was here listening to the old man talk. But no. *Making up memories.* It sounded like so much hocus-pocus. Plus, it didn't pass the smell test.

"What if your driving people crazy?" Doug said, looking Doctor John in the eye. "They go senile on you, and you get the house and car and the insurance money? A nice little living for you and your girlfriend, huh?"

Doctor John unexpectedly cracked a smile. He actually laughed. "Wow. Okay. I see."

Say what you will, Doug thought, *Doctor John is a friendly old con man.*

"Looking at pictures won't make you senile, Doug," the doctor said. "Made up stories that make you smile can rescue a soul drowning in sorrow. Know what kills though? Sensory dep. *Sensory deprivation.* Picture the aging process: your body changes, friends die, you get sick, can't walk. Then add on isolation, abandonment. People here have kids but you'd never know it from the support those brats gave them. It was plain non-existent. Imagine, you're vulnerable and all your connections are cut-off. Would you like that? No. Well, look around the room, because that's the life story here.

"I'm a medical doctor. I should have practiced, but I didn't. I started a company and it went big just like I hoped. I mean, a cash avalanche. Money rained down. Still does. But there's grief in the world. It ain't about money. Money doesn't touch your soul. This does." He gave Doug shoulder a squeeze. "Say! Where's Milly?" Doctor John spread his arms. "Ahhh! Miss Milly!"

Across the room, a familiar-looking old woman rose from her chair. She leaned on a walker. It was the rocking chair lady from the dirt road.

"Stay there! We'll come to you, darling!" said Doctor John.

"Well, I'm up now!" Milly lifted the walker and dropped it a few inches farther on. "That's what your shouting gets you, John . . . something you didn't want, when you could have done better just waiting."

Milly crossed a throw rug at a tedious pace, smoothing it down between each step. How had she gotten to the road, for God's sake? Doug wanted to pick her up and carry her just to get this slo-mo procession over with.

"This young man," Doctor John said, "wants to know about senility."

Milly came to a stop. She looked at Doug and straightened up. "Tell him to wait. He'll find out."

Doctor John laughed. "Sure. But I thought you might give him a preview. She lived in Rapid City, Doug. Thirty years, wasn't it, dear? Milly has a son and a daughter-in-law. She had a big house, and they all lived there. But Milly started setting the table for imaginary company. Her boy, turns out, had a low opinion of shenanigans like that, see. Next stop for Milly was a nursing home. Right?"

"Yes. But I cooked imaginary food. Donny took it real serious. You'd of thought I was trying to burn the house down. But it was imaginary food."

"I'm interested to know, Milly, did Don—did anybody—get you treatment?"

"You know they didn't, John. Donny got me hauled off. But you sent for me, and that boy came to the sanitarium—and I was glad of it!"

"That right there! That's the culture, Doug!" said Doctor John. "Polite as hell, but there's that emotional gulf! It keeps things clean! I bet Don didn't even blink sending mom away. Convenient, low-cost, clears up space. What's not to like? Thank you, Milly!"

"You bet, Doctor."

Doctor John grabbed Doug by the elbow and steered him toward a window. "And in the nursing home, she was *worse*," he said.

Tanya appeared and was immediately crowding Doug. Suddenly Amanda was there too.

"Milly withdrew completely. She wouldn't talk to anybody until we took her. And she's still not perfect! Hell, she was probably eccentric from day one! A difficult woman. But she's relating real well now! Cooking real dinners. Was she senile? No! That's too easy! But the goblins got her!"

"*Goblins?*" Doug felt tired, spooked. His fact-sorting organ hurt and he needed an aspirin. "What was that you said about 'taking her'?" he said, in a shaky tone. He was startled when Amanda started to talk.

"When Doctor John started all this, he said, 'Every human being is an exploration. Every individual is a search inside. Withering of the body may be inevitable but the soul is irrevocable, and its discovery is the goal!'" Amanda had a loud, loud voice, Doug noticed. Also, there were long, white hairs on her chin. "And with the soul's *discovery* comes spiritual *recovery*!" Amanda said. "The pain-wracked brain can bloom again!"

Chapter 28

The evening deepened. The deep-blue sky lost all color as Tanya and Doug sat alone on the front porch. "There's a story here," Doug said. Something made a sound, maybe a cricket. The night was starting to take charge. "What do you suppose they're *hiding*?"

"You could get them in real trouble, Doug," Tanya said.

"That's a problem for who? You forget I saw you bring down Councilman What's-his-name."

"Hammer. And he's still in office."

"See? That's a problem with women. One minute you're a great attack-dog—and more power to you—then your hormones act up and—*whoosh!*—you're all mushy and softhearted and consistency's out the window! Where's your killer instinct?"

"You're embarrassing yourself."

"Oh! I am!"

"If you could see how transparently this aggressiveness is rooted in your greed, your hunger for praise and prestige, your need to win because you think can, you'd be embarrassed. Yes. That's why there's war, by the way. Talk about hormones."

"How long have you been saving up to say something like that? You're never happy unless you're the teacher, and I'm playing the underling who doesn't know shit."

They were on familiar ground. Their relationship was one big power play. Why hadn't Tanya seen it? She watched the moon behind the clouds and the shadows shifted on the white chalk cliffs.

"Somebody's hiding something. These old duffers hardly even move," Doug said. "How're you supposed to come up with video if they only sit?"

Tanya laughed. When had she changed, she wondered. She wouldn't have noticed Doctor John's face softening as he talked to Milly, nor the simple joy in his voice, as he described her transformation, no, not when she was working at the station, not in a million years.

"Where's your objectivity, Tanya?" Doug said. "You got your butt kicked in Minneapolis, but you're still a reporter."

That's it! Tanya thought. She'd lost her objectivity! She felt a sudden pity for Doug Pepper. He had a man's body. And he was brave. Perhaps she'd even caught a glimpse or two of an unsuspected capacity for openness in him lately. Maybe, someday, maturity would develop and a centeredness someone could lean on. But not now. And Tanya wasn't a baby sitter!

"Are you staying up all night?" she said.

"Maybe. Why not?"

"Cool. Amanda probably has extra blankets. You're going to need something out here," Tanya said. Doug would not be crawling under her covers tonight.

Amanda was in the kitchen. "You kids don't ever seem to sleep. Talk, talk, talk," she said.

"Well, what about you? It's after three. The sun will be up soon."

"Hah! Guess that's how I know about you two," Amanda said.

"I'm going to bed. Do you have some blankets Doug could have for the porch? He's in a mood."

"Surely. And there's plenty of bedrooms if you need your space for a night or two."

"It isn't like that, Amanda. There's really nothing between us."

Amanda sponged some dishes.

"I don't know how it looks from the outside, of course," Tanya said. "But we're colleagues, not anything else."

"Oh, honey, I don't even know you two."

Amanda led Tanya to the laundry room. On a shelf beside folded sheets, there were blankets.

"A relationship with a strong-willed man is devilish," Amanda said. "I love John, and that has to be enough. 'Cause if not, I either have to sue the son-of-a-bitch, or get the bus to Shreveport."

"I don't love Doug."

"No?" Amanda looked hard into Tanya's face. "Well, you're like me. You're going to have to . . ." she pulled some blankets from the shelf. "Have you ever been in love, Tanya?"

Tanya didn't need to be interrogated, not here, not anywhere. But what the hell, she thought. "Her name's Marlene," Tanya said. "She was my college roommate. I followed her to Minneapolis. That's how I got there."

Amanda nodded. "I've sometimes wondered if that would have worked for me." She shook her head. "Why aren't you with her?"

"Because I wanted a man. Not Doug. That was old news a long time ago."

"But isn't it the damndest thing," said Amanda. "Men. You can't live with 'em and you can't live without 'em."

"Hah. I've got to find my own way. I kind of lost it and got off track," said Tanya. "I have to work on that."

"Good for you! It's tough finding your own way. If you've got to include a man, well, that's worse!" Amanda laughed. "They don't fit too well."

"Thank you, Amanda." Tanya took the blankets and walked down the hallway.

* * * * *

DOUG BRUSHED HIS TEETH. He went back to the porch. He found his cache of cigarettes and had a few. He brushed his teeth again. He wracked his brain. It took over an hour, but he got things straight in his mind. He marched up the stairs and opened the door to the bedroom. It was dark but not too dark. He did a dive and bounced hard onto the bed. It shook and sagged and then settled back with a loud smack against the wall.

"Good! You're awake!" Doug said. He'd taken his shirt off. He'd removed his gym shorts. It wasn't warm enough, so he joined Tanya under the covers. "Here's what we got," he said. "A monster kind of guy who kidnaps all these old duffers and locks them up miles from anywhere. And then what? You know what? He gets their money because insurance, and then he has them write wills and shit! Of course they *do* because he has the power! So naturally they're under his power."

Tanya was quiet for quite a while. But then she had an opinion. "Quite a scenario, Doug. But you better hire accountants and track down records from courthouses and attics all over the place. There have got to be witnesses, too. Because stories like that? You're way out on a limb, Doug. Journalistically. It's tough. And, in this case, you know, just fucking not true. And those blankets? They need to go back to the laundry room. When you're done with them. There's plenty of bedrooms here."

"Okay. But on the porch, some guy comes out to smoke and I pump him for facts about this place! He got *asked* to change his will! John asked him! So he's leaving all his money to the doctor! And he's not the only one! They all do it. I'm getting that guy on camera! Right away!"

Tanya rolled to her other side and pulled the covers up. "Tell me tomorrow."

"Yeah. I can see how they work this. He wouldn't let us go upstairs. The senile old wrecks probably get stored up there in those rooms. Breathing through a tube, and all. Meanwhile he gets their checks. Then they kick and he cashes in *again*! *Big*. Oh, man, this has got to stop."

"Okay," Tanya said, from below a comforter. "You better have a real clear paper trail, otherwise they'll sue your ass. Probably me and Cat, too."

"Oh, I'll make him show me. Where's their phone, Tanya? You know cells don't work worth shit here. 'Cause no towers! That old man John practically broke my arm when I snuck up to that floor." Doug rubbed his shoulder. "Where's the nurses? No nothing. You think him and Amanda can handle all their needs? Ha! They're storing people for the cash plain and simple. Probably starve 'em."

"Seemed pretty healthy," said Tanya, "the ones I saw."

"Yeah. But not on that upper floor!"

* * * * *

DOUG WASN'T IN BED when Tanya opened her eyes. She enjoyed lounging for a change. She went to the window and opened it. The strange white cliffs were very bright. The boulders made the setting a magical place. Tanya realized she'd made good her escape from Minnesota. She was free now. She didn't need TV, or Minnesota, or Connecticut, didn't even need family except, maybe, for Christmas. California, she thought, that's where she should be. In media, perhaps. A Silicon Valley start-up. Learn to tweet.

She could see the van. It was filthy. She should write "wash me." Doctor John must have a hose. Speak of the devil, there came Doug. He was in shape, for sure. That was why no shirt. God, he was an asshole, Tanya thought. How was it possible to look like a god with no workouts and no character? Doug opened the back of the van.

He meant business. He pulled out a blue bag and brought out the big camera he said was back in Minneapolis for repairs! He put it on his shoulder.

"You crook!" Doug yelled, standing in front of the house, like an old west gunfighter.

"Doug!" Tanya shouted. He was a few feet below the window. Tanya could have jumped and tackled him.

"Crook!"

"Goddamn you, Doug!"

Tanya pulled on jeans and a shirt. She raced downstairs and pushed open the door and sped across the porch. Doug had attracted a lot of attention. People were gathering. It was a very elderly crowd and it included John and Amanda.

"You in the white slave trade? Is that what's happening?" Doug looked through the eyepiece.

"Don't play his game," Tanya said to Doctor John and Amanda. "Just go back in. There's no need to talk to that buffoon."

Doctor John squinted in the glare. He put a hand up. "Can't see you too good, Doug. Not out here in the sun. Damn it. You're young, more power to you," John said. "But maybe you haven't seen what it is to be cast off."

Doug kept the camera steady on his shoulder.

"You take the world personally. Okay, I know." Doctor John made a sweeping gesture with his right hand, "Huh. But, these little towns—store, grain elevator—and then you're back on prairie. Check the upstairs hotels above the hobby shop, or one of those new coffee bars. That's where they turn up, you know. Who knows where they came from? Sent there to die, I say, when they're no good to anyone!"

"Shut up, John," Amanda said, shoving Doctor John out of the way and moving in on Doug until she almost swallowed the lens. "He's an old poet. He won't get through to you. He's too dumb to know you're just mean. He thinks you're trying to get at the truth." She spat in the dirt. "Me, I don't care about you, or what you think. What I know is Doctor John's a saint. The pope never got the word. What else is new. Sure, he's a fanatic, too."

"Amanda," Doug said, in a no nonsense tone, "let's look at the facts. You both know Tanya and me are fugitives, but you don't call a cop. You've got something to hide! Isn't that right?"

"We don't want publicity!" said Doctor John. "We're under the radar." Doug stepped back as the big old man advanced. "We turn you in, what do you think happens."

"No kidding!" said Doug. "But you know better than to call attention to your little scam!"

"Shit-o-dear," said Amanda. "You should have kept that press guy you had in Santa Cruz. He could handle this."

"What was his name?" said John. "He was a weasel."

"Weasel or not, he'd know about this," said Amanda. "You know we're on video, now."

"I'm handling things fine," said John.

Amanda laughed. "Depends."

"On what, Amanda? It's not funny."

"It depends on if Doug here puts down that big camera and has lunch or not."

"No. I think he's planning on putting us on YouTube. Or wherever this goes," Doctor John said.

"Well, then we might as well sell the furniture and move back to Palo Alto, because the jig's up."

"Defeatist! Shut up."

"Will you two please focus, please?" said Doug. "I'm the one interviewing, so let's let me ask the questions! Right?"

"I've heard nothing from you but hypocritical blather!" said Amanda. "Ask away!"

"Tanya!" said Doug, "get in here. This is where you come in. Tanya? No? Okay. Then how so, Amanda? 'Hypocritical'? When you two are the obvious perps?"

"See, now, that's why I'm laughing, here, John," said Amanda. "Because of his stupid, stupid talk. 'Perps.' Except on some law show!"

"Oh, don't act like I don't know what's going on," said Doug. "Tanya!"

"What? You're embarrassing yourself, Doug," Tanya said.

"Which is so right," said Amanda.

"She's as much in this as I am," said Doug.

"That is impossible to believe," said Amanda. "For all I know she's a kidnappee in need of rescue."

"Tell her, Tanya. This is getting unprofessional on your part."

"Get your face out of that eyepiece for a minute and tell me what you see," said Tanya. "Look around! Are these people victims in your opinion?"

Doug took the camera from his shoulder and cradled it. "It's hard to be the shooter," he said, "and then the reporter at the same time. Since you stopped working."

Angry elderly residents surrounded Doug. The porch was packed too.

"The doctor ain't no crook!" somebody said.

"We're fugitives too!"

"Not one of these people is in danger of jail," said Doctor John. "They escaped their prison. Sometimes it was their own home!" Doctor John's face went white. He stepped forward, blindly clutching at something that wasn't there.

"Okay, John! Back in the house with you!" said Amanda, putting his arm around her shoulder. The big man sagged against her, and she steadied him, guiding him to the porch swing. He took the wooden seat gingerly. "Give him some air," Amanda said.

Doug stared. The camera dangled at his side.

"Damn it!" someone said. "You be careful with that old guy!"

"Pipe down, now!" Amanda said. "Give him some peace. You just need to rest now."

"I was just . . ." said Doug, but Amanda waved her hand.

"He's got a bad pump," she said. "Not that you'd guess it with him coming on like the savior of all mankind! Something he sure as hell is not." John tried to lift himself from the swing but Amanda pushed him back. "You stay put!" She pulled out a bottle. She stuck two pills in his mouth. "That'll hold you. But you're going to go to the clinic, mister!"

Doctor John pushed her away. "Oh, fuck you, Amanda," he said.

"That's more like it," she said. She stood straight and looked down at him. She shook her head. "One of these nights, you're going to wink-out like a candle—poof! Everybody'll be blue. But I'll know you did it to yourself. You didn't listen. Do you?"

Doug saw tears in Amanda's eyes and wondered if he should've ratcheted down his tone when confronting the old man.

"Well, I'm still here. You can save your blather," said Doctor John.

"There, there. There, there." Amanda leaned over the old man and patted his heavy arm. "Somebody get a pillow!"

"Call Barry," John said.

"Barry!"

"Yes, Barry! He's not the devil, Amanda. He's what we've got for continuity. And maybe sooner rather than later, too."

"You never said that!"

"You weren't listening. He's youngish. He knows the ropes."

"Like you said, though. You ain't dead yet. Jesus Christ!"

"True enough. But we got this other problem, now," John said, glaring at Doug. "I'm not up to it. Neither are you."

"John. Listen. Barry *is too* the devil. Besides, we just had a little misunderstanding. Didn't we, Doug?"

"Maybe," said Doug, nodding. "We could of."

John shook his head, disgustedly.

"I wish you'd have reined in your boyfriend," Amanda said to Tanya. "Now we've got real trouble. Look, John, here's an idea! Put these two young people on salary. Barry can do the accounts, sure, as long as someone's looking over his shoulder. We go on with Doug and Tanya 'til we're gone! That's fair!"

"Just a minute," said Doug. "We're journalists, or mainly Tanya is. Or was. We've got jobs."

"Oh, brother," said John. "Get Barry."

"Don't go trying to buy us off, Amanda," Doug said. "Or you, either, John. I stole a Roving-Eye van and sunk it in the Mississippi River. That's a prisonable offense. Sooner or later—probably sooner—I'm through. But I did it to find a little truth out here in America. Maybe I did a little. The Tree-lunking was good. And I still say you and him and all these old people right here are a story! And, Tanya, you know it, and I know it!" Doug put the camera down on the porch as if it were a rifle, or a spear. "Though I'm willing to be wrong in some of the details."

"What was it you did again?" said Amanda. "You sunk a vehicle?"

"He's goddamn Robin Hood," Doctor John said. "That's what."

"Your Barry? A lawyer? You trust him? We're vulnerable," said Tanya.

John shook his head. "Barry's more loyal than honest," he said. "Makes him worth every cent."

"Oh, my god, the time!" Amanda said, and left. The residents, lured by frying chicken, dispersed in twos and threes. Doug and Tanya sat by Doctor John on the swing.

"Lunchtime, you know," Doug said.

"Right. But we've got to talk turkey here," Tanya said.

* * * * *

"These beans are good," said Tanya.

"Refried," said Amanda. "That's the secret."

"Yummy."

"How do you get all this food?" Doug said, "Out in the middle of nowhere."

"Supply chain, my boy," said Doctor John, finishing a drumstick. "Supply chain."

"Yeah, because you're not raising chickens or beans or anything or here in this chalk, I see."

"Let me digest, will you?" Doctor John said. "We'll get to all that. I've been stressed enough for today."

"That you have," Amanda said. "And it's good you see that." Tanya joined her at the sink and picked up a towel. "Where's Jesse?" Amanda said. "He's on clean-up!"

"Out there!" said Tanya.

Through the kitchen's bay window a couple walked hand in hand among the huge white boulders. Jesse, and an elfin, white haired woman. They'd been bantering during lunch. "I didn't peg that as a romance," Tanya said.

"Oh, it wasn't, at first," Amanda said. She rinsed a stack of dishes and put them on the counter. "It's been a pleasure to see it, though. John! Jesse got to first base with Loe, John!"

"Oh, give 'em their privacy, Amanda!" said Doctor John.

"You're in a mood, John. I'm understanding because of what you've been through. But, John, when are we going to get that new Bosch?"

John laughed. "I thought you said you liked washing dishes."

"Well, but they say it's real quiet."

Amanda took off her apron and left Tanya at the counter drying dishes. Doctor John stood and stretched. Amanda followed him down the hallway.

"So what's the story?" said Tanya over her shoulder to Doug, dipping morning pancake in his coffee.

"Don't know. Hal Parsons wants meat," said Doug.

Amanda came back as Tanya finished the dishes. She pulled a pie out of the oven and put it on the table. "Pack that away," she said. She sat down and had a piece herself.

"Wow!" said Doug, chewing.

"Huh?" said Amanda.

"The pie! It's good!"

Amanda looked at Doug for a second. "Yeah? Oh, good."

"Did you make it, or is this something that Doctor—"

"Oh, hell," Amanda said. "Why he left me to baby sit, I'll never know." She headed for the hallway. "Both of you come on! I might as well show as tell ya!"

The stairs were dark. Tanya and Doug followed Amanda down into a part of the house they hadn't seen on the tour.

"Great ironwork!" Doug said. "Who did that?"

"I don't know," said Amanda. "Maybe the sisters."

"Looks new. Shinier."

"Maybe. John has expensive tastes."

Their feet crunched along a passageway a shop-vac could help. A yellow bulb above them failed to penetrate. The cavernous space seemed limitless.

"Very atmospheric!" said Doug.

"Hah!" said Amanda.

The floor was uneven—rock or cement was covered with a fragile, oily crust of some sort.

"Creosote," said Amanda. "It's a filthy place, this. But private."

She led them to a dim alcove, cluttered with mops. Behind a stained commode was a door. Amanda unlocked it with a key from the wall.

"What the nuns did down here, I don't have a clue. Store potatoes? Careful where you step now."

They entered a tunnel. It led into the distance with a walkway of wooden planks lit at intervals by naked bulbs. The walls and ceiling were the same white chalk that dominated the landscape for miles. The tunnel widened into a grotto, and the walls were hidden in the gloom. Mud-stained sheets hung alongside the plank pathway forming a kind of hallway in the measureless expanse. Finally, a fluorescent glow shown ahead.

Amanda pulled away a final sheet.

Doctor John sat at a table with a microphone in front of him. A row of red lights on a radio scanner rolled in continual sequence. A loudspeaker squawked.

"Jesus, what's all this?" Doug said. Tanya moved into the room.

"Where's your phone?" she said.

Doctor John wore fancy padded earphones. He looked up and frowned.

"It's okay, John," said Amanda. "You know that as well as I do."

A table under the light was piled high with phone books, street atlases and other publications. Much of the assortment was covered with a layer of white dust. Doug picked up a yearbook dated '42. "What's this for?" he said.

A voice barked over the radio. "We got her! Got her! Talk to me!"

"Wah-hoo!" Doctor John shouted into the microphone. He grabbed the mike stand off the table and waved it around like a war club. "Bring her on home! Now!"

"Roger that, sir!"

Amanda slapped the doctor on the back. "Oh, my god!" she said. "I've got to get to work!" She disappeared behind the sheet and her footsteps clattered along the planking until they were lost in the blare of the radio.

"You're right," said Tanya, examining an ancient yearbook, "this is a story. You don't have to know *where* this is happening to know it's cool it *is* happening! No matter what it is."

"Yeah," Doug said. "Doc just rescued a senior citizen and my phone's on the kitchen table!"

Doctor John pulled off the headphones with a flourish and stood up. He gave Tanya a smile. "They should all be like that!" he said.

* * * * *

THREE HOURS LATER, an extravagantly huge black helicopter landed near the patio at the back of the house. The noise was almost intolerable as it echoed off the boulders.

A few onlookers from the front room stood on a raised deck. Somebody took a shot with a flip phone.

"She's a beaut!" Doug said.

"What?" said Tanya.

"Nothing!"

The machine shut down with a lengthy whine and four long blades drooped as they slowed. Doug raced closer. Crewmembers in impressive jump suits jumped out as the engines stopped. Behind them, identifiable by her bright pink dress, was the passenger.

"My God! I love extractions!" said Amanda. "Careful!" She shouted, heading toward the craft at a half-trot. The new resident smiling ear to ear, was lifted to the ground by a crewman. "Welcome, Miss Helm!"

Doctor John put his arm around Miss Helm as she was placed gently in a wheelchair. "Excuse the dust," he said. "It's really only when the wind blows. You'll see. The croquet court is lovely!"

"My, my," Miss Helm said, taking in the activity with bright eyes. "My, my."

"Your room, 3B in the east wing, is ready!" Amanda said.

A crowd enveloped the welcoming committee, each individual trying to take part in the simple act of directing the wheelchair up the ramp.

"Is it always like this?" said Tanya.

"No," said Amanda. "Sometimes the rescue is late. They arrive on stretchers." She shook her head. "No time left. Still, it's better. And we've got plenty of room. We're learning."

"I thought this place was small," said Doug.

"It's the angles," Amanda said.

A crewmember carried two suitcases and a covered birdcage into the house. The craft fired up and unleashed another whirlwind. Doug covered his eyes. The big chopper rose and dipped to the west, leaving behind an eerie silence.

"Whose helicopter?" said Doug.

"This one? This one I don't know," said Amanda. "I'll ask John. It looks new, damn it! I've told him about that. They're all French."

Doug felt stupid. Maybe it was all the noise and then the sudden silence. "Oh," he said. He felt a hand on his arm. It was Doctor John. He was glowing. He didn't look like a man with a heart condition.

"What do you think?" he said.

"Hell of a nursing home, I guess," said Doug.

Doctor John laughed. "Is that how it looks? Sure. I see that! Mind you, I've got some of those." He looked around with a grin. "This place—it's special. This place is a club for souls on the mend."

"'Souls on the . . .'" said Amanda in an exasperated tone. "Normal speaking terms, John. He means to say loving families don't need this. But sometimes people get lost, often it's the old ones. They lose love. The people around them cease to be family. They come here. Or should. We're getting better."

"That we are, Amanda," John said. "That we are."

"You see, the doctor here is on a long-term guilt trip. He made a fortune on a *switch*. Now he acts like a rich Jesus. But it's his blessing and his curse. He worries too much."

"Thank you for that unenlightening bio," Doctor John said. "Shut up."

Amanda held up a silencing hand. "In a minute, John. I just want to say this old man's a saint. Saint Francis would have done the same if he had his money. Only maybe with birds."

"Christ, woman," said Doctor John. "You talk like a loon. Doug, where's your camera? You should be taking pictures."

Doug nodded then shook his head. "I . . . don't know," he said.

"C'mon. There's something you should see on the second floor."

"You were going to get the camera," said Amanda in a helpful tone. "I remember saying you should get the camera."

"Later, woman," said John. "There's time."

"One second you're serving us pie and the next you're dragging us into Mission Impossible, Amanda," said Tanya.

"Oh, you get used to it. He's a medical doctor who wasted his God-given talent on switches. But it's better now." She used the rail to help her climb the stairs. "So much better! His hands! He can radiate love like an electric current! You'll see!"

They followed Doctor John along the second floor corridor. He opened a door. "Here's Anna," he said. "She's packing. It took her a while to get up the nerve, but she's strong enough now. She'll leave by morning."

An old woman lay on the bed breathing slowly, calmly, almost imperceptibly. She might have been cast in bronze or chiseled from fine, dark wood. She didn't move—seemed not to know they were there.

"What do you mean, 'packing'?" Doug said, warily.

"She opened up plenty of old experiences to look at for the last time, and then she put them in their proper place. Looks like she's about done. She's sure of what she left—and she's sure of where she's going. Memory is the last stop before the river of eternity."

"She's dying," whispered Doug. And Tanya felt her eyes fill with tears. She wasn't horrified though she knew Doug was right. Death just seemed a simple step, one to be made gracefully. She didn't know this woman. Yet, somehow, she was filled with admiration for her. And she felt gratitude—gratitude toward life, gratitude toward Doug. He had approached the bed and put his fingers on the comforter covering the woman. He stared into her face. Tanya wondered what he was thinking. She was very, very glad he was there.

She grabbed his arm and steadied herself. Was he curious? Was he sad? She moved her body closer to his and held on to him. She wasn't anything like this old woman. She wasn't ready for whatever she was facing.

Doctor John put a hand on Tanya's shoulder. He smiled gently and led her and Doug from the room.

Chapter 29

Tammy Bailey waited for a break in the conversation.

Her little studio apartment was buzzing. Soon she would call for order, but she could afford to wait. They were all there. *Good*, she thought. Her place was cozy enough—more womblike than cramped.

Oh, but she was nervous. Yet something about the scene made her smile. Along with the butterflies flittering around in her tummy, she felt a growing sense of duty.

Her friends were sprawled along every available inch of the lush purple carpet. They propped themselves on the jumbo throw pillows, colored turquoise and blue, her favorites.

Ted Haley lit a cigarette, seemingly planning to use his palm as an ashtray. Oh, well. His hand was big enough. He just needed to stay away from her Navajo pots. They weren't ashtrays. If he didn't observe that unspoken rule, she'd cuff him upside his cute little bristly head.

"Hey! How about doing that on the porch!" said Seth Peterson. Ted stepped onto the balcony with a sheepish grin on his face.

Stellges and Barnum looked stoned, but it was hard to tell. It didn't matter. Tammy was pretty sure they could still function. Seth was eating the peanut M&Ms by the fistful. It was lucky she'd made a Costco run.

"All of us here," said Tammy, at last, her voice rising above the gentle murmur, "share a, well, a lot of friendship. And so I guess that's why we're here. Because friends know each other, and we know what we have to do if we want to protect each other. Right?"

"That's right!" said Brewer Dunn, new to the station, though she was just as committed as everybody else.

Tammy opened a *Pioneer Press-Dispatch* and folded it over so everybody could see the Bud Vanderpein ad. "This ad is a shame! You've all seen it! It blots our reputations every time it runs, since it supposedly speaks for us!" Tammy shook her head in disgust. "We're journalists, aren't we! Everyone here is! It's not just about Vern Balstad! He's made a big mistake thinking it's about him and his money because it's all he cares about!"

People cheered and clapped. Tammy almost started to cry but she didn't. She took a moment to think. "I love you! You're very important to me!" She squeezed a Kleenex in her damp left hand. She waved the newspaper like a flag. "And don't forget our poor Bob Tratcher! His poor broken heart is so bad he's still in the hospital. I went to see him. He's pretty doped up. But I saw it in his eyes, him being with us one-hundred percent!"

"Didn't Bob write that Bud Vanderpein ad, though, Tammy?" said Dexter Hughes. "Or give Bonnie Lee Thayer, the idea, at least?"

"No. Maybe so," Tammy nodded. "That could be right. But I don't think so. He's sorry about it, because it was a huge mistake." She looked around the room in case there was going to be argument. "He's real sorry. I went and saw him. And he's fighting just like us. Only he's fighting from Abbott-Northwestern. And he's glad we've got our health.

"Because we're probably going to lose our jobs, of course." Tammy felt like tearing up again. Luckily, Ted Haley stared at her with that look he sometimes got, and his cute eyes made her feel better. "But looking back, I bet we all say, 'We made this world a better place!'"

"Yay, Tammy!" said Cat Barnum, clapping. Everybody took it up and gave her a big hand.

"Oh, I was forgetting about Bud!" said Tammy. "His life is at risk every day. But what does Vern do? He gives those gangsters seventy-five seconds on the six o'clock every damn night! Pretending that's supposed to save Bud when we know it's nothing but ratings he's after!"

"Where's Tanya?" said Seth. "She should be here!"

"She left town," said Cat.

"That was quick."

"Yeah."

"A job?"

"Yeah."

"Good for her!"

Cat shrugged. "Sort of," he said, in a low voice.

"I wish she was here," said Tammy. "I'm only up here because she's not."

"Don't be modest, Tammy," Ted Haley said. "You're doing great."

Tammy turned red and smiled and looked at her bare feet. "Okay," she said. "Thanks." She was getting teary. "Okay. But we've got to remember Bud! You know? He's the one we have to think about! And Bob Tratcher! They tried to do what's right! But you know Vern Balstad, so they got in trouble. Don't forget that! So we're here to fight. No matter what! Okay! We don't care if it costs us! Because we're duty-bound! And we've got pride and truth on our side anyway!"

* * * * *

VERN BALSTAD SAT in front of the TV. He was watching the competition though he knew it was bad for him. His blood pressure always went up. By rights, the best thing for him was PBS "On Demand" and the Patty Page special whenever it was on. She sang, "Moonlight in Vermont," in a way that was so sweet and perfect it took him back to the good times.

Instead, though, Vern gripped his chair. WISK-TV was starting a newscast. Vern could feel himself tensing up because he knew what was coming. Hal Parsons had promoted the hell out of another Doug Pepper story. In a way, all those promos showed that Doug Pepper was old news. Old Hal had to hype the hell out of him to maintain interest. But Vern couldn't help himself. He had a perverse desire to see what Doug Pepper was up to. He wanted to know how the bastard who stole his Roving Eye van was screwing him this time.

Channel Five's fancy news open played, and then there was the anchorman with a picture of Doug Pepper over his shoulder. Doug Pepper was their *lead* story! Vern watched in fascination as that creepy Northern Minnesota voice started talking.

"We were going to do a story about people who climb around in these huge oaks here. Big, aren't they? But to tell the truth," Pepper said, "there was something more interesting on the ground. Pretty amazing."

Vern was sipping a drink but now he gulped it down and reached for the bottle. He knew he needed some clarity. Those people rolling around on the ground looked familiar. After a couple of close-ups he was sure. Greta B. Jones and Red Bertram were trading blows in a death match. She hadn't mentioned any of this on the phone!

"Look at the fur fly!" said Doug Pepper. "Watch out, Red! Greta's about to—ouch! That must have hurt! As you can see, people finally pulled them apart. But look—Greta's not done! Oops! Our microphone was pretty far away or we'd of had to beep all this. Go ahead and read Red's lips! It's pretty funny, people!"

It was awfully violent for TV news.

Vern clicked off the set and poured another shot. He paced around the room, glass in hand.

WEE-TV and WISK-TV, he thought, had been neck-and-neck in the ratings. But Greta B. Jones beating up Red on video was a disaster! It was a game-changer! Hal Parsons would play it and play it and play it again, the bastard! True, Bud Vanderpein was still captive, thank God! The Skull Crunch Gang was terrific at using FaceTime on various phones—and sometimes Periscope—to elude cops. But fat old Bud was fading in public interest even with the fortune Vern spent on ads!

No, Vern thought, it was time to go to the next level. He phoned Steve Cooney at home. Suddenly, he felt better. Vern was a desperate man. But he felt better.

* * * * *

IT WAS RAINING. The streets and sidewalks had been dry for weeks but now they were coated with a filmy sheen. The air smelled clean and the reflected light on every surface made the gleaming city unexpectedly festive and bright.

At 5:00 p.m. most employees at WEE-TV, including the news crew left. Hours passed. The old building was quiet and dark except for the bright lobby, where, as usual, Theresa sat at the reception desk taking occasional calls and watching the giant OLED (organic light emitting diode) screen Vern Balstad had installed just for her.

Sometime around seven a funny thing happened. One by one, people from the newsroom returned. Theresa buzzed in Tammy Bailey, Brewer Dunn, Ted, Sally, Dexter Hughes, and just about everybody else. Then, suddenly, seemingly out of nowhere, there was Bud Vanderpein standing at the glass doors!

Theresa buzzed him, of course, but she couldn't just sit there, not after all he'd been through, so she jumped up and raced around the desk and hugged him tightly. "Oh, Bud, 'How wonderful are His ways,'" said Theresa.

"What? Oh."

"You're free. Nobody bothered to say a word!"

"All of a sudden the police came," said Bud. He dropped his hands from her back. "Well . . ."

"'And the weak shall be made strong!' Bud I'm so happy!"

"Me too. Obviously, of course. I mean, thanks." Bud shifted his weight to his left foot, and Theresa let him step back. "They're going to want me," he said. "I mean, in the lounge."

"God bless you! I'm just so happy."

"Oh, they were just kids. I don't know why it got to be such a big thing. You'd think they could have . . . anyway. Thanks." He walked past the elevator along the hallway.

At 8:30, Theresa routed the commercial lines to the service and Pop James took over the switchboard to handle the night. She told him he should stay awake and that news was seemingly having a staff meeting and that Bud Vanedrpein was back.

The newsroom was dim and quiet downstairs with only a night producer and a few writers and editors on duty in the dungeon-like space. They put the final touches on the 10:00 p.m. news.

Directly above them on the first floor, just beyond the elevator, the dusty old lounge was hopping. Not since the days of the afternoon cartoon shows was there such an excited crowd in here. Shadowy figures whispered to each other. Nobody had figured out how to turn on the lounge overheads.

"I can't read my copy," said Brewer Dunn.

"I thought you were going to practice at home, honey," said Tammy.

"I was, but—"

"Then go out in the hall and work on it," said Tammy. "Quietly."

Lou Banciato followed Brewer out into the hall. Then Ted Haley joined them. Soon the half-lit hallway was filled with nervous, murmuring people.

"Please keep it down out there!" said Tammy in a whisper that reverberated down to the water cooler. "Jesus!"

Pop James, only a few steps away jerked alert momentarily then relaxed.

"Are you all ready?" Tammy said to Bud Vanerpein, gently.

"Everything's right here." He pulled a paper sack out of his backpack.

"Okay everybody!" said Ted Haley, looking at his watch, "Rehearsal's over, come on!"

Deep in the belly of the building there was a groan. Ted stopped and listened. It was the elevator complaining steadily as it began its nightly nonstop climb from the basement newsroom to the fourth floor studio, carrying the staff and anchor team for the WEE-TV 10:00 P.M. Report. The gears gave a metallic shriek.

"This is it," said Ted Haley.

Everybody stopped breathing.

Ted walked to the far wall of the lounge and opened the metal electrical box. He flipped a circuit breaker and the groaning stopped. There was dead silence. In a few moments, understandably, a chorus of shouts came from the crew trapped in the elevator. It was a shame to treat them that way, everybody agreed. Still, it was in the service of a higher good. That couldn't be denied. The pounding and shouting seemed to come from a great distance. It really wasn't relevant to the task at hand.

Lou Bancioto strolled to the switchboard. Pop James was nodding off. Lou tapped the old man on the shoulder. "Hey, Pop, got a little something for you." He set a bottle of Jack Daniels Premium Blend on the counter. "Go home and enjoy yourself. We'll handle this tonight." The old man took the bottle and got to his feet.

"Okay," he said. "Okay."

The old man left the building. Lou watched him moving slowly down the street with the bottle tucked at his elbow. *He'll probably be fired,* Lou thought. *Like the rest of us.* Pop didn't deserve his fate, though. Lou shrugged. He was collateral damage. Lou blocked the remaining lines on the switchboard and cut contact with the outside world.

* * * * *

"C'MON! HURRY EVERYBODY! Upstairs quick!" Tammy Bailey said. It was seven minutes to ten and the studio was on the fourth floor. She watched her friends disappear at the landing. Her heart was beating. *This is such a great way to get fired,* she thought.

One last time Tammy put her ear to the metal elevator door. Nobody was shouting down there in the shaft, though someone pressed the alarm bell. Maybe they thought it connected to the fire station or something. Ah, well. It had to be done. Michelle, "The Weather Girl," and Jean-Claude, and Ned Storm, plus some new people Tammy didn't know were stuck in there. They'd be okay.

* * * * *

THE FLOOR DIRECTOR GAVE his cue and the show was on. Tammy Bailey sat in the anchor's chair and opened the show. She looked at the teleprompter and did a pretty good job of reading what was there. Cat Barnum had written the script.

"For several months now, WEE-TV has drifted farther from true substance and closer to a superficial appearance of same. It's true that tonight we make no pretense of presenting you the news. But we may come closer to honesty because in the past months, unfortunately, all the news we brought you has mostly been pretense. And we're sorry."

Tammy was squeezed between Dexter Hughes, Brewer, Cat, Seth, Stellges, Ted Haley, Lou Bancioto, and several others. The anchor desk was a little crowded for anybody trying to spread out.

"And now," said Tammy, "it gives me great pleasure to welcome back a special guest. He's been gone a long time, but he's certainly not forgotten. We're glad he's here tonight. We know his life has changed in the past few weeks—for the good—though the experience, itself, wasn't good. And now, without further ado, a man who has a special message for us . . . none other than our own Bud Vanderpein!"

People at the anchor desk applauded. The camera went to Bud standing alone in front of a studio curtain with a puppet on his hand. Bud was a lot thinner. He seemed intense. Everybody was quiet and watched him. "People have good inside them that has to come out," Bud said in a loud voice. "If they keep it in, then it goes bad. They get infected with their own feelings! It makes you crazy!"

Lou looked at Stellges and raised his eyebrows. Tammy swallowed nervously.

"Anyway," Bud said, "I brought this puppet here to explain what I mean." The little hand puppet was a cow. It had a ring in its nose and a bell around its neck. "Excuse me, Bud," Bud said, in a squeaky voice he provided out of the corner of his mouth though his lips moved. "You're using me as a metaphor for relating to people, right?"

"That's right, cow."

"Well, I have to be milked every day or I'm in agony." Bud said, making the cow bob its head. "You could say I have to give of myself or I suffer. I presume that's the connection you're looking for?"

"Yes, cow, that's the connection," said Bud. "Don't you see, folks, it's easier to be nice—to smile, talk to people, relate—because you have it in you! It's no trouble to be friendly. And if you bottle it up inside, then it goes sour."

"But," said the cow, "what about smiling when you don't feel like it? That's phony!"

"Well, if they milk you when you're dry, cow, you get sore tits. So it's up to you to keep those excellent feelings welling up from your heart through generosity, and relating honestly to other people." Bud smiled and his eyes seemed to glow. Sweat rolled down his freckled forehead. "And that's it," he said. He wiped the puppet across his forehead and then he walked off screen.

"Well," said Tammy, when the camera came back to her,

"Is that news?" said Brewer Dunn.

"I think it was darling, Brewer," said Tammy. "Glad to have you back, Bud! Best of luck!"

"Nut case," said Lou, in a low voice not intended for the microphone. "I've always known that."

"And now a word for our sponsors," said Dexter Hughes, reading from the teleprompter when his red light went on. "They spend a lot of money bringing you this show, or, rather, to have the show bring them you." He chuckled. "They have to keep your head percolating with detergents and deodorants you've just got to have! But ever wonder who these people are who pay for commercials? Well, we wrote a little play that should help you understand sponsors!"

* * * * *

"THAT SHOULDN'T BE ALLOWED," said an engineer in master control, to his boss, who was sitting next to him.

"Yeah?" chief said, "What would you like to do about it? Read the log. There it is, 'news,'" He pointed with a stubby finger. "That don't change. Unless I get orders, that don't change."

The silence of the phone confirmed the chief's steady hand.

* * * * *

THE COMPUTER PLAYED THE STORY. The scene was a military barracks. Rows of men stood at attention. They wore Army green. Lou Bancioto stood in front, a drill sergeant's Smokey Bear hat on his head.

"Okay! Louder!" said the drill sergeant.

The troops yelled back. "Every day, in every way, I'm getting better and better!"

"Hold it!" the drill sergeant said. "What about you, Smith?"

"Every day in every way I'm getting better and better!"

"How's that?" the drill sergeant said, cupping his ear.

"EVERY DAY IN EVERY WAY I'M GETTING BETTER AND BETTER!" Smith shouted.

"You sick?" said the drill sergeant.

"No, sir!"

The drill sergeant shook his head, disgusted. "That's not better and better! It's worser and worser! Carlysle!"

"Yes, Sergeant!"

"Go ahead!"

"Every day, in every way," said Carlysle in a loud voice, "I'm getting better and better!"

The drill sergeant stepped an inch from Carlysle's face. "Tell me how, Carlysle."

"Sergeant?"

The drill sergeant got closer still. "How? How are you getting better?"

"Well . . ."

"Lost any weight?"

"No."

"No. That's obvious. Any better at push-ups?"

No. I . . ."

"Can you run better, think better—do anything at all better?"

"I . . ."

The drill sergeant spat. "Everybody! Again!"

"Every day, in every way, I'm getting better and better!"

"Finlay!"

"Sergeant?"

"You getting better, Finlay?"

"Yes, I certainly am!"

"Than who?"

"Every single one of these Bozos, Sergeant!"
"Walker! You better than Finlay?"
"You bet I am, Drill Sergeant!"
"You're damned right! You're both dismissed! The rest of you losers stay at attention 'til you learn to think positive!"

The camera came back to the studio.

"Well," said Tammy from the anchor desk. "That was quite something, Dexter. Thanks! Do you think you could tell us a little bit more about what it maybe could possibly mean?"

Dexter Hughes nodded nervously.

"Okay. Commercials try to sell you a positive image of yourself. But first they have to cut you down pretty bad so you'll think you need their products to be good enough. Is that it?"

"Okay, Dexter. Good enough," said Tammy. "Okay. That's really something to think about."

* * * * *

At first Vern Balstad was just puzzled. The wrong people were on his TV. There was little Tammy the newsroom babe. There was Seth Peterson whom Vern had personally fired a couple weeks back. Then he noticed the words weren't right. It was some kind of airy-fairy shit.

Unbelievable.

"I've been robbed," Vern said. "I've been goddamn robbed!"

The switchboard didn't answer though that old drunk should have picked up. Bob Tratcher was in the hospital. Calling him made no sense. Flo didn't answer, and 911 put him on hold. He scrambled for his keys, which had fallen behind the cushion. He raced to the car waiting for 911 to pick up and do their job. The Beamer glistened. Somehow Vern's shirt got soaked opening the door. He barreled down the drive and onto the parkway ignoring the stop sign. The road was empty, and he had priority.

He fishtailed some in the wet. He turned on the wipers, which blurred the road. Again 911 dropped the call. What the fuck! Vern gritted his teeth. He tried to dial again but missed a number.

He looked up suddenly and the familiar arrows were pointing right. He tossed the phone and turned the wheel to do the sharp curve but the Beamer slid. He broke through a wood fence and was suddenly airborne.

He saw it coming. It looked like a storm cloud somewhere. It came closer fast and it got bigger and blacker. He recognized it with some kind of terrible feeling he'd never had. This wasn't a storm cloud at all. No, it was something else. The Beamer landed on it's grill and rolled onto it's top and Vern had an airbag in his face.

And then everything went dark.

Epilogue

Tanya Thorpe was feeling strange. Domesticated. Doug Pepper slept between the sheets now—next to her.

In the bad old days, she and Doug had fucked a lot. It was a sexually gratifying but joyless connection. Maybe the Twin Cities were at fault because somehow out here in the middle of nowhere they had discovered common ground and a depth of affection she, at least, had never known before.

Now, when Doug came to her, when he lay on her, she let herself sink into his hard body and somehow she knew they were melding into the same being.

She stood in the shade at the back of the house watching old Milly digging a garden. The awkward old woman wore a sunshade, and she scratched at the chalky dirt with a trowel. The sun would be overhead soon, and there would be no choice but to go back inside. The helicopter ferrying Miss Helm had brought Milly some flowering plants. The blooms were red, yellow, orange, and blue. They rested in their flat in pert good health.

"Those are awfully pretty," said Tanya.

"They're succulents!" Milly said, fingering the leaves of a plant with a bright blue flower. "Like cactus."

Milly turned and smiled at Tanya and Tanya felt a wave of warmth. The old woman was a gangly creature. She was difficult, too. She had a penchant for pushing her wheelchair out to the main road, such as it was, and roaming for miles through the badlands, and frightening the hell out of Doctor John. She had a homely, almost mannish face. Her body was angular and hunched. Her hair was thin. But she radiated an infectious sense of ease.

"You seem happy," Tanya said.

Milly looked at the white cliffs in the distance and her arms fell to her sides. She smiled. "I feel nice," she said. The sense of relief in those words made Tanya's eyes burn.

Milly fell to all fours and began digging again.

The garden hose at her side spat and gurgled. "Shush, you!" Milly said.

It seemed to Tanya that Doctor John was hosting an extended party for the failing members of his generation. If he was a genius it was surely related to his capacity for loving, really loving, those who lacked his blessed vitality and health. He'd invade a person's space with his big body and loud voice, blissfully violating their boundaries so he could touch them and love them. They all—like Milly—were the better for it.

Tanya walked along the polished hallway into the bright living room, crowded as always, with people chatting, wearing earphones, watching more of those silly still pictures. Doctor John had cornered a group by the window, and they bantered and laughed, Doctor John, of course, the loudest of all.

There were daily helicopters. They explained the opulent furnishings, the cleanliness, the fact that nothing ever seemed to break down. Workmen came, did their jobs efficiently, then left.

"Is that why you love him?" Tanya said, joining Amanda, who was taking in the gentle murmur of the gathering from her preferred spot against a wall.

"What?" Amanda said.

"Doctor John, Amanda—is he a saint?"

Amanda smiled. "Oh, charisma's his thing, Tanya. If I cared about that, I supposed I'd be sitting at his feet like the others. But I don't love him for being that way."

"But you do love him? Is he just another loud, friendly guy—like Doug?"

Amanda laughed, and led Tanya by the arm back to the kitchen. She cut two pieces of pie.

"Underneath it all, John's a needy man," said Amanda. "And mostly what he needs is me. You can love a man for his weakness." Amanda put a hand on Tanya's arm. "I think you know that."

"Oh. Well, I'm not sure I love Doug. If that's what you mean."

"I always thought the best reason to love Jesus wasn't that he healed the sick, or turned water into wine, or died for our sins. You wow the customers with that kind of trick. Though naturally I won't know about the salvation part until I'm dead. I love Jesus because he *wanted* to heal people, make the wedding a success, save us all from Hell. If he pulled it all off, great! But I can't love that. I just watch with my jaw slack. You see?"

"No."

"Your man Doug aches with the need to do what's right, just like the doctor. I love John because he *needs* to help. I can't tell you what it is that gnaws at him. Maybe he's just hungry for love. But it's enough for me, even so. I guess I love a man that needs me."

"But maybe he doesn't need you. Maybe it's only the crowd. Like an actor."

"Yes. But that's something you've got to decide for yourself."

"But Doug is all fucked up," Tanya said.

Amanda picked up Tanya's hand in her two big hands. "Yes, ma'am," she said slowly. "That's part of it."

* * * * *

DOCTOR JOHN AND DOUG were smiling. Dinner was over and Tanya could hear the piano in the living room and a few strained voices trying to sing, "Danny Boy."

Doug's cell interrupted her quiet contemplation with the first irritating bars of "Stars and Stripes Forever."

"That's it!" Doug said, touching the screen. "Mr. Cooney? Yes, sir! Doug Pepper at your service!"

"WEE-TV Sales Manager Cooney?" said Tanya.

Doug nodded and motioned for her to be quiet. She would have protested, but the very concept of Doug and Mr. Cooney talking was a terrible shock.

"That's right, sir, Lansing," Doug said.

Tanya could hear the buzz of Cooney's voice, but the conversation made no sense. Doug grinned at her in a smug way and shrugged.

"Just where is Lansing, sir? Oh, well, sort of upstate, central, I think—maybe a little more eastern. It's real nice. Lots of—trees. Parts of it."

Doug winked at her and made a face. He was no genius. His ignorance of geography and the exact location of a second-tier Michigan city wasn't, in itself, remarkable. But why it might be pertinent was beyond Tanya.

"The weather? It's kind of rainy—mostly—and then sunny, also—today. Anyway. That is, partly sunny, chance of rain. You know what I mean." Doug laughed.

Tanya bit her lip.

"Yes, sir," said Doug, shaking his head. "I know—a real tragedy. Vern—I mean, *Mr. Balstad*—he wasn't so bad. He was a real good man. Loved by many. He was real young to retire."

"How in blazes did anybody know Doug was here?" said Amanda.

"Quiet, Amanda!" said Doctor John. "Cooney doesn't know anything. He thinks these guys are in Lansing, Michigan. Their friend, Cat, arranged this. To tell the truth, Doug wasn't sure it was a good idea. Obviously that's changed."

"What idea?" Tanya said.

"This Cat," said Amanda, in a low voice, "sounds like he's stirring up trouble."

"*What idea?*" Tanya said.

"What's your role in all this, John?" said Amanda.

"Please, Amanda! You're interrupting."

"Yes, sir," Doug said. "Yes, that's right, Mr. Cooney. She's here. You can always rely on ol' Cat, sir! He's got the facts. Hey, Tanya! Mr. Cooney wants to talk to you!" Doug handed her the phone. She gave him a severe look. He looked away with a smile. "Go on, go on!" he said. "Take it!"

So, she did.

"Hello?"

"Tanya Thorpe! How are you? It's wonderful to hear your voice! Frankly, we've missed you terribly on the air!"

It was Steve Cooney, all right. He was a glad-hander, for sure. Nonetheless, it was nice to know she'd been missed.

"I'm fine, Steve. How are you?"

"Good! Good! Cat Barnum tells me you've been a wonderful influence on our Mr. Pepper!"

"I don't know," she said. "I guess, maybe, I . . ."

"I know things have been happening a little fast—with our beloved Mr. Balstad leaving us. He's bought property up in Moorhead, believe it or not. Frankly, I miss him. When the Kleizer sale is complete, my first act as general manager here, will be to name Vern Balstad as a consultant."

"Okay," Tanya said.

"Okay!" said Mr. Cooney. "Your Cat Barnum was kind enough to put me in touch with you folks, and it's a real privilege, let me tell you. But I have to confess we wouldn't be talking right now but for Vern's wonderful plan to capitalize on Doug's fame—or should I say 'notoriety'!" Mr. Cooney laughed heartily. "Doug and Cat can fill you in, Tanya. I know how very busy you are. But let me say, I couldn't be happier with the arrangement. And just because he'll be getting the airtime, don't think of Doug as our star attraction. Sure, research shows he's huge. But it's you who brought our boy up to journalistic snuff! So kudos, Tanya. You're the producer. I think you'll be pleased with your compensation."

Tanya didn't know what to say.

* * * * *

TANYA WAS AT A CROSSROADS. She sat on the porch swing late into the night. She kept waiting for Doug and Amanda and John to go to bed. But they stayed with her.

"I was hoping you two would stick around," Doctor John said at last.

"Mr. Cooney's plan isn't going to tear us away from here," Doug said. "I've said that."

Doug said "us," Tanya noticed. True, she'd provided him with generous and unrestricted access to her body. But her mind was off limits. It always would be.

And yet, she didn't want to leave this place. She could have wept. For the first time in her life she felt complete. Or nearly so. By letting Doug close—but not closer—she'd found a way to include him in her life, at least for a while.

Without Amanda—and Doctor John—the arrangement couldn't go on.

Cooney wanted her to be Doug's producer? It had been the transgressive nature of their fugitive reports that had kept them pure. With WEE-TV footing the bills, she'd be producing a reality show. She'd face the same seductive mix of fame and dollars that had corrupted her before. She felt a darkness rolling in that had nothing to do with the moonless night.

Tanya looked at Doug. He was just a silhouette but even in the dark she could feel his energy and excitement. She was envious. But this couldn't be for her. Perhaps there was no such place. She'd move back to Connecticut, live with her parents for a while, be a good girl.

She would lose her connections to this place. She might send Amanda a Christmas card once, twice, and then she and John would fade into irrelevance.

* * * * *

DOUG OUTLINED THE DEAL Cat Barnum had struck in Minneapolis. Cat, acting as agent for Doug and Tanya, had negotiated a fat contract that guaranteed them a lot of money to do a few news stories every month.

"News?" said Tanya. "Try reality show on a newscast. You know that, don't you?"

But nothing seemed to dampen Doug's enthusiasm and sense of accomplishment. The viewers identified with him. The precious eighteen- to thirty-five-year-old demographic loved the "On the Road" vibe Doug brought to Vine and Twitter and YouTube. and the rest. He was believable in an awkward way. Steve Cooney was going to monetize that rebel appeal.

* * * * *

Lost in earnest discussion, Doug and Doctor John sat on the porch. They were alike, Tanya thought. Both ego-driven dreamers. Silly men. She doubted the Cooney-Balstad plan could work long term. Almost certainly, it wouldn't.

But Amanda was a wise and powerful woman. In the face of her own doubt, Tanya suspected she'd do well to defer to that store of knowledge.

"You can't get rid of us! This is home base!" said Doug to Doctor John in a cheery tone.

Doctor John nodded. "Maybe so. But you'll be gone so much! We won't even know you anymore!"

"Doc! We've got an expense account! We can fly places! And your chopper has room, doesn't it? We can hitch a ride!"

"True, true," said Doctor John, lighting his pipe.

Amanda had left for a while but she rejoined them. She moved across the porch and sat down on the step. Tanya sat beside her. The old woman put her arm around Tanya's shoulders. Grateful for the human contact, Tanya leaned against Amanda's large, warm body. Where did the helicopters come from? Where did they go? Tanya didn't really need to know, she realized. Not now.

Perhaps, someday soon, she'd hitch a ride somewhere and be gone. She would miss . . . this. Was it family?

Amanda leaned closer and whispered to Tanya. "They're going to do what they're going to do," she said. "Neither one of them knows enough to be scared."

Then, clucking about John's health, Amanda roused herself. She stood over Doctor John and playfully badgered him until he allowed her to usher him off to bed.

Then, it was peaceful except for the occasional call of some animal nearby. Tanya couldn't identify it. It might be an owl. Perhaps it was only a spirit.

Doug joined Tanya on the porch steps. Quietly he nuzzled her neck, breathing his warm breath into the night chill that had stolen into Tanya's unprotected bones. "You're awful important to me, you know," he said. "You're a goddess."

"So much has happened," she said.

"Well, it's pretty simple."

"No, it really isn't." Tanya looked at Doug. She felt cold, even though his body was warm.

"Yes it is. You'll see."

"It is? Tell me how."

"Come on. I want to talk to you. Ever heard of a Foster Kleizer? Good friend of Doctor John's. They share a philosophy. We've got a mission, Miss Tanya. Seems like a door is opening. I can't walk through it, not without you."

He kissed her lips. And Tanya, wondering what Doug was into now, went with him, hand in hand, up to bed.